Stain on the Earth

Louise Dawn

To sign up for Louise Dawn's newsletter, go to:
http://www.louisedawnauthor.com

◊ ◊ ◊

To the ones that are stuck and
to the ones who fight to get un-stuck.

Success requires getting a little dirty.
Get muddy.

◊ ◊ ◊

Prologue

Somewhere near the South Sudan/ Uganda border

The black stallion skittered sideways, and the rider brought him harshly back into line. He couldn't blame Atheas. Temperatures soared into the mid-forties and they'd been here too long. He patted the sweat-soaked stallion's coat and called out to one of the men.

"The horse needs water. How long does it take to clear a damn village?"

"We're almost done, master. I'll find something."

"Fuck it. We've gone too far north. We'll backtrack to the church we passed."

The church they'd ransacked. The Scythian adjusted his soaked hood, feeling perspiration chafing his already raw skin. This was the price he paid for being the most notorious extremist on the African continent. A woman started wailing, and her shrieks added to his already irritated mood.

"Someone kill the bitch."

The Scythian led Atheas to a miserable patch of shade, then observed the carnage from a distance. His men were well trained. They'd better be after all the slaughtering they'd done—it had been a productive year. They'd concentrated their efforts on remote outlying villages in East and Central Africa. Working near borders meant his army of mercenaries could easily slip into new territory when threatened by local military. Recently, they'd focused on new Sudanese refugee settlements in North Uganda. The newly built thatched settlements were easy pickings for his well-trained unit.

Aside from two of his men contracting malaria, the past month had been uneventful, and Scythian hated to admit that he felt a little bored. The same thing every week—accept a contract, then spread Scythian terror. Extremist organizations tripped over themselves to use his legendary services and they paid well. This being aside from the other businesses he ran, he was constantly traveling, splitting his time between his old life and his new Scythian persona. Growing his unique persona took consistent work, and he'd reached the apex of infamy. Now that he was a wealthy man, it no longer felt like a challenge, and the Scythian needed a new interest. But he had personal business to complete and business contracts to fulfill over the next month before he could even consider a different life path.

His soldiers separated the men from their families. They lined up the last of the stragglers and waited for his final commands. He nudged his horse and walked it over. In a weary tone he ran through a speech that he chanted on a daily basis.

"I will eat your harvest and bread, I will eat your sons and daughters, I will eat your sheep and oxen, I will eat your grapes and figs. The Horse Lord is coming."

One of the men began to sob and pointed to his wife and young boy.

"Your woman will be sold. Your son will work for me, and you will die. Accept your fate." The Scythian switched to Dutch and Arabic and repeated his statement. He dismounted and drew a machete, pausing to revel in the thrill of the moment, imagining how imposing he must look to the prisoners trembling before him. Over six feet of honed muscle clad in a pointy, red leather mask, with a sleek stallion snorting at his back. Yeah, his brand was a striking and glorious one.

He raised the machete and swung with all his might.

◊ ◊ ◊

Three months later
Johannesburg

James "Johnny" Cane topped the hill, raising his Smith sunglasses while looking down at the park revelers below. He'd dressed to blend in, wearing tan cargo shorts and a black shirt. His size drew attention. In his line of work, Johnny used that to his advantage—especially when working an asset. Too many people were clustered near the giant oak tree to make out the target, but he'd find her soon enough.

Joining the Facebook group Americans in Jo'burg and accepting the invitation for the outdoor picnic had been as easy as apple pie. He had a feeling that seducing Lizette Steyn would be just as easy, and judging by her photo, she might just taste of apples with a side of sunshine. He hadn't met any of the Americans yet, but this was what today was about, specifically befriending the airhead princess who would eventually lead them to their primary target. He wouldn't play the game too hard, flirt just enough to string Lizette along.

The picnic was being held at Emmarentia Dam, a scenic spread of water surrounded by botanical gardens and tranquil lawns. He headed for the shady tree, marking his destination. A grocery bag nudged his leg as he loped down the hill. Rug rats chased each other, screaming as they ran circles around him, and Johnny paid them little heed. An eighties ballad blasted through a portable speaker as he greeted the outlying couples and worked his way into the center of the chaos. He laid out the pasta salad he'd bought among the rest of the wares. Still no sign of his blonde target. A group of teenagers and fathers were gaping up at the oak as Johnny wandered by, pausing to scan the perimeter. A couple of kids played down by the water as their mothers corralled them in. Lizette Steyn wasn't with them at the water's edge.

A woman shrieked, gazing up while pouncing too close to Johnny. "That has to be the most idiotic thing you've done to date!"

He sidestepped and glanced at the excitable woman, who waved her manicured hands in the air.

"Holy shit!" a pimply teenage boy shouted as the crowd scrambled back in a wave.

His only warning was the sound of wood cracking from above. A body crashed through the leaves, bouncing off branches on its downward trajectory.

Johnny catalogued the missile as he lunged to catch it. A skinny kid dressed in dungarees, approximately a hundred pounds. Thanks to gravity, this was going to hurt like a mother.

Out of time, he situated himself as the body slammed into him. Johnny staggered and tripped on a raised root, and they both crashed to the ground. He sheltered the kid as best he could. Heads knocked together in a jarring thud as they rolled down a grassy hill.

When they finally came to a painful stop, Johnny took note of aches and pains. He'd tweaked his shoulder and it burned like the blazes, and his wrist felt a little sore. Nothing broken. The kid lay over him, head tucked into his shoulder, hair smelling like a bowl of ripe peaches.

Johnny rolled them over, and his brain came to a screeching halt. Lizette Steyn's wide blue eyes stared up at him. From the stats in her file, he knew she was petite—but fucking hell, she was tiny in every way. He studied her delicate features, wanting to trace his thumb over her bow-shaped upper lip. A knot formed on her forehead and instead, he swiped at the swelling egg.

"Fishsticks! That hurts, stop bloody touching it!"

He grinned and immediately apologized as a crowd gathered.

"Don't move, where do you hurt?" Johnny asked as he scanned her limbs, taking note of the cute dungarees paired with a white tank top.

Lizette ignored his question. "Where the heck did you come from? Who are you?"

"Ja—John Calaway." Shit, he'd almost said his actual first name. That had never happened before, must be the knock to the head. At least he'd used his fake last name.

She stared at him like he was an alien, so he elaborated. "I joined your American Facebook group a couple of days ago."

She reached out to touch the tiny scar running from his temple to the corner of his eye, then reconsidered the intimate action and pulled back. "I must've not checked out your profile, you're beautiful!"

He felt his face heat at the compliment and concentrated instead on the task at hand. "Wiggle your toes, tell me if anything hurts."

"I would except you're still lying on me—not that I mind a giant hottie man-blanket but it's getting kind of warm under here."

Johnny quickly rolled to the side, and Lizette grinned. "I'm Liz by the way. You can call me Lizzy."

A pretty brunette knelt next to Lizzy and swiped a muddy smudge off her tanned shoulder. "Cuz, you're damn foolish. You could've broken your neck! Don't you dare move, we're calling an ambulance."

"Don't be ridiculous," Lizzy grumbled, trying to sit up. He pushed her back down. "Wait for the paramedics. You may have a concussion or a neck injury."

"And ruin a perfectly good picnic! Stop standing round and gaping, everyone, get back to the barbeque."

He jumped into a crouch, shaking out his sore arm. "Those were some hard hits while bouncing down that trunk."

"Other than the two of us de-braining each other, I'm perfectly fine."

"I used to be a medic, lie still while I check you out." After two minutes of checking pupils and asking her about dizziness, nausea and a headache, Lizzy was done.

"Stop fussing," she said, slowly climbing to her feet. "I've had worse."

"Damn right you have, silly girl." A minuscule older woman slapped at the leaves clinging to Lizzy's back. "You're too old for tree climbing. Those tomboy adventures will be finishing off the rest of your father's gray hairs."

Dust clouds rose as slaps increased. "Ouch. Mom! Stop. I'm fine—I have hard bones just like you."

"More like a hard head—a stubborn one!"

They both had the same Californian accent, which made sense as Lizzy grew up in San Diego. Her father—a South African—met her mother, Tina, while managing a boron mine in the States. Twenty-six years later, Daniel Steyn was now an influential mining magnate who managed two coal mines just outside of Johannesburg.

"Hey, Carl!" Lizzy called to a gang of teenagers. "I won the bet. Pay up."

A gangly kid broke off. "No way! The bet was if you climbed the tree, that also means climbing back down, and you fell out."

Lizzy refastened an eighties-style bandana in her curly blonde hair. "That's so bogus. The bet was if I got to the sixth branch, and I did. Now either you pay up, or you'll have to climb way higher than I did."

Johnny frowned at the crazy female standing before him. She'd climbed the tree for a bet?

Carl stared up at the top branches. "There's no way I'm climbing up that thing."

"Then you owe me twenty bucks, in dollars—not rands."

The kid grumbled before shelling over the cash. Lizzy shoved the bank note in a back pocket.

He narrowed his eyes. "You nearly killed yourself for a twenty?"

Lizzy grinned over her shoulder before walking away. "I've done it before for a ten. Sorry about the head-bashing thing, big man. Put some ice on it."

Okay, so maybe he'd profiled her all wrong, he thought as the tiny blonde flitted among the picnickers. Definitely not a high-maintenance rich girl. More like a Madonna-wannabe hellion.

Johnny's shoulder ached, so he walked behind a hedge to stretch out his back and arm in private. When he turned, a gang of women were watching him with a predatory gleam. *And here we go.* His build got him unwanted—and sometimes wanted— female attention. At 6'4" with 230 pounds of Ranger muscle,

Johnny didn't exactly fade into the background—which was sometimes a hassle as a member of a black ops team.

Johnny was trained to work targets and assets—and he'd work around the distraction. The really pretty distraction. A red-haired vixen broke off from the group and sauntered towards him. Damn. He'd always loved a tall and shapely redhead. He preferred not to date short women. He liked to stare in a woman's eyes when they worked up to fucking—an Amazon who could give as much as she got and wasn't afraid to get a little rough. He preferred women who weren't afraid of his brute strength.

His dick stirred just thinking about the she-devil standing in front of him. If he wasn't working…

They chatted for a few. Her name was April and she smelled like ripe jasmine and sex. So what if his eyes watered slightly at the overwhelming scent as she tucked an arm in his and led them back to her gaggle of friends.

When the conversation turned to designer handbags and other first-world neuroses, he lost interest, homing in on Lizzy as she prepared the lunch. She ran back and forth to the men crowded around the smoker. Did she ever stop smiling? One of the men made her giggle as he waved a pair of tongs in the air like a sword. Goose bumps crawled over his skin at the sound of that melodic laugh.

Lizzy ran back to her mom, who pointed to a rental trailer in the parking lot. Johnny broke away from the high-maintenance band of women and walked over to offer his help, which Lizzy accepted.

"Are you sure you're up for the trek to the car? How's your giant head feeling?"

"Just a small bump. How's your noggin, any nausea or dizziness?"

"Nope and too busy to care." Pulling out her phone, she tapped away. The music blaring through the speaker changed over to a U2 ballad. She adjusted the volume on the speaker. "Sorry. I'm the resident DJ. What were we talking about? Oh yeah, chairs—we'll need to grab a dozen more fold-out chairs from the trailer—thank God I rented a whole stack. Can you help my mom with that? I'm reckoning a hulk like you can carry at least ten."

Johnny easily carried the full dozen down with Tina protesting as she ran alongside. By the time they'd laid out the extra seats, food was up and Lizzy flitted off again.

After lunch as the party simmered into the late afternoon, Lizzy chatted with a couple of moms near the sandpit. He planned his next move, needing to worm his way into her inner circle. Lizzy was the closest link to Abigail Evans—a suspected terrorist. A little girl shoved a toddler off a swing. The boy wailed as his mother and Lizzy tried to comfort him. Nothing deterred the kid, and his cacophony doubled in volume. Lizzy ran and grabbed the portable speaker, selected a new playlist on her phone and cranked up the music before bouncing up to the kid. It took him a minute to place the vintage song. "Circles in the Sand" by Tiffany. Nope...Belinda someone or other...Belinda Carley...Belinda Carlyle.

Lizzy pulled the wailer into her lap and started singing along. Johnny walked over as she put actions to the words, interspersing the song with kisses and tickles. The tyke started to listen.

Lizzy held his stubby finger and traced a figure eight in the sand along with the chorus. The kid smiled and kept on squiggling circles in the sandpit.

Lizzy tickled the youngster's neck as he laughed hysterically. They were darn cute together and Johnny settled in the sandpit opposite them, enjoying the interplay. He couldn't hear her clearly over the music or the crowd of Americans spread out across the field, but it sounded like she had a pretty voice. Lizzy Steyn wasn't self-conscious in the least, she just did what made her happy, and that was a refreshing change from the selfie-obsessed generation in Johnny's dating pool.

Soon the other kids joined in, drawing shapes in the sand. She tickled the lot of them, rolling around, before shifting onto her stomach and setting her sights on Johnny.

"Well, well. If it isn't my fellow head basher."

He laughed along with the older kids.

Lizzy grinned, never taking her eyes off him. "Kids, what do you call a woodpecker without a beak?"

The youngsters threw out some possibilities and Lizzy shook her head, still staring deep into his eyes before yelling out the answer. "A headbanger."

He snorted and Lizzy threw sand on his stretched-out calf.

"Hey, easy, hellcat! I liked the tune by the way. Aren't you a little young for that playlist. What are you, like twenty-three?"

"Twenty-five. As a kid, my dad got me hooked on the eighties. Freddy Mercury beats out anything from this decade."

"What's your name?" one of the older girls asked.

He played up a Western drawl. "Well howdy, ma'am. It's Johnny, John Calaway."

The children giggled and he smiled, still staring at the blonde pixie sizing him up from across the small sandpit, a smudge of dirt streaked across one pretty cheek.

One of the boys waddled up on his knees. "You're He-Man, aren't ya?" Now it was Lizzy's turn to snicker.

"How do you know about He-Man?" Johnny asked the freckly kid. "He-Man was around long before you were born."

The kid sighed dramatically. "They still play it here. I prefer Skeletor. He has an awesome castle. He-Man has a cool sword though. We can't afford Netflix so I have to watch the other, stupider channels. Anyway, *He-Man* is always playing on the television. You look just like him. My daddy is much smaller than you, but I still think my dad could kick your butt—even though you're bigger, my daddy is meaner—he'd actually kick you in the karunas—sorry. I'm not allowed to say 'balls,' cause my mom says that's a bad curse word."

Lizzy tried to stifle an unladylike snort. Mirthful tears filled her ocean-blue eyes. Johnny's heart pounded once before turning over. His hands curled into fistfuls of sand because just like that, Lizette Steyn slid into his battle-scarred heart.

Chapter One

Lizette Steyn disengaged the slide, pulled up the door handle and swung the aircraft door outward. Frigid air swept in and she barely repressed a shiver. "Freezing fudge buckets," she muttered before greeting the ground agent at the top of the stairs. The miserable structure that was Bacha Khan International Airport looked archaic—with all the developing nations Lizzy had visited in the past five months, that was saying a lot. Peshawar, the wild west town of Pakistan, felt as cold as a dead man's nose.

"Well isn't that just grand," Brianna muttered, stepping out of the wind. "All I bloody packed was a vest and a sleeveless shirt."

Lizzy refrained from rolling her eyes. The two other cabin attendants had as much sense as two rolling hamsters. Brianna, a hardy Irish girl who started flying for JetHaven around the same time as Lizzy, was a workhorse in the cabin, but loved to go on partying benders the minute they arrived at the hotel. Then there was Suzie. This was Lizzy's first flight with the high-maintenance Capetonian. Thanks to her lax attitude onboard, Lizzy and

Brianna worked their asses off. Lizzy didn't mind. Suzie was still new to the job, although Lizzy doubted she'd last out the month.

Had she ever been that juvenile? The past six months had affected her in so many ways. Lizzy now felt like a mother hen, especially with Tweedledee and Tweedledum whining behind her.

"How hectic is this weather! Aren't we supposed to be in a desert?"

Lizzy turned to Suzie. "You'll need to get into the habit of researching weather conditions on future flights. Early March is barely spring in Peshawar. It snows in Afghanistan in the winter and we're east of the border."

Suzie rubbed her goosey arms. "But we're nowhere near Afghanistan!"

"Hun, where do you think Peshawar is situated?"

"Um. Somewhere in Asia?"

Lizzy gave up on the conversation and readied herself to greet their disembarking passengers. They carried a smaller contingent than they were normally used to, thus utilizing a smaller Airbus—the A318 Elite.

The six male passengers looked somber as they gathered their sparse belongings. Definitely a team from an American three-letter agency, Lizzy thought. Possibly CIA, FBI or NSA. Throughout the flight the hardened men had kept to themselves, shut in the boardroom at the front of the aircraft, only pausing for the breakfast service. Lizzy had worked on a number of clandestine flights that flew into high-risk regions. She'd also ferried diplomats and their families, military personnel and news correspondents. After some gruff thanks at the door, the men drove away in a black Hilux into the early morning light.

The crew bus pulled up and Lizzy covered her hair with a scarf before teetering down the wet stairs and dragging her trolley bag to a seat. She was the first onboard the musty coach and settled her tired ass on a window seat in the middle. Brianna popped up through the door. "We have a twenty-four-hour layover. I'm heading into town after I've cleaned up. I hear the Khyber Bazaar has the best Persian rugs. On her last flight to Peshawar, Jane got a fierce Pakistani Persian that is fucking unbelievable."

Jane, a fellow crew member, was an interior designer wannabe. Indigenous knickknacks filled her Kenyan apartment, and it smelled like a damn Brazilian rainforest. Lizzy had no inclination to replicate the jungle-style Zen that Jane strove to create.

"Sweet cheeks, you should know better than to venture into Peshawar on your own. There are travel warnings in place for good reason. I'm going to hibernate in my room, order room service and watch the first Bollywood movie I come across."

"Oh, come on." Brianna tossed her suitcase onto a seat. "That hotel isn't even a two-star, never mind a three-star. The last time I stayed in Peshawar, I thought one of those stinky-ass street donkeys wandered into my room, and then figured out it was just a fucking cockroach the size of a damn stallion. You really wanna spend your afternoon in a cockroach motel? Plus, you know what Captain Stuart is like—he'll be knocking on your door in no time, trying to drag you down to the bar for a virgin martini."

Brianna had a point.

"Besides, Suzie is coming along. It's her first layover and the girl needs to live a little. It's not like we're going out on the lash! It's a dry town. Hell, not even the hotel has a mini bar!"

"Tell me about it, doll," Suzie swung herself across from Lizzy. "I need a tall glass of chardonnay, like ASAP."

Yip. Good luck with that. Lizzy swiped lip balm over dry lips. "Just chill, you'll be back in Nairobi by tomorrow night."

"Thank fuck!" Suzie sighed. "A white wine followed by a macchiato. At least Kenya has stunning coffee."

Kenya was the base of operations for JetHaven, and all the flight crew lived in Nairobi. The private security contractor provided specialized and tailored services to accommodate VIP, diplomatic and crisis flights across Africa and the Middle East.

The bus driver's brief glance reflected disdain at the girls' antics.

I feel you, buddy, Lizzy thought as they waited for the cockpit crew to disembark. She felt herself caving in to the whims of dee and dum. Apparently, there was a fabric bazaar near the Khyber area. Lizzy could grab some pretty materials and keep an eye on the girls at the same time.

"Here comes Captain Stuart and his sad-ass swagger... definitely thinks you're a hottie." Brianna winked.

Lizzy sniggered. "Don't be ridiculous."

Suzie leaned over. "I bet he's going to make a move in 3...2...1—"

The American captain crab-walked up the aisle, his eyes immediately swinging to Lizzy before landing on the open seat next to her. Suzie casually jumped the aisle and slipped in beside Lizzy, giving him an innocent grin. It didn't deter the man.

"Thank you for looking after me, Lizette. You make good coffee."

"Not a problem." Smiling politely didn't dent his ardor.

"You should have popped into the cockpit for a chat."

"Busy flight, what can I say."

Stuart narrowed his eyes. He knew the crew had been blessed with low-maintenance passengers on this leg of the journey. He liked to think that because they were both from California, it gave him a leg up. Lizzy might have the same accent and have spent her first decade in the sunny state, but Johannesburg felt more like home. That was until a brawny soldier with a fake name broke her heart, and she chose to run like a coward. Suddenly she felt bone weary. So damn tired. The pilot was still yammering on and Lizzy forced herself to listen. "Even when the flight is quiet, you still dart around like a dynamite Barbie. Such a little thing with so much energy."

"Did you just call me Barbie?" Lizzy glared, and Stuart backed away. The first officer climbed onboard and the captain used that as an excuse to take a seat.

Lizzy simmered as she stared out the window. She dragged that awful stereotype along as a shadow wherever she went. She'd dynamite-Barbie his arrogant ass. She didn't even look like the stupid doll. Lizzy glanced down. Her chest was on the small side, 32 C. Fair enough, she was blonde and slim, but definitely not tall or willowy or even Marilyn Monroe-like. So maybe she did bounce more than walk, but that didn't warrant the comparison. She hoped she wasn't perceived as an airhead. She liked to have fun, but still held an interest in the world around her and tried to be thoughtful and kind.

The bus pulled off.

The only human—aside from her parents—who really knew the real Lizzy was John. Not that "John" was his real name. She'd bet Calaway wasn't his last name either. Lizzy wondered what other shitty covert names he used in the field. John had swept into her life, caught her in his strong arms under a shady tree, then pretended to like her. After meeting at the picnic, they'd dated only six weeks, but it was intense and Lizzy thought it was the real thing. He treated her love and trust like they were grapes in a barrel, stomping all over them with his giant feet. All of his charm had been a ruse to get close to her friend.

First Ivan—her ex-fiancé—had kicked the shit out of Lizzy both mentally and physically, bruising her young heart. Then John had come along and picked it up off the floor to finish the job, slashing it into tiny pieces. Yet she still missed him so much, it hurt.

Six months had passed since she discovered their relationship was one huge lie, that her best friend—Abigail Evans—had covered up for her covert friends, and left Lizzy out of the loop. Lizzy had a lot of time to think things over. Abby still emailed her every week, Lizzy opened up a couple of the messages but never replied.

Abby spoke of her sweet family; of how proud she was of her strong husband and his brave friends. Of John's loyalty and kindness and how torn he was over what had gone down in Johannesburg. How he'd destroyed any chance with Lizzy.

The anger still raged, but her love for Abby was slowly winning out, and so was the confusion and indecision that defined her life. John's team of clandestine bad boys had used her to get to Abigail, with no consideration for her family's safety.

If it were just Lizzy involved she could forgive them, but her parents could have been hurt. Forgiveness was off the table but a conversation with her friend was on her radar. Maybe once she returned from Peshawar she could sort out the details of her aching heart.

Once they'd checked in, the girls decided to meet at Lizzy's room in an hour. She collapsed for a twenty-minute nap before taking a quick shower. By the time she was dressed, there were shrieks at the door. Oh boy. This was going to be an interesting day trip.

Lizzy swung the door open. "Son of a biscuit! You're not wearing that!"

Brianna stepped in wearing a teeny black tank top and jeans. "What? All my bits are covered. I'm rocking the *Tomb Raider* vibe."

"Barely! We're in a Muslim town, you crazy Irish beserker. Don't move, I'll find something in my bag."

Suzie slipped in the room next. At least she wore a loose T-shirt. It still wouldn't cut it.

Lizzy threw a black, long-sleeved, Nike shirt at Brianna. "Try that on. Let's hope you get it over those giant boobs."

"Leave my tits alone! The ladies are a perfect size. Cost a lot of money to get them to look this pretty." Then Brianna groaned as she stared at the tiny piece of material. "Like I'll fit in this. You're like a tiny bad-ass snow fairy...with attitude. Do you shop in the bloody kid's department?"

Lizzy had in the past. It was fun buying the occasional My Little Pony T-shirt covered in pink glitter.

Suzie traced Lizzy's shoulder. "Look at what you're wearing—you look like a Pakistani fashion model in your waistcoat thingy."

"It's called a scraf."

Lizzy wore a dusty pink kurti—a loose, long blouse—over fitted blue jeans, paired with a soft cream waistcoat known as a scraf in Asia. Her favorite brown sandals finished the look.

Brianna wiggled and groaned as she pulled the shirt over her head. It was a tight fit. Her breasts pressed together, threatening an escape. Lizzy yanked up the front and draped a large pashmina over Brianna's "girls." At least she wore a tank underneath.

Now for Suzie. Lizzy had nothing left in her trolley bag of tricks, but she was pretty sure the front desk would help. "We'll pick up a scarf for you at reception."

"I'm not wearing some used smelly-ass scarf!"

"Then you're not going. This is Peshawar. You need to cover your hair—out of respect for the locals. There's always the telly." Lizzy picked up the remote.

Suzie huffed out a breath. "Fine. But I get to choose."

The rickshaw dropped them off in Clock Tower Square. Brianna scurried into the first rug stall and the other girls followed. The locals seemed friendly, and the store owner immediately offered them a traditional green tea. Lizzy loved the sweet tea native to Pakistan so she gladly accepted. Suzie turned her nose up and Lizzy quickly drank it to ease her companion's faux pas. Lizzy had brought her digital Canon along and snapped photos along the way. The expensive camera had been a gift from her father on her last birthday and she loved it, thinking maybe someday she'd write a travel book.

The narrow streets crammed with wares were an overload on the senses. Donkeys clattered among bearded men in turbans selling their textiles. A pakol hat maker tried to sell her a hat as she dodged a moped bike. The decaying Sikh architecture littering the gray and brown streets was fascinating. Unstable wooden buildings were stacked together in grimy colors. Wires, phone lines and old Bollywood signs hung from above. She snapped away.

Brianna couldn't find the right rug for her apartment and the day wore on. After they left the third bazaar, Lizzy put her foot down.

"Sadar Road!" she yelled at a driver as they climbed in yet another taxi.

"Apparently they have the best kebabs and fried fish. I'm not doing this without food in my stomach, plus I need to buy some fabric, so your Persian rugs need to wait."

"I could eat a reverend mother," Brianna said. "Lead the way. We'll rest our asses while you buy your materials and shit."

Lizzy left the girls at the café and bought a mix of bright fabrics in the square. She returned to Suzie giggling at something Brianna said.

"Asses up. We need to finish this gig. I'm running out of steam and need a hot shower."

Brianna pulled a face. "We're checking out that donkey."

Lizzy turned to see a mule with its front hooves flailing in the air. The overloaded cart strapped to its tiny frame pulled the poor beast off its feet. Lizzy's heart clenched at the cruel sight, and she looked away.

Brianna lurched to the side, her phone swaying erratically. "I need to snap a photo." Suzie guffawed with laughter.

Something was definitely up. The girls were acting sillier than usual. Suzie swayed as they got up. They linked hands and stumbled ahead of Lizzy. Brianna dragged Suzie's scarf off her head before trying to strangle her with it. Where they drunk? Or high?

"I'm too racked to look at anything else," Brianna yelled over her shoulder. "Let's head back to cockroach city."

They lurched into a shadowed alley and Lizzy ran to catch up. "What's going on?" She grabbed Brianna's arm. "You're acting crazy."

"And you're acting like a Muppet. What's wrong with a bit of fun?"

Lizzy smelled alcohol. "You've been drinking."

"Relax, we smuggled a few minis off the plane. We've even saved some for you!"

Brianna opened her satchel. At least twenty unopened bottles rolled around inside.

"Are you freaking crazy!" Lizzy's screech met their disappearing backs as Suzie dragged Brianna down the alley. If the local police found alcohol on their person, it could mean imprisonment—there would be zero leniencies for westerners. Respecting laws in other countries was essential to the job.

"Don't be a party pooper. This looks like a shortcut to the taxi rank. Beat you there!"

This wasn't good. Lizzy hesitated. Then she ran down the empty alley to catch up. Rounding a corner, she came up empty. The girls were gone. She should leave their stupid asses and head back to the hotel. A distant giggle led her up a hill. The roads were quieter on the back end of the bazaar. A shrouded woman watched from a doorway before shaking her head. A couple of kids paused to stare as she hurried past. Lizzy rushed past a fenced hedge, an iron gate leading to manicured gardens hung open. Brianna's shriek came from behind the hedge. Stepping into the private park, Lizzy called out to the women in a whispered shout. When no one answered, she made her way off the path towards a rustling thicket.

"BOO!" Suzie jumped out, staggering sideways in a fit of giggles.

"Son of a bucket!" Lizzy stumbled back. "Where's your silly sidekick?"

"Trying to untangle my scarf. It got caught up in a rose bush."

"For Pete's sake, lead the damn way."

Rounding a tree, Lizzy looked up and slowed. A towering mosque stood centered in the gardens, gleaming in the midday sun. Arabic yelling had her glancing back down and she slammed to a stop. A group of men surrounded Brianna as she held the scarf to her chest. Her handbag lay on the ground, glass bottles lay strewn across the grass. One of the men grabbed Brianna's sleeve and Lizzy leaped into the fray. "Leave the bag. Let's move."

The angry crowd quickly doubled in size and men screamed in Arabic. The horde shoved the three girls among them. Someone grabbed Lizzy's hair, and she screamed in terror. Bruising hands tried to tear them apart and Lizzy hung onto Brianna like a leech. If they were separated, they were done for.

Her screams were met by a slap to the face, as the growing swarm of men shoved her to the ground. Panicked regret turned to what could've been, as an image of John came to mind, then dissipated among the rabid shouts of violent men.

Mogadishu

There would be nothing left of them but crispy eco-skeletons if this heat continues, Johnny thought as he emerged back into the scorching shade after a cool shower. The rest of the team sat sprawled under the awning, also recovering from the intense morning training session. They'd shipped off another contingent of Somalian soldiers, trained and ready to fight rebel forces to the south. They occasionally worked alongside AFRICOM to stabilize the region, but as Tier One Operators they worked for a taskforce called MIT—Mobile Intelligence Team—which sat under the Joint Special Operations Command umbrella.

MIT targeted and quietly removed extremist leaders before their regimes had a chance to grow. Reduce an enemy's capacity to mount terror operations on US compounds or interests.

There were six MIT Teams situated around the globe, and

Johnny—a former 75th Ranger and medic—worked for MIT2, whose focus was East and Central Africa. Somalia, Kenya, Ethiopia, the Congo and Sudan. In almost three years, his team—under the command of Team Leader Erik "Max" Andersen—had dismantled three international extremist syndicates and provided intel on numerous targets. By eliminating the threats and extremist leaders, the region had a chance to stabilize.

His team had just finished a six-week round of teaching battlefield logistics within the Mogadishu compound, and he was ready to escape the arid military base that had been their home for almost two months. They shared the locked-down facility with four thousand sweaty soldiers and operators.

MIT2 would leave the compound to head to Rwanda for a couple of days before hitting their home base in Nairobi.

"Zero-beer-thirty. We're officially off-duty, big man, at least until Rwanda." Derek "Slater" Banez threw Johnny a water, followed by a beer, and Johnny slid onto a bench before stretching out his aching muscles.

Max tapped away furiously on his phone, probably messaging his pregnant wife back home. Donnie propped up his legs and watched two SAS boys working out in the sun. *Crazy British bastards.*

Slater took a long draw of his beer and settled back, closing his eyes. Johnny glanced worriedly at his usually jovial friend. His call sign had been given to him for good reason—he was named after the jock A.C. Slater in *Saved by the Bell* and was the quick-witted jokester in the group.

Over the past few months, Slater had changed. He looked burned out, still working through PTSD issues after rescuing teammates and civilians in the Black Friday bombing a couple of years before. And then three months ago, Slater's long-term girlfriend, Kathleen Flynn broke things off. Johnny and Slater had both commiserated through the past few gloomy months. Unlike Slater, Johnny would get his shit back on track and didn't need the headache that women brought to his already full table. He'd been foolish enough to think it would work out with Lizette Steyn. It hadn't, and it was time to move on.

Johnny watched as a pretty female walked past the tented courtyard. He recognized her as one of the new CIA operatives on base, and he kicked Slater's foot.

"What the hell, dude?" Slater cracked open an eye.

Johnny turned the top of his bottle towards the slim brunette who'd stopped to talk to the British contingent. "That's your kind of woman."

"How is that?"

"You like the ambitious, sophisticated, composed type—hell, you hit on Abby when you first met her."

Max's fingers paused.

Slater bristled. "That's bullshit. I felt bad for her—she's like my sister. Besides, Abby has a whole load more to her than just ambition and sophistication. She's cool and artsy and elegant and darn funny."

Max glanced up. "Easy on the wife compliments. I'll beat that soppy crush right out of you."

"Well, she's my type." Donnie nodded towards the agent. "My wife was classy, just like that. French girls are smoking hot."

Donnie mentioned his deceased wife more often these days, and Johnny wondered if the quiet operator was ready to dip his toe into the dating pool. It'd been a couple of years since her passing.

Johnny sat back. "She reminds me of Kat."

"Don't mention Kathleen's name, I'll pound you into the burning sand," Slater said.

"I'm just saying—"

"I know what you're saying. I screwed it all up, stay out of it. Besides, she's doing just fine without me. Probably in New York chasing her dreams. That was our problem. Kat's ambitious, I'm ambitious. It never worked out."

"I saw Kat the other day—shopping with a friend." Donnie said, crossing his legs.

Slater sat up. "Where?"

"Salt Lake, two months ago."

This was getting interesting. Slater was already considering moving to the city to be closer to Max.

"As in Salt Lake City, Utah?"

"Apparently she's living there now."

"The hell she is!" Slater shifted to the edge of his seat.

Taking a sip, Donnie stretched out his legs. "She's looking damn fine."

Slater launched to his feet.

"Relax, I'd never break the bro-code. She has a cute friend though. Blonde hair with pink highlights."

"Casey? Stay away from my cousin. Next thing I know, she's riding on the back of your motorized dick—"

"Relax, Slater, Donnie's not interested in Casey—he's yanking your chain." Max pocketed his phone.

"I am." Donnie grinned. "But next time, leave my Harley out of it."

Johnny's phone buzzed in his pocket just as Slater threw an empty water bottle at Donnie's head.

He stared at the number. His lips suddenly felt numb, and his hands, clumsy. *No fucking way.*

"You okay, buddy?" Max's voice penetrated his foggy brain.

"It's Lizzy. She's calling me."

Slater swore. "Well, answer!"

When she'd first moved to Kenya, he'd tracked down her number. He'd even used it to ping her phone a couple of times while covertly checking on her in the dangerous city of Nairobi. He'd gone so far as to hack her monthly flight schedule, downloading it to his phone. He hadn't spoken to her in six months and now he was about to hear that beautiful voice. He took a breath and pressed the screen. "Hello, angel."

"Is this John Calaway?"

The Middle Eastern male voice on the other end had Johnny's blood freezing. Not Lizzy.

"Where's the owner of this phone? Who is this?"

The men were on their feet as he struggled with a safe scenario of why a strange man had Lizzy's number. He ran over her schedule in his head. *Peshawar.* She was in fucking Peshawar. He was at least a six-hour plane ride away.

The man's next words were a punch to the gut. "My name is Javid Ibrahim, and Lizette Steyn is with me."

◊ ◊ ◊

Cold seeped up from the rough cement floor, and Lizzy wiggled her toes, trying to warm up the ice blocks that were now her feet. She shivered like a tuning fork, and her body thrummed as a cold breeze shifted the air. The sun had set hours ago, and the shouts outside the barred window had finally fallen silent.

The women were placed in separate rooms. Lizzy hadn't seen anyone since the phone call to John. That seemed like hours ago. Lizzy ignored the scuffling in a dark corner of the room—not wanting to know which critters crept in the shadows. Instead she focused on the grimy wall in front of her. Aside from smaller scrapes, her thigh throbbed in time with her racing heart. A well-placed kick from one of the attackers would result in a bruise the size of a plate.

She'd allowed them to call him, and if he came, he'd see her like this—weak and dirty. That was not how she'd imagined their next meeting. Instead, she'd imagined running into John in a market in Kenya. With a handsome stranger on her arm as she strolled in the bright sunlight looking tanned and happy.

In her nonsensical fantasy, John would pull her into his arms and beg for forgiveness. He'd drag her mouth to his; her legs would wrap around his strong waist as his large hands gripped her ass and settled her… Okay, that was so not what she should be focusing on, while huddled on a broken stool at the mercy of angry strangers in piss-ant Pakistan.

Lizzy gingerly adjusted the metal cuff that chained her sore wrist to the table. Her mind wandered back to Johannesburg—to the last time she'd seen John. The day she'd sent him away.

"Lizzy, I'm so goddamn sorry that I lied, that I didn't tell you sooner. If I could take it all back—"

"This isn't about us. I was in trouble long before you came along. I need space, maybe I'm running away, but it's what I need to do."

John pressed his business card into her hand. "That's my international number. If you ever need anything…"

Lizzy nodded as angry tears ran.

He led her to his car. Too soon they pulled up to her drive and Lizzy tamped down the heartbreak. She chose her last words carefully. "You're a good guy. You deserve someone great in your life. I hope you find peace."

He stared straight ahead as she studied his handsome profile. This gruff Samson was supposed to be her first. John should have been her

27

first and last. Instead he'd fallen between deceitful cracks and all that was left were bittersweet memories. Lizzy kissed him on the cheek. "For what it's worth, I loved you too."

In a haze, she climbed out, shut the door and walked out of his life.

The willpower to fully exorcise him from her world failed her at the first turn when later that same night, she'd dug out his business card, stroked his name and memorized the number.

Now her willpower failed her again—months later—when she gave John's number to Javid Ibrahim the man who had rescued the women and had crouched in front of her and asked who else she wanted to call. Apparently, Ethan Matthews, the CEO of JetHaven and the man she worked for, wasn't answering his cell, and the JetHaven office phone went straight to voicemail. Captain Stuart and the first officer weren't answering the phones in their rooms. Her father could never know. He worried enough about his daughter living so far from home.

The only man who could get her safely back to Kenya was John Calaway. All she knew about John was that he worked for an American covert team stationed in East Africa. Lizzy was betting on his spook connections. John was probably out in the field. If he didn't come, perhaps he could send a rescue team of sorts.

If help didn't arrive soon, the women would be transported to a holding facility, and Lizzy had a feeling that the prison system would suck them in like quicksand.

Javid entered the room, placing an open bottle of water in front of her. Lizzy drank while studying his white Punjabi suit— traditional Pakistani clothing that looked like a pajama set. Spotless and clean compared to her now torn and sullied outfit.

"Have you heard anything?"

"Not yet. We are running out of time." Javid adjusted the pakol perched on his head. "Once the news reaches Inter-Services Intelligence headquarters, they'll send police officers to pick you up. My fear is that the men who come will be corrupt." Tension in the room ratcheted up.

The two drunk girls wandering into the local mosque's gardens had gotten Lizzy into this mess. It was considered sacrilege for female non-Muslims to trespass on holy property. Brianna's satchel full of alcohol ramped up the charges.

The mob of men that attacked Lizzy, Suzie and Brianna intended to stone the girls to death. Thankfully, they had been shoved aside by Javid and his class of moderate scholars. Javid taught at the Dar al-nur Masjid Madrasa, an Islamic school for religious instruction, which sat next door to the mosque.

Javid and his men had raced the women to an older abandoned seminary three blocks away, before the growing crowd of protesters could catch up.

Two officials from the local town council insisted on detaining the females until law enforcement placed them under arrest. Now it was a waiting game. If the mob had their way, Lizzy and her partners in crime could be jailed or put to death, and those morbid possibilities had her shaking in her chair.

"Why can't I see my friends?"

"It is not up to me. I am trying to help as much as possible, but you are considered to be detainees. Risking that phone call to your man friend earlier may get me arrested."

Loud voices in the passage had Javid on his feet.

"Mr. Ibrahim," Lizzy called. "Regardless of what happens, thank you for your help."

Javid nodded once before stepping out the door.

Straining her ears, Lizzy made out an American accent. The

voices switched between English and Arabic. Lizzy's stomach somersaulted, and her palms grew damp. Was John on the other side of that door? A part of her prayed he was, another part screamed no. Lizzy wasn't ready to see him again.

Time dragged as negotiations rose and fell. Finally, the door opened and a man stepped through, carrying a bottle of water.

She registered cargo pants, a black T-shirt and gray hoodie. The large build seemed fleetingly familiar until the man stepped into the light. Not John, but a soldier with the same hardened look, like he owned the small space and any other territory his alpha boots stepped on.

Inky eyes assessed her, seeming almost black in the dim light.

"Are you injured?"

Lizzy swallowed back the relief at his American accent and he repeated his question.

"Are you hurt?"

"No."

He spoke over his shoulder. "They cuffed her, and they've used a Darby 121. He won't be happy about that."

A second man stepped through the doorway. His white-blond hair glowed in the dim light and contrasted with the sooty-haired giant standing before her.

"Yeah, well, there's one of him and four of us. We'll calm him. Is that table nailed to the floor?"

"Yip. We'll retrieve the bolt cutters from the truck if this shit isn't resolved."

"What's a Darby 121?" Lizzy asked.

"Discontinued handcuffs only used in a sprinkling of third world countries," the brute said, twisting off a cap and handing her an open water bottle. "You need to keep hydrated."

"Are you with John? Are the other girls okay?"

He ignored the questions as he examined her wrist, before speaking again to his teammate. "It's interfering with circulation—fastened way too tight."

Lizzy tried again to get his attention. "What's your name?"

"Ryker."

"And your angelic friend standing in the doorway, looking like he's gonna sprout wings?"

"What the—?" Choir Boy stepped forward.

Ryker snorted. "That's Phoenix. Under all that angel dust, he's one tough mother. We've both got your back…even though you and your tipsy fucking friends got yourselves into this."

"I didn't know they had alcohol on them."

Ryker stood up. "Yeah? You should've just stayed at the hotel."

Her eyes burned with unshed tears.

"Don't get your pink panties in a knot. Be patient. We're on the other side of the door if you need us. I need to make a few calls to smooth the way. Phoenix will check on your two cabin mates and find the official with the key to that." He pointed to the cuff.

"What time is it?" Lizzy asked, shifting her numbing ass.

"2100 hours."

She'd been locked in this room for six hours. Trust didn't come easily, but the two big warriors were all she had. Lizzy reached out with her free arm and grabbed Ryker's hand. "Thank you. I'm darn terrified. If I get out of this, I'll hunt you down and buy your team a lunch. Complete with Heineken beers and double malted milkshakes, and whatever dessert you want. I can bake. I'll make a Malva Pudding. It's a South African recipe that's all syrupy and—"

"Enough." Ryker released her hand, smiling. "It's a deal.

Regardless of pudding, we're not going anywhere." He paused at the door. "Do you want us to call your family?"

"No. They'll just worry."

Ryker stepped out. Phoenix winked at Lizzy as he closed the door. "Later, Puddin'."

Ten minutes later, Phoenix looked on as a surly local pulled out a key and loosened the cuff. After they left, Lizzy waited and waited. Despite the cold permeating stiff joints, she dozed off, waking suddenly to a warm hand on her knee. Oh, God. John was there. So solid and male as he filled her vision. His hand cradled her cheek as his rich brown eyes blazed with savage fire.

"You feel like ice. Where's your damn scarf?"

First words in six months and that's what he says.

"I—I don't know. I guess at some point it was yanked off?"

"Max, she's shaking like a leaf. Find an asshole with a blanket, robe, jacket. I don't care, find something, she's a mess. My jacket is in the car."

A shadow moved. Max was here? And apparently Lizzy looked like a "mess." Just the impression she was going for.

"I'm fine," she said as she drank in the man before her, almost wanting to run hands through his thick brown hair.

"You're fine?" John's voice raised an octave, as he yanked up her thin sleeve. "You're littered in bruises; your clothes are all torn up. Look at your wrist, look at it!"

Lizzy spoke carefully. "I'm aware of what I look like—feel like—believe me. Considering the circumstances, I'm just peachy."

"Peachy, Peachy!" He stood and towered over her.

"You don't have to yell."

"Do you know where they wanna take you? The next stop is an ISI interrogation room. You don't have a clue what that is.

32

It's like a medieval torturing facility in the middle of bum-fuck nowhere! One of the town idiots out there thinks you're an American spy."

"I know this is bad—"

"That doesn't begin to cover it. You've literally caused an international incident." John pointed at the closed door. "I have four agencies and the Pakistani Police Force involved. I've dragged fellow task members into this mess, men who were trailing a high-value target in Afghanistan and instead had to race here to rescue a spoiled only child. A little girl who's up for a Darwin Award for staggering around Peshawar in a drunk haze!"

"That's a rotten thing to say!"

"Oh, I'm sorry, princess, when I get a phone call from some random guy telling me that you've been attacked by an angry mob, and then I sit on a goddamn plane for six hours wondering if you'll still be in one piece by the time I get here, I kind of lose my shit!"

"I wasn't the one drinking! I didn't even know they had the bottles. I tried to get us back to the hotel." Lizzy kicked him in his perfect shin.

He swore, turned and paced the room. "I know, Ryker told me."

"Then why did you say—"

"Because if we can't extract you tonight, then I might as well toss my life away. I'll infiltrate every facility I can to find you."

"It won't get to that." Max entered the room, rounded the table, and gently placed a large jacket over Lizzy's chilled arms. "IG Kashmir is in the other room."

"Thank God." John ran frustrated hands through his hair.

"What's an IG Kashmir?" Lizzy asked.

"Here, drink." Max jammed a straw into a juice box. "IG

stands for Inspector General—Inspector General of Police. Faisal Kashmir heads up the KP Police. He's an ally."

Lizzy took a long sip of the mango-flavored juice. John stared through rusted bars onto the street below.

"Johnny, a word?" Max said.

"I'm not leaving her."

"In the hall, now. This isn't our jurisdiction. We'll need to cooperate."

John stepped out. Lizzy finished the juice. Played with the straw as time dragged by.

Max walked in followed by John, Ryker, Javid and a man she didn't recognize who wore a navy jacket and matching beret decorated with ranks and insignia. Crossed silver swords decorated his shoulder. He gave her a gruff look before tossing a file on the table and taking a chair opposite. This must be the IG Kashmir guy. Lizzy remembered his name because it sounded like the word *cashmere*.

He opened the file and threw her passport on the table. They'd removed it from her person earlier. A photocopy version lay in the file along with a thin pile of paperwork. He grumbled as he sorted through documents.

"Lizette Steyn. You've caused a great headache for me, this night. What do you have to say for yourself?"

Lizzy looked at him blankly. "That I'm sorry?"

He raised a thick brow.

"No, I really am. It has to be like one in the morning, and I'm sure you have a family waiting for you at home. Please apologize to your lovely wife. If you're not married, well then, I apologize for saying that you are. In any case, I'm sorry for keeping you—"

"Lizzy, enough." John growled.

IG Kashmir raised the other brow before bursting into laughter. "I'm married with three children, so I take no offense. You're a funny little thing, aren't you?"

Great, of course her diminutive size was mentioned. Lizzy flashed a polite smile as he extracted a form and handed it over.

"You will need to sign this statement."

Lizzy looked to John for confirmation and he nodded. Arms crossed, he looked formidable standing in the shadows.

"What does it say?"

"Firstly, that you were unaware of the mini bottles of whisky, or that the other two cabin attendants were consuming the alcohol. Secondly that you did not intentionally wander onto holy ground." Kashmir handed her a pen and showed her where to initial.

Both statements were true enough, but Lizzy paused before signing her name.

"Lizbug…" John warned.

"What happens to my friends?"

"They are not your concern." Kashmir nudged the paper.

"Sign the damn thing," John snapped.

"What will happen to them?"

"They are in measurably more trouble than you. Intoxication in public, trespassing on mosque grounds while inebriated, comes with serious charges."

The pen trembled. "I can't leave them."

"I swear to God—" John erupted and Max stepped into the foray, touching her shaking wrist. His pale gray eyes pinned her with a magnetic stare.

"We've contacted their respective embassies in Pakistan. Your boss—Ethan Matthews—is flying into Pakistan tomorrow. His legal team is landing in Karachi tonight. Refusing to sign this statement will not make one ounce of difference to their situation. In fact, it will make it more difficult. The legal counsel needs to focus on just two of them."

Lizzy held back hiccupping tears as she placed the pen down, needing time to think. "This was Suzie's third flight." Lizzy grasped the IG's wrist and he looked up. "She's sheltered and naive, and so young. Don't let them lock her away for one stupid decision."

"People make stupid decisions every day. My overflowing prisons are evidence of that." Kashmir pulled his hand back and picked up the pen. "Don't let me add your name to that list, Lizette Steyn."

"Promise me you'll protect them best you can."

"I have a town full of angry citizens demanding justice, but I will try my best."

Lizzy signed her name in a blur, and Kashmir gathered the papers. "I don't want to see you in my city again, Miss Steyn. I suggest you bid for other flights in future. You've been flagged by Inter-Services Intelligence."

John stepped in the IG's way. "Get that cuff off her. Now."

Kashmir nodded. "I'll send someone in."

The men left. John sat down in the chair opposite. She ignored him. Frustration at the girls' predicament had her simmering.

"Once we've transported you to a safe facility, we'll get you checked out. Aside from feeling a little battered, are you okay to walk?"

"Look at you, sweeping in to rescue me—again—even when I don't want you anywhere near." Lizzy regretted the words the second they spilled from her acidic mouth. That was a mean thing to say and she flinched at the sudden hurt in his eyes. "I'm sorry I sa—"

He spoke carefully over her apology.

"We're never going to get past Johannesburg, are we?"

"Don't bring up South Africa. This isn't the place."

He studied the table. "I can't do this anymore."

"Do what?"

"Care. Worry about your life, worry about your soul. This is too hard."

"What are you talking about? We haven't seen each other in over six months."

He rubbed a thumb over a knuckle. "Your last flight was to Rwanda. Before that you flew to Iraq. I have your damn roster memorized. You took a vacation two months ago in Mauritius, with your parents." He looked grim.

"John—"

"I know it seems stalkerish, but the reality is that I want you safe. Your job isn't anywhere near safe, and it kills me not knowing where you are." His mouth turned further down at the corners as he shrugged. "I can't be your guardian and move on with my life—or meet someone else. I need to let go of us."

He stood, and panic took hold. Her eyes welled. He refused to look up.

"You're leaving me here."

"Never. I trust my task-force brothers to look after you. We'll get you home, and then it's all up to you."

"What I said just now, that was unfair, and it was a lie." Lizzy tried to stand. The handcuff stopped her, her thigh locked up and she cried out from pain.

"Fuck!" He clenched a fist, raising it to punch the wall, instead he lowered his arm and paced the room. His muscles quivered with tempered rage.

Lizzy wasn't scared. The realization had her sitting back

down. She'd never been afraid of this man, only of the hidden possibilities of their unknown future. The past six months were a hiatus, where she slowly found her way back to forgiving him. Ironically, he'd used the time to find an escape from her.

She'd pushed away this beautiful warrior, with good reason, and now it was too late. She'd never see him again. That hurt more than anything Ivan or any other human could ever do to her.

John slid down and crouched against the wall. She searched for the right words, her mind still stumbling for rationality after struggling through the past eight hours.

John stood. "Be safe, Lizbug."

"Please don't go."

He walked away, and she lost it.

Lizzy shouted his name to a closing door. Her shout turned into a wail and Lizzy wept, shame ripping her heart from its foolish position, her sobs ringing through the lonely space.

She despised herself in that moment. John was right; she was a sniveling and selfish princess who'd learned nothing since moving to Kenya. Still demanding of others—still pathetically lost.

Ryker came in and unlocked the biting cuff before shuffling her out. Her thigh muscle spasmed from sitting for so long, and her leg collapsed. Phoenix swept her up, carrying her to the vehicle as Lizzy gritted her teeth from the pain.

Chapter Two

Not much got to Johnny. He liked to think he was a balanced soldier who'd seen a lot in his military career. Any challenging experiences in the field usually got resolved by physical work when Johnny returned home to his Wyoming cabin. The empty solitude had a way of flushing away the blackness of war from one's soul.

Looking into those troubled blue eyes and the sound of Lizzy's sobs echoing in that dingy room had him wanting to put a fist through the wall. Johnny paced the hallway, waiting for the local men to liberate her from their obsolete confinement.

Javid Ibrahim watched him carefully from down the hall. Johnny paused, then approached him. "Thank you for rescuing them." He swallowed before continuing. "Without your help, they would've been stoned or beaten to death."

Javid nodded once. Johnny reached into his back pocket. "If you ever need any—"

"I need you to look after Miss Steyn."

"Excuse me?"

"I see the way you look at her, and the way she looks at you."

"I won't be seeing her again."

"Well, that's a shame. Her soul is a rare one, she is pure of heart. She deserves nothing but peace and kindness."

Johnny agreed but didn't know how to respond. Max walked up and thumped him on the shoulder. "Ryker has the key. They'll be slipping out of the rear alley. I'll meet you at the truck."

Johnny looked away. If he hesitated, he'd storm in there and carry her out like a territorial caveman, so he left the team to their job and exploded down the stairs, slamming through the back exit.

Once inside the vehicle, he scanned for potential threats.

Lizzy's American citizenship saved her from the same fate as the others. If she was from any other country it wouldn't have been that easy. Pakistan's good relations with America had played a major role in the negotiations.

Thankfully due to her passport origin, MIT headquarters had been given the green light and assigned the closest team to the rescue. MIT3, under the command of Devon "Ryker" Stone, operated out of Afghanistan, had flown in their assistance.

Without MIT3's interference, Lizzy would've been thrown into a local prison and Johnny would have arrived too late. It would have been weeks or even months before they'd gained access to her.

Peshawar prison conditions could easily break a trained operative, never mind a civilian. And God only knows how they'd treat a Western woman. Johnny wouldn't relax until she was out of country.

MIT3 were transporting her to an undisclosed location for the night, a safe house they occasionally used. Johnny had the coordinates. In the morning, she'd fly out to Kenya on a private jet.

Max approached the truck and slipped into the passenger

seat. "Any potential threats in the area?"

"Nope. Looks like the zealous troublemakers have retired for the night. There are a couple of stragglers out front, across the way."

Max grabbed a gummy worm from an open packet and shot Johnny a look that had him glaring back.

"Don't look at me with those zombie-ass eyes, I'm about to lose my shit."

"I wasn't gonna say anything." Max shoved fruity worms into his mouth.

"Sure, you weren't, just spit it out." He waited impatiently for Max to swallow.

"The last time you'll ever see her, and that's how it goes down?"

"I can't do this roller-coaster shit anymore. That woman lights a bonfire in my brain. No one has ever burrowed that far into my head. I haven't had contact with her in months, and she still has the ability to trigger every caveman instinct that I possess."

Max looked out the window. "Hell, I'm not good at this touchy-feely stuff. What do you want, Johnny? Where do you see yourself in five years? Sitting on the farm in Wyoming? Who's sitting next to you?"

"Don't ask me that, because I want something I can't have."

The door opened, and Ryker emerged. Phoenix followed behind, carrying a fragile Lizzy. It should be him, not Phoenix holding her. Her skin was still as soft as he'd remembered. One stroke to her cheek in that dark room, and he'd wanted to drag her into his arms.

That option wasn't on the table, not since Johannesburg. Lizzy was right. He had neglected to protect her. Because of his failure to tell her who he really was, or to warn her of the potential risks surrounding her friend, he'd almost gotten her killed in a gunfight. Her choice to banish him from her life wasn't unwarranted. She deserved to be safe.

The remaining MIT3 members watched their six. The alley remained quiet as the team settled her in the back of a white van. Once the vehicle pulled off, Johnny pulled in behind, planning to follow them out of the square, and then circle away towards the private airfield they'd utilized earlier in the night.

Max wouldn't let up. "You're working with a team, yet you're living in a separate space in that giant macho head."

"I know. Lizzy has a hold on me, and I'm trying to move on. I can't do this anymore, it's unhealthy."

Max snorted. "Well then talk to the lady."

"It's my fault she took the job with JetHaven and moved to Kenya. If I'd told her sooner who we were, then maybe she wouldn't have run away."

"So, you're saying this is just about responsibility? That you flew here on a six-hour trip because of guilt?"

"Ah, shit. Screw you." Johnny punched the wheel, then turned left instead of right, ignoring Max's resulting grin.

◊ ◊ ◊

Phoenix laid her on a soft mattress. Lizzy protested and immediately sat up. "I need to shower."

"Don't you want to eat something?"

"I can't think of food, I need to get clean."

"We're here for the next five hours. Get some shut-eye and I'll wake you an hour before we leave."

Lizzy ignored him and shifted to the side of the bed. Phoenix laid a hand on her shoulder. "Easy, Puddin', the shower isn't going anywhere. You need to rest."

"If the lady wants a shower, she gets a shower." John stepped in the room and Lizzy stilled then turned away.

"You left me there."

"I never left, I was there the whole time."

Her leg ached, and Lizzy stretched it out gingerly.

Phoenix sat on the edge of the bed and grasped her thigh. "Where does it hurt?'

"What are you doing?" John moved around the bed.

"She has muscle spasms from sitting so long."

"You mean sitting in the freezing-ass cold. Because no one on your team thought to find her a damn jacket until I arrived. Take your hands off her, I've got this."

"I'm the medic on 3."

"Well then, make yourself useful and look at her wrist. I've got the leg."

"The two of you are like mother hens. I have a bruised leg and some cramps, big deal. I sat on a chair for eight hours, I didn't go to fricking war! Get out of my way, I need to use the bathroom."

John and Phoenix reluctantly stepped back as she hobbled to the bathroom. "Don't you boys have soldiery things to do? Climb a fence? Crawl under barbwire? Go do that and leave me the hell alone!"

◊ ◊ ◊

"Well, that went smoothly," Phoenix said, rocking back on his heels.

Johnny walked to the bathroom door. "Max is swinging past the hotel to pick up your things. When he gets here, I'll leave your bag outside the door."

A grunt was the only response.

"You're not her most favorite person. What did you do? Dump her ass in a past life?"

Johnny rounded on the cocky medic. "I'll dump your ass at the bottom of a ravine if you don't back the hell off."

"Why should I? She's cute, and…available."

"She's been through a shitload and I'm not referring to Peshawar. If you exploit that vulnerability, you and I will have more than just words."

"I can still hear you!" Lizzy yelled. "Vulnerable, my ass! Take your posturing somewhere else and leave me in peace."

Phoenix grunted and slapped Johnny on the back as he walked out the door.

Johnny sank onto the comfy duvet and rested his worn-out head.

Thirty minutes later and the water was still running. Max walked in and deposited the trolley bag on the bed. "Is she still alive in there?"

"Hell, if I know." Johnny rolled his ass into an upright position.

"When you're ready, there's a whole spread of food in the kitchen. I'll be out there, with the boys."

Johnny ran a hand over his head and nodded.

"Lizbug, are you doing okay?" Nothing. He tapped on the door. "If you don't answer, I'm coming in."

The water turned off. "Hold your giant horses, I'll be out in a minute." The sink faucet turned on. "Fudge berries! I need my damn stuff."

Johnny was grabbing her luggage when the bathroom door swung open behind him. "Just hand it over."

He froze. A large towel engulfed her tiny frame, leaving just her arms and shoulders exposed. The scratched-up skin had his attention. Marks inflicted by men intent on killing her, beating her into the ground. It had been so close. Red-rimmed eyes challenged him to look away; instead he lowered the carry-on and stepped forward.

Lizzy narrowed those same eyes, snatched the bag away and scuttled back into the bathroom.

"Oh no, you don't. Get back here. Those lacerations need to be looked at."

"Hand me antiseptic ointment through the door. I'm sure swarthy warriors like you carry medical kits the size of small tanks."

"Please let me help."

"John, for the love of God. I need a moment to myself, without large men looming over me. I need space."

Her voice broke on the last word and he gritted his teeth in frustration. Yeah, being mauled by a gang of rabid men would justify her claustrophobic freak-out. *Space* was what he gave her. He popped the heavy military-issued medical kit through the door. Plenty of ointments and antibiotic salves lined the pockets.

Lizzy knew what to do. She'd almost completed a nursing degree a few years back, until her ex-fiancé, Ivan Chasov, flew off the handle and tried to kill her. The psychological damage from the incident must have had her spiraling into a lost haze. Johnny didn't know the details of that night.

Out of respect, he'd stayed away from investigating her harrowing past; it was her story to tell. But three months ago, Ivan Chasov had been released from prison, and the bastard was on Johnny's radar. Intel indicated that Ivan had moved up to Nigeria, and was currently working with a subcontractor for an oil rig near Lagos.

Finally, Lizzy emerged, looking washed out. Her skin shone

pale against a neon pink off-the-shoulder sweatshirt that spelled *RAD* on the front in giant lettering. It hung mid-thigh over black leggings. She still had an obsession for the eighties and nineties.

That quirkiness was what attracted him to the blonde bombshell in the first place. Lizette Steyn was a puzzle he could never quite figure out.

An energetic tomboy one minute, then a retro fashion model the next, adorned with flashy jewelry and happy colors. Sparkly, then serious. Kind yet highly strung, with a fragility that ran parallel with a tough-as-nails streak. His Lizzy was a messy ball of twine made up of contrasting colors and textures.

Hell and shit. Lizzy was not his, not by any stretch. Six months ago, she'd made very sure of that.

◊ ◊ ◊

Standing awkwardly, Lizzy tried to ignore the larger-than-life operator and concentrated on drying her hair. That steamy water had felt like heaven—she'd never felt so grateful for a warm shower. She considered herself the luckiest person in Pakistan that night. Which made her think of Brianna and Suzie. They were the unluckiest. She should've stayed with them, but Max was right. She'd have just gotten in the way. Worry for their safety sat heavy on her heart.

"Do you want me to leave?"

Lizzy shook her head. "I'll probably be asleep in five." She pulled damp locks over her shoulder and dried them with a towel.

"I'll bring you some food. It's all local—"

"I like local. Thanks."

John turned to leave.

"I knew you were watching me," she said.

He paused, and she climbed on the bed and continued.

"You were at a market in Kenya once. I swore I caught a glimpse of you. There were a couple more times after that. On a layover to Tanzania. I liked knowing that you still looked out for me. I played silly games, thinking that you'd be around for good."

"We both played games. Mine were of the deadlier variety and I nearly got you killed. You were right, I dragged you into a shitstorm in Johannesburg. You almost died."

Playing with her sleeve, Lizzy looked up. "That's why I called you, because I knew you'd save me from this Pakistani shitstorm. Save a foolish girl who doesn't deserve saving."

"You've never been foolish. Brave, lost, but never foolish." John sat on the edge of the bed. Brawny arms rippled as he resituated himself.

"You've grown. I mean in size. You were defined before, but you're now seriously all muscle."

"The team has been working long hours—training long hours too."

He tucked a curl behind her ear, his warm hand felt good against her still chilled skin. "I miss you, Lizbug. This suspended state isn't good for us."

"I know. I'm sorry that I was so mean—back in that miserable room. You came for me, you actually came."

He sat so close. She ached to trace the small scar on the edge of his eye. She missed that familiar face and his direct regard. His coppery eyes stared back with glowing intensity. "Why are you still so angry with me?" he asked.

She lay back and stared at the ceiling. "Because you threw us away. You chose your dangerous job over my safety. We were just getting started, with what I thought was an incredibly real relationship. Instead it was all based on deceit, and everyone was in on the macabre joke but me." Anger swelled as she thought back on the heartbreak.

"Lizzy—"

"Don't! Before you snuck into my life, I was engaged to a man who lived a lie, and when it caught up to him, he turned on me. You were the first man I trusted after that, and you played with my healing heart. I don't even know how much of that was you. Was it all an elaborate act?"

John rubbed his neck. "I intended it to be that way, but the instant you landed on me, like a missile falling from that giant oak, that moment you fell into my life—I knew I was screwed."

She closed her eyes and took a breath.

He rose. "I'm hurting you again. You and I both need sleep. Let's table this for the morning."

Lizzy rose to her elbow. "How about a reset?"

"A what?"

"A reset. We start fresh. I let go of the anger and we get to know each other again—as friends." She ignored his frown, stood and stretched out her hand. "Hi, I'm Lizette Steyn. I'm from Johannesburg—well, actually I was born in California. I'm in Pakistan on business. Bad business. You seem nice. You're super tall, what should I call you? Tank? I have a feeling you'll probably end up calling me something odd like Lizbug—that's okay—I don't mind the nickname. I hope we can be friends. I need a friend, around about now."

He chuckled. She waited with her arm dangling between them.

A broad hand engulfed hers with a firm shake. "My name is James Cane."

Her eyes widened in surprise. "Sheez kebab! Is that your real name?"

"Yes, ma'am. The one my mama gave me."

She dragged him by the hand and crawled onto the far side of the bed. He followed, situating himself alongside her.

"James. It suits you. I could call you Jay Jay."

"Jay Jay?"

"Yes. Short for James Johnny." Lizzy unscrewed a water bottle.

"Don't be a smart-ass."

"Why do they call you Johnny?"

"It's how I'm known in the field. The majority of the time, that's my name. It's an integral part of who I am."

"But why Johnny?"

"It's pretty obvious…"

"Big John? From Robin Hood?"

"Yip. My previous team leader slapped me with it." He yawned and took a sip from her water.

"I think it suits you, but why not a crazy call sign like Crash or Wookie or Big Dick."

John spewed water.

"What? I've felt you up before. Granted we didn't get far enough for me to actually see it, but it felt really, really generous. Don't you remember our groping sessions? I'm thinking you're hung like a dinosaur."

"Holy moly, Lizbug!" He swept water off his lap, trying to cover the obvious woody tenting up his pants.

"What?" She grinned innocently.

He narrowed his eyes. "I remember running my hands over your hot little body, and I've thought about that many times since."

She shifted uncomfortably at his words.

Clearing his throat, he then explained, "Covert teams need to blend in, adopt names that sound real enough. If I'm interacting with a suspect—a target—I use an effective alias that provides a solid cover. Crash Cane won't exactly cut it."

"Where does Max get his name from?"

John resettled. "He does everything to the max. His brain is a machine, and he's incredible with languages. His real name is Erik."

"And the cocky ladies' man on your team? The one who seemed all handsy with Abby in Johannesburg?"

"Slater. From the eighties TV show—"

"Oh my gosh! *Saved by the Bell*, I can see that."

John raised his brows.

"Hey, I don't just listen to eighties music. My dad made me watch all the old shows as a kid. He has a whole library of eighties paraphernalia. That's how I got hooked."

John yawned again. "Honey, we need to rest."

"Aren't there four of you on the team? I've only caught a glimpse of that other serious dude. The one with the goatee."

"That's Dave, known as Donnie in the field. We're all proficient in martial arts but Donnie takes it to another level. Because of his combat skills, he's named after Donnie Yen Chitan—an actor and multiple-time world wushu tournament champion. Dave is our analyst."

"Will you leave again?" Lizzy asked sleepily as she settled onto her side, hugging a soft pillow.

"My team is heading to Rwanda for a couple of days, but I've been reassigned. I'll head back to our base in Kenya to set up some meetings for next month. I'm hitching a ride on the flight to Nairobi in the morning—with you."

"I'd like that. We're friends—on reset, remember? You won't leave me?"

"No. I'm just down the hall. We'll talk later. Sleep for a few."
He switched the light off and left the door ajar.

Alone in the dark, she thought about the other two flight
attendants awaiting their fate behind bars. Then her mind turned
to John and how tempted she'd been to run into his arms. Except
that embrace was dangerous. He would never hurt her physically,
but her heart? That was a different story.

◊ ◊ ◊

At six in the morning the streets were quiet. Two vehicles pulled
out; Lizzy sat in the back of the truck next to Johnny, and Max
sat up front as Ryker drove. The rest of the MIT3 team trailed
behind in a black SUV. Their plans had shifted. Lizzy would be
flying back on the MIT2 transport with Johnny and Max.

They'd take off from a private airstrip, land in Mogadishu to
drop Max off to meet up with the rest of the team and, once
refueled, Johnny would head on to Nairobi with Lizzy.

She'd snuggled up beside him, and dainty snores filled the
subdued space as her head lolled against his arm. Itching to wrap
that arm around the tiny blonde, Johnny turned instead to stare
into the dawning light.

Peshawar and its neighboring war zone wasn't Johnny's
favorite place. Too many violent memories, losing team
members over his earlier years in Afghanistan. He hated that
Lizzy was here. He wanted them gone.

"Thanks for the escort." Max said.

Ryker turned onto the main road. "No problem, bro, the
assignment includes a successful exfil—ensuring the asset is safely
on a plane. Once Lizette Steyn is airborne, we'll head back to the
Stan."

Johnny yawned into the ensuing silence, barely an hour's

worth of sleep had the men eager to get some shut-eye on their respective flights.

A foreign ringtone pierced the air, and Lizzy jerked awake.

"It's my boss calling. Gosh darn it." Lizzy mumbled cute obscenities as she scratched around in her bag for her phone.

The phone stopped ringing as she produced it from the satchel from hell, which had to contain the *The Da Vinci Code*, Johnny thought as he stared at what had tumbled out.

Lizzy repacked a mix of tampons, lipsticks, nail polish, carabiners, lollipops, teabags, fuzzy dice and a lucky troll keychain. "Ethan will be mad if I don't answer," she said as she shoved a pair of pantyhose into a front pocket.

Johnny frowned. Was she really calling Ethan Matthews by his first name?

Ethan Matthews ran JetHaven, a private security firm that provided tailored services to VIPs and diplomats in high-risk areas. Matthews ran a fleet of eleven luxury aircraft for ferrying top-paying dogs. When Lizzy first started working for the billionaire executive, Johnny had run extensive background checks on Matthews. By all appearances, he ran a relatively clean operation.

The phone rang again.

"Hand me the phone, Lizzy," Max said.

"Why?"

"I need to speak to Matthews."

She hesitated.

Max pushed. "Do you still want to work for JetHaven?"

"Of course."

"Then hand me the phone."

"Mach 1, not Mach 5?" Johnny said to Max.

"Sure," Max said as he took the phone.

"What does that mean?" she asked.

"It means Max will dial it back."

"As opposed to?"

Max settled back to answer. Ryker shot him an amused glance, turning onto a dirt road.

"Mr. Matthews, nice of you to finally call…It doesn't matter who I am, let's just say, I'm involved in the extraction of Lizette Steyn. Tell me, are you still enjoying the spoils of Paris?"

Lizzy gasped and surged forward.

Johnny pushed her back. "Trust us," he whispered.

Max rubbed the back of his neck. "I know exactly where you are. I also know that you neglected to answer any calls for over four hours, neither from the men who held your cabin crew, nor from three different agencies." He spoke over tinny shouts. "Your captain and first officer never answered calls either, instead enjoying a visit to a whorehouse. Aren't they supposed to be your first line of defense? The crew is the captain's responsibility."

Lizzy gasped, and Max held up a hand as he listened to the asshole.

She turned to Johnny. "The flight crew were with prostitutes?"

"Their taxi driver confirmed it."

"You guys are thorough."

Johnny grinned. "We have to be in our line of work."

Max sat forward with sudden tension. "That's your defense? It's the women's fault for getting themselves into this in the first place? Where are your contingency plans for incidents that occur in foreign countries? Most major airlines have procedures in place. Cabin crew are humans—humans can behave erratically." Max snorted as Matthews ran on, then cut in. "Your legal team might be in Karachi, but Brianna Walsh and Susan Vorster are still in Peshawar. Would you like their exact location? I've had men watching the facility all night."

Lizzy looked at Johnny for confirmation and he nodded.

"Don't worry about Miss Steyn, she's been taken care of. She contained the incident as best she could. Without her common sense in the mix, you would be simmering in hotter shitting temperatures. Threatening her job or my team would be extremely unwise. JetHaven would be grounded within twenty-four hours, I'd make sure of that."

Johnny gave her a quick squeeze as she stared at Max with wide eyes.

"Matthews, I expect you to be in Peshawar by lunch. If not, I'll ensure that your company is nonoperational for the foreseeable future...Oh, and lastly, Lizette Steyn will need at least a week's worth of recuperation. Paid leave will be appreciated."

Max hung up.

"That was dialing it back?" she almost screeched.

Max twisted, handing the phone back. "Ethan Matthews is now worried about covering his shit-don't-stink ass, instead of focusing on using you as a scapegoat. He would've blamed and fired you for the whole fiasco—you were the easiest mark. Firing you now will cause him a potential headache, especially now that a covert agency is invested in the outcome."

Johnny agreed. "He thinks he's a big turd in a little bowl. He now knows he's being observed."

"Thank you. I think." Her eyes flitted uncertainly between the men in the truck.

Turning in his seat, Max grabbed her wrist. "I don't give a damn about Ethan Matthews, but you? Different story. You're one of us, been that way since Johannesburg, even though we acted like a bunch of dicks. If your boss gives you any problems, you call me."

Johnny chuckled. "Close your mouth, Lizbug, you're gaping."

Rallying, Lizzy narrowed in on Max's light eyes. "You told Ethan you have someone looking after the girls?"

Ryker spoke up. "A couple of informants who work with my team. It's temporary, pretty soon it will be out of our control."

"I don't know what to say. Thank you."

They rolled up next to the runway, and relief shot through Johnny. He was taking his girl home, away from dingy cell blocks and shady oblivion.

He climbed from the vehicle, assessed their surroundings, then turned towards her. "Time to go, princess." She hesitated before grasping his hand, and Johnny pulled her into the bright sunlight.

Chapter Three

Nairobi
Two days later

Lizzy loved the view from her balcony. The small apartment on the second floor of the complex looked out onto manicured gardens and a field. City buildings and treetops spanned the horizon beyond the perimeter wall. Kids played soccer below. She took a sip of coffee and yelled out a greeting, feeling once more like a functional human. A human with a date—with a significantly larger human. It wasn't technically a date, just two friends going for lunch and treading carefully around the minefield of their past.

The trip back to Nairobi had been an awkward one. After takeoff, as Lizzy internally celebrated her successful release from the Peshawar nightmare and John snoozed in the corner, Max had slipped into the seat opposite.

"As far as Johannesburg goes, I'm sorry you were caught in the middle, but I wouldn't have done anything differently. We removed a dangerous terrorist, and shortly after, brought down his entire cell."

Lizzy nodded. "Abby's been emailing me constantly. I

haven't been ready to reply to her emails."

"I know, she's worried about you. We all are."

"She wrote that she's pregnant. That's fantastic news."

"Yeah. Four months." Max looked solemn.

"What aren't you telling me?"

"Due to her traumatic history, it's a high-risk pregnancy."

"And you're here—not there with her."

"That about sums it up." Max had turned away but not before she saw the flash of fear.

The capable soldier loved her friend. She was glad for Abby. They deserved a happy life. Lizzy worried over Abby's health, and a possible phone call to her estranged friend lay in Lizzy's future.

She splashed the pot of long-dead carnations with the last of her coffee and stretched before walking inside. A quick cleaning spree might be in order, she thought as she surveyed the untidy chaos. Not that John would notice, he was as messy as she was. She didn't consider herself dirty; she cleaned the place regularly with a mother-load of bleach, but she was messy by nature— leaving clothes and magazines scattered about.

The place still looked cheerful, thanks to her color scheme. Indigo blue, yellow and white accents gave the living area a sunny feel. Ever-changing light shining through the two floor-to-ceiling windows made it seem larger than it was.

She'd woken up late, so after stuffing clothes into messy drawers, she leaped into the shower, then threw on black fitted pants with a khaki green button-up shirt and matching wedge sandals. Kenya's warm climate meant that she usually went out sans makeup, but she wanted to look pretty, especially since the last time he saw her looking like a "hot mess." She played up her blue eyes with burnished browns and coppers and added a lashing of mascara to finish the look.

Ten minutes later, John knocked at the door. When Lizzy let him in, he immediately walked her entire apartment, including the attached bathroom, which she hadn't bothered to tidy.

"What in daisy blazes do you think you're doing?"

"Checking out your security. I didn't get a chance when I dropped you off the other night."

"My security is just fine! I live in a compound."

"A lightly guarded, sub-par compound. An eight-year-old could get past those two inept guards." He pointed to her bathroom window. "You need security bars on this."

"Boy, you know how to rile a girl up. How about 'You look pretty, Liz. Ready to go, Liz? Let me escort you to my car, Liz.'"

John grinned. "You look pretty, Liz. Tighten your security, Liz. I want you to be safe, Liz."

Lizzy stuck her tongue out and turned to grab her bag.

He grabbed her arm and pressed her into the wall. "You do look really pretty. So pretty that I want to lick that lip-gloss off those lips." He paused before rubbing a thumb over her lower lip and touching his lips to hers. "You taste like passion fruit."

She groaned, and with one hand he lifted her up and shoved his tongue in her mouth. Wrapping her legs around his waist, Lizzy registered the heat thumping through her veins as he ground her slowly over his engorged crotch, their layers of clothing preventing his dick from finding a new home. He nibbled on her bottom lip and rolled his hips. "God, I missed the taste of you." Grabbing the back of her neck with his hand, his expert tongue tangled with hers as he growled in frustration.

She opened her legs wider, and he slammed them into the wall. *Holy cannoli!* He'd always been so careful with her before. She liked this rough warrior side to him, and her nether regions felt the same as she pulsed in time with his urgent thrusts. Even through his jeans, she could tell how huge he was. Her bruised thigh protested but she ignored the niggling pain.

"Yes, just like that." Lizzy moaned as his erection ran over a sensitive spot. "Again. God, do that again." They were dry humping in her hallway and she had never felt so beautiful—or so turned on.

John swore, and in two steps had her on the bed. "I've wanted to touch you for so long." He nuzzled her neck. "I want you so badly."

Firm fingers stroked, scraping fabric, and she jerked at the erotic vibration.

"We can't—I want it too, but we're supposed to be friends."

He stilled at her words. Her body screamed for release as her brain pulled her from her thrust-worthy fantasies.

He groaned into her shoulder. "Friends with benefits maybe?"

"John—"

"You're right. Resets don't start in the bedroom." The hulking man still didn't budge.

"Um, John—as delicious as your giant pole feels nestled against my bits, we have made an executive decision to go to lunch."

"I know," he mumbled. "Just give me a minute, you smell so good, all peachy and—"

"What you're smelling is apricot. I use an apricot hair perfume."

"Shit, babes, it makes me want to eat you up."

"Well, I want to eat a juicy hamburger so roll your brawny carcass off the bed."

With a last neck nibble, he was up. Lizzy took a moment to

appreciate the sinewy man standing over her. It wasn't his powerful body that took her breath away; it was those tender eyes that gazed at her with soul-stroking embers. The "friends with benefits" option suddenly seemed tempting. Could she be physically intimate with him, yet still preserve her newly discovered independence? John held out a hand, and for the second time in as many days, she took it.

◊ ◊ ◊

The place was a hovel in the wall. A relatively clean hovel, but it still emanated a definite shanty vibe.

Lizzy insisted on coming here—that was the thing with her, you never knew what to expect. Most women would insist on a fancier lunch—a place that served salads and wine. Not Lizzy. Nope.

The questionable neighborhood kept Johnny on his toes. He watched their six for the hundredth time, as she inhaled her double whammy burger. His firecracker could eat, and it was damn sexy. Johnny had an adventurous palate and loved to eat. If he hadn't joined the military, he would've trained as a chef. He liked that Lizzy wasn't afraid to try the local foods. She seemed to seek out the lesser-known foodie spots and he was happy to comply.

The meal tasted good and the local owner, Fadhili—Fadi for short—was apparently a friend. Lizzy greeted him smoothly in Kiswahili, the local language. When she turned and introduced Johnny in the foreign language, he did a double take. Her command of Swahili was impressive; she wasn't by any means fluent—like he was—but she knew enough to get by on a rudimentary level. Remarkable considering she'd only been a resident for five months.

Wedged up in a corner with the best view of their surroundings, Johnny eavesdropped on their conversation. They'd switched to English, and Fadi asked her how Valentino was doing.

"He's good—improving every day. Thanks for your help with building the new extension, it's much appreciated."

Who the hell was Valentino and what had Lizzy gotten herself involved with? Johnny zeroed in for any more clues.

Fadi smiled. "I'll always make time for such a brave and kind woman, and for your fine friends."

Lizzy thanked him again. "*Asante*. On Friday, we're cooking up a large stew. You're welcome to stop by. Valentino misses you."

"He does? I appreciate the kind hospitality. I'll bring along a large bowl of chicken wings."

"I love your wings. Thank you."

As the conversation jumped to the unusually warm weather, Johnny mulled over what he'd just heard. When Fadi moved off, Johnny moved in as she polished off her fries. "I'd sure like to come around for Friday's stew. Where exactly is this happening?"

"Calm your covert butt down. I knew you'd be all over that. What? Do you need to scope out all the corners of Nairobi where I lay my feet?"

"Damn right, I do."

Lizzy sighed and pushed her plate away. "I knew I couldn't hide my little haven from you for long. I need to swing by anyway. Are you up for a small road trip?"

Five clicks out and with Lizzy's direction, he pulled into a dusty lot. The place fell slightly off the beaten track, a little too isolated for his liking and he wasn't quite sure where they were.

"What is this place?"

"We're not about to get jumped if that's what you're asking. We've parked around back."

She led him to the front, and he found himself staring up at the rusty sign secured to the front of the main building. Teens & Tots Haven.

"It's a children's village," Lizzy said as she stopped beside him. "There's not many like it. There are plenty of orphanages popping up in Kenya. They're needed, especially with a severe AIDS epidemic and lack of food in the drought-affected areas. Except some children's homes use the kids in commercials—to gain foreign donations. They don't use the money for the orphans. Instead, they raise them on the poverty line, afraid that if they ran a beautiful orphanage, donations would stop coming.

"Teens & Tots is run by a local family who is improving the children's lives on a daily basis and trying to bring in new legislation against the greedy pop-up charities. It's still fairly new, but we're making great progress."

Hands on hips, he looked around the dusty playground. Indigenous bush surrounded the humble facility. "How did you get involved?"

"One of the flight attendants I first flew with brought me along. She volunteered a couple of times, then moved on, but I was hooked. I think I'm making a difference."

"How?"

Lizzy flinched like he'd slapped her, and he tried to self-correct. "I didn't mean—"

"I know what you meant. What value would a silly princess like me possibly have to offer."

"Goddammit, Lizbug, that's not—"

"I have some nursing experience, and I've recently completed an Immunization and Injection Training Program in Kenya. I'm certified. I also run non-medical projects with the children. I hold sewing classes once a fortnight and teach them about music."

He pulled her in for a stiff hug. "You're freaking amazing, baby. I was only curious as to what you do every day and what programs are on offer."

"Oh. So, you're not mad?"

"Why would I be mad? It sounds amazing. The perimeter needs securing—my team can help with that—but I'm all in. Show me around."

His words were met with an infectious grin as she grabbed his hand and pulled him through the front door with hurried eagerness. With no one in the foyer, they winded their way to the back. He took note of the layout. Single-story structure with a fresh coat of yellow paint, offices leading off a central hallway that split at the end. They turned left. More doors to the right.

"Who's Valentino? Does he run the place?"

"He's a little young for that. He's one of the orphans. Valentino's been here from birth. He was a newborn—found in a dumpster on Valentine's Day, three years ago."

"Hence the name?"

"Yeah. He's at the general hospital though; he has bronchitis and breathing difficulties. We've just discovered he also has severe asthma." Lizzy walked him into a large lunchroom. At least seventy small faces turned their way. Children, ranging between approximately four and sixteen years of age. Deafening squeals had him stepping back as a horde of tykes ran for Lizzy. She gathered as many to her chest as humanly possible. *Fucking adorable.*

An older Kenyan lady bustled in, yelling at the kids to get back to their benches. She spoke to them in English, and with

Lizzy's help, the kids disbanded and returned to their food.

Lizzy bounced up and introduced Johnny as "Jay Jay" to the fearsome lady. "Esther and her husband, Denis, run the home. Denis is staying in Tanzania for contract work. He should be back in eight weeks. I haven't met anyone yet who can outwork Esther. This is her life's work, and it's an honor to work with her. She's my dearest friend in this crazy city."

"Wow! Lizzy, you know how to introduce a girl." Esther pretended to blush, and Lizzy giggled. "Welcome to Teens & Tots Haven. We are greatly blessed to have you with us."

"I'd like to help," Johnny said, stepping forward. "It looks like a wonderful place. The kids look happy and well fed."

Esther fanned her face. "Look at you—looking like you punched your way out of the earth's center and landed on my humble doorstep!"

Johnny felt his eyes bulge, but Esther didn't slow.

"Where do you hide your cape, young man? Even if you had one, I doubt it would hide much of that fine-looking specimen standing before me. If ever a large as life lady like me interests you, please lay that cape on my pillow." Esther turned to a laughing Lizzy. "Well done, lady. You've landed yourself a good one, keep him close!"

"He's not mine," Lizzy said. "For now, he's a good friend."

Not if Johnny had anything to do with it. He followed the two cheerful women out back, plotting his next move.

◊ ◊ ◊

The flame tree was in bloom and Lizzy couldn't resist walking out of the front gates of her apartment complex and plopping down beneath the scarlet tree. She crossed her legs and picked up a bright flower as she waited for John.

Lizzy loved people-watching, and this was the perfect spot for it. Locals ran for the bus stop, mopeds sped by, and cars negotiated through the morning bustle.

The previous day had been a pleasant surprise. After a quick walk around the children's home, Lizzy excused herself, helping in the kitchen by chopping up vegetables for the evening meal as John thoroughly walked the property, listing potential improvements.

It shouldn't surprise her; John took everything in stride, and his easy adaptability was one of the star qualities that attracted her to the man.

By the end of the day, he'd accrued a workforce of teenage boys as a gang of wide-eyed little girls trailed his every move, peppering him with questions. "Mr. Jay, do you have a mommy? Do you have a sister? Why don't you have a sister? Mr. Jay, do you have a pink teddy bear like this one? Mr. Jay, why is your leggys so big? Is Miss Wizzy your girlfriend?"

When Lizzy walked up to him on the soccer field, a kid sat on his shoulders and he held two others as he watched the boys play.

"Are you ready to go?" she'd asked.

"Why are there so few boys at the home?"

"We need to build an add-on to the boys' facility. We don't have enough beds. When they first opened, Esther and Denis focused first on rescuing girls. There are at least thirty thousand street children in Nairobi. While boys survive on collecting garbage and unloading goods, girls are forced to resort to prostitution from a young age. Also, girls with disabilities are marginalized and are at the highest risk for abuse. Of all the little ones rescued at Teens & Tots, around thirty percent of the girls living here have some form of disability or suffer from disease."

Lizzy remembered the look in John's eyes at hearing that, as he'd tightly hugged the little girls perched in his arms. Her warrior had a heart as big as the bright blue ocean.

She wasn't able to see Valentino yesterday as he was with a lung specialist. Soon she'd introduce John to the kid. She couldn't wait. Valentino held a special piece of her heart. Those tight little toddler hugs and the way he snuggled into her neck whenever he saw her. Such trust.

The crunch of twigs jerked Lizzy from her reverie. An old man leaned tiredly against the trunk of the tree. Lizzy dug in her bag of tricks and produced a boxed juice, handing it to the homeless man along with asking how he was in Swahili. *"Habari gani?"*

"Nzuri ahsante."

He didn't look fine, and Lizzy waved him over to sit beside her on the blossom-strewn earth. A brief chat revealed that he collected recyclables and hauled them across town on the rickety wheeled pallet secured to the tree. At seventy-six years old, he supported a sickly wife and their grandchildren and lived in a shanty village a mile from Teens & Tots. Lizzy gave him the address for the children's home, telling him to drop by for a medical check-up and collect a food parcel for his family.

As she slipped a rosy flower behind her ear, John's silver SUV turned into the drive, swerving around to roll up beside them. In a flash, John was standing over her, concern evident on his handsome face.

"Are you okay?"

"Yeah. Why wouldn't I be?" Lizzy introduced him to the old fellow and asked John if he had any food supplies hidden away in the shiny 4x4. She knew how much John ate, and her assumptions were on the mark as he produced a handful of granola bars and energy drinks.

The elderly traveler took the snacks but refused a ride, saying he still had collections in the area. He stuffed his pockets with the goodies, promising to visit the orphanage. With that, they pulled away.

Lizzy hummed as she rezipped her tote, stowing it by her feet, only noticing John's angry, jaw-ticking profile as they maneuvered onto the main road.

"Any news on Brianna and Suzie?" She asked him every day, and the answer was always the same. It was a waiting game.

"Not yet. Sorry." John shifted—his body stiff.

"What? Say it."

"You have as much sense as a damn cow in a thunderstorm."

She regarded him stonily. "Excuse me?"

"Lizbug, I get that you have a bleeding heart, but why in the living blazes were you squatting on the pavement outside of your secured compound? You'd be safer waiting inside."

"Let me guess; we're suddenly living in Afghanistan? I felt like sitting under a pretty tree while I waited for a grouchy oaf."

He scrubbed a hand over his face. "You wander around in a fantasy world filled with rainbows and fucking fairies—chatting to random strangers—never thinking about the potential risk to your safety."

"The guards were a few feet away," she said, glaring. "Would you prefer that I ignored that frail man? I'm sorry I don't see the world in shades of doom and gloom."

"Jeez, no. I want you to be aware of the risks. What would you have done if a vehicle full of men pulled up? This is a big city where violent crime and rape are on the increase. A woman was raped last month in broad daylight—in the business district, at eleven in the damn morning!"

She'd heard about that, but she refused to live like a prisoner. Like any city, Nairobi had its safety issues, but it was a vibrant and exciting place.

"This is my life. I'm an independent woman who makes her own darn decisions. Get off your soldiery stallion and live a little!"

"I've lived a whole hell of a lot. I've seen a whole hell of a lot. That's the issue. I know what's out there. I've seen firsthand what a gang of thugs can do to one tiny woman."

Gosh, wasn't Mr. Big, Rough and Raw as cheerful as a cricket. Lizzy needed to turn this conversation around. "Okay, grumpy pants. You've made your point. What time do we need to leave the orphanage? What's on your work agenda for the day?"

John sighed and his hands relaxed at the wheel. "I have a late afternoon meeting, but the rest of the day is yours. I brought supplies along to fix the border fence. We'll need to swing by a hardware store on the way, and I need breakfast before we get started."

"Well, crikey all mighty, let's get cracking, Mr. Jay Jay!"

And she had him smiling again. Mission accomplished. The man was warm putty in her sneaky hands.

◊ ◊ ◊

He'd sweated off half a tube of sunscreen in the baking Nairobi sun. Johnny stepped back to admire his handiwork and congratulated the crew of boys that helped. They were all covered in dust and grime, including Johnny. They'd run a new strip of fence along the left perimeter and ditched the old torn-up boundary fence. The temperature soared into the mid-nineties by mid-morning; it was time to get the kids out of the midday sun.

"Now that's an incredible piece of handiwork," Esther said from behind.

Johnny turned to face the woman, staring at him like he was Sunday lunch.

"You like the fence?" he asked warily as Esther's eyes ran over his shirtless torso.

"Sure. The fence looks good," Esther said, not taking her eyes off him.

Johnny smiled nervously as she swayed up to him. Her generous assets peeked out her shirt, shimmying for attention. A swift step backward had him tripping over the toolkit, and Esther chuckled in amusement.

"Relax, John. I am only messing with you. I know your heart is locked down on our sweet Lizzy. I came to offer refreshments and the use of our guest shower—so you can clean up. The fence looks wonderful. Thank you for your hard work. We could not have afforded to do this ourselves."

Johnny grabbed his go-bag and headed indoors. Thirty minutes later, he systematically searched the home looking for Lizzy, eventually finding her on a bench under a shade tree outside the clinic.

A harried smile greeted him as she rocked a wailing toddler.

"This little munchkin is from the nearby village. She broke her ankle playing with her rowdy brothers. They set it this morning; her mother is inside getting her medication sorted. I'm on babysitting duty."

Sitting down, Johnny examined the small cast as the tyke paused to regard him warily, tears running down fat cheeks, and suddenly the cacophony was back. Lizzy shifted the little girl and tried to console her.

"Why don't you play the sand circles game?"

"I never thought of that—she doesn't understand English."

"Music is universal. Any fun lullaby might help."

Lizzy sank to the ground and sang Belinda Carlisle to the babe. Johnny felt a knot claw at his throat. He'd missed that angelic voice. One night at Abby's home, Lizzy had produced a guitar and sang a mix of tunes. He was floored by her talent and by her second song, he'd secretly recorded her on his phone. Listening to that incredible voice, as he'd lain down every night over the past six months, was blissful torture.

As she traced a figure of eight, the youngster sniffled and began to watch. Lizzy wiped the last of the kid's tears, hugging the kid playfully as she sang. Squidgy fingers pulled at the coral blossom in Lizzy's hair. He blocked out the soft breeze blowing through the leaves and the thick sounds of the African bush, alive with swarming creatures. The delicate sprite sitting cross-legged in the dust had his full attention. Lizzy looked up and spotted the child's mother strolling their way. Johnny lifted the tyke as Lizzy sprang to her feet. He handed the kid back, and she ran over, eventually walking the family over to the exit.

He knelt back down, staring at the bruised, red flower crushed on the earth. Rough fingers traced the circle she'd drawn. The sad fact was, he loved a wild and flighty girl who'd broken his heart and would do it again in a heartbeat. Johnny was fucked, and he knew it.

◊ ◊ ◊

The next day, Lizzy decided to swing by the hospital to see Valentino. She waited until John was free, and they headed to Nairobi's central hospital.

Kenya had some of the most advanced medical facilities in Africa—private hospitals that rivaled those in the West. This selection of impressive hospitals was available only to those who can afford it, with fees beyond the means of most Kenyans.

In contrast to the millions who relied on severely overcrowded and under-resourced government facilities, the central hospital tried its best to cater to the hundreds of patients who sat in the waiting rooms every day, under tremendous pressure to meet the needs of the Kenyan people.

John seemed as saddened by the overcrowded wards as Lizzy was.

It was times like these when Lizzy regretted not finishing her nursing degree. Every bit helped. Standing on the periphery didn't feel natural or very helpful.

Little Valentino sat in a sea of chaos on an overly crowded children's ward. His huge eyes lit up, and he tried to pull the nebulizer off when he saw Lizzy rounding the corner.

"Easy, little man." Lizzy gently pulled his stubby fingers away and slid onto the bed, pulling him into her lap. Those same fingers clutched at her shirt, then her hair as he snuffled with excitement, babbling into the face mask.

Lizzy laughed as a nurse walked by.

"You can take it off. He's been on it long enough," the nurse said.

John leaned down and slowly slid the mask off Valentino's chubby cheeks. Freedom from the mask released a chattering diatribe. Lizzy couldn't understand much of what was said. All she caught was something about candy and a "twuck with big wheels."

She grinned at John. "Hand over his gift—that might slow him down."

Valentino's excitement at the Spiderman backpack and coloring book and pencils brought a lump to her throat. These kids had so little to look forward to. Like the other children at the orphanage, Valentino would treasure those two small gifts for years to come.

He deserved so much more. A home with loving parents, food on the table, new shoes and clothes that fit, and a toy box all of his own. Instead, he was a lost little boy. A number in a system. A tick on someone's checklist in an overcrowded ward.

John saw her swallow back tears and distracted the tyke by opening up the coloring box as Lizzy turned away. When she'd gathered her composure, Lizzy turned back, kissed Valentino's sweet face and helped him color in a picture of the Transformers.

◊ ◊ ◊

The kid got to Johnny. Correction—the kid and Lizzy's reaction to the kid—got to him. His immediate protective instinct towards the tender scene took him unawares. He wanted to sweep them both away from the chaos. Take them to his Wyoming cabin far away. Far from the harsh realities of a world Johnny was all too used to.

And leaving that sweet boy in the room was like a kick to the gut. Lizzy stood, and panic lit Valentino's wide brown eyes. She leaned down and spoke softly in his ear before singing a quick lullaby. The toddler lay back with such a resigned, flat look that Johnny had to turn away.

Sadly, Valentino knew what to expect in his tiny world. People left. Came back, then left again. Then new people took their place.

Johnny knew the uncertainty of that parentless childhood. He knew what if felt like to be alone at such a young age. He swallowed against the ache in his chest, took Lizzy's hand and led her out of the bleak room. They sat in the darkened space in the underground parking, saying nothing.

Lizzy took a breath and placed her purse on the floor. "I hate leaving him there; he's just so tiny."

"Are they checking him out in the morning?"

"Thank goodness, yes. The Teens & Tots resident doctor will pick him up at seven. God, there are so many orphaned kids out there. How do I help them all?"

"It's impossible, but you're doing your best."

"It's not enough."

Johnny picked up her hand and kissed her palm. "I love your big heart, but you need to pick your battles, otherwise it will break you."

She stared back before tracing his temple with a tiny finger.

"Why do you do that?"

"What?"

"Touch my scar?"

"Because I want to make it better."

"Jesus." He grasped her wrist and pulled her onto his lap. They paused, staring at each other before he crushed her lips to his. Her hair fell over Johnny's hands as he grasped the back of her head, seeking a better angle. He stroked her temples, in time with his tongue stroking hers, and she moaned against his mouth. She tasted like spearmint gum and glossy strawberries.

Lizzy sucked his bottom lip before pulling back. He loved that she was as out of breath as he was. "What are we doing, John?"

"What we do best—loving on each other."

"There's no love in this equation if we're going to continue…whatever this is."

"Don't say that."

"I mean it. You won't break my heart again."

He lifted her off his lap and reached for the ignition. "You think that's what I'll do?"

"I have no idea. I thought I knew you, but I don't know anything anymore."

Not trusting a reply, he backed out and circled to the exit. Lizzy latched her seatbelt and he looked away. Then he opened his mouth, as surprised as she was at what came out.

"I want you. I want to bury myself in your tight little body. If you don't want the candles and poetry thing, then let's just screw like rabbits."

"Gee, that's romantic."

"That's honest. Just being friends with you will be too tough. I want to touch you every second of the day. No games, Lizbug. That's me, putting it out there."

They pulled up at a red light.

"Fudge buckets. I'm speechless…"

Johnny said nothing, just gave her a heated stare, letting her know what he wanted to do to her. Lizzy licked her lips and his pants grew tight.

The light changed.

She turned in her seat. "If we do this, it means no commitments and no promises. What we do in Kenya, stays in Kenya."

"Yes, ma'am."

"We're strictly friends—with benefits."

He placed a hand on her leg and squeezed. "Whatever you say."

She nodded, seeming happy with that arrangement, and he smiled to himself as his fingers stroked her thigh. Lizzy had just made a deal with the devil. Once he got her between the sheets, she was never getting out.

Chapter Four

A surprised Lizzy opened the door. "What are you doing here?"

"A guy can't see his girl for four days in a row?"

"I'm not your girl."

Johnny pushed past. The strappy dress she wore revealed tanned limbs, and he ached to kiss the couple of freckles dotting her right shoulder. Instead, he laid a pizza on the counter. "Want some?"

"It's nine in the morning."

"I've been up since five, sorting out the team's week. They're rolling in late tomorrow, and then we'll be heading out the following day."

"How long will you be gone?"

"I'm not sure."

MIT2 were heading to the Kenyan territory bordering Somalia. They planned a joint training exercise for Kenyan first responders and law enforcement professionals to support efforts concerning extremist activity. MIT worked closely with PREACT—Partnership for Regional East Africa Counterterrorism—a US-funded multifaceted program designed to build counterterrorism capacity across East Africa to fight extremism. Al-Shabaab had a hold on the region, and PREACT needed all the help they could get.

Lizzy pulled a couple of plates from the dishwasher; the dress rode up revealing the backs of her thighs. "I have a flight scheduled for tomorrow evening. I baked some blueberry muffins if you prefer those instead?"

"Are you serious? Where, baby?"

"Are you asking where I'm flying or where the muffins are?"

"Muffins. I already checked your schedule. You're heading to Cairo."

"In the Tupperware next to the sink," Lizzy said. "Instead of hacking the JetHaven database like a covert ninja, I can print off a copy of my schedule for you."

"Whatever you want. That's a cute dress, by the way." He popped open the container.

She looked down at the turquoise sundress with a yellow African motif. "Thanks, I made it."

"You made that?"

"Me and the older girls, back at the orphanage. They sell the dresses they make and have caused quite a stir in the Kenyan fashion community. We're sitting on loads of back orders. I'm looking for additional second-hand sewing machines, at least three more. We might switch to just cutting dresses and slow down on the industrial clothing sales."

"Wait, you make and sell safety overalls?" Johnny asked as he munched down half a muffin. It tasted damn fine, a warm center with a toasted sugary crust.

Lizzy half-jumped, half-wiggled her ass up onto the counter next to him. "We work with construction companies in the area. They require flame-retardant overalls for some of the mines. The cool thing is that all profits go directly to the orphaned girls, and we've opened savings accounts in their names. Esther is recruiting other volunteers to take turns guiding the girls."

"How do you know how to make industrial workwear?" He couldn't resist slipping her hair off her shoulder and rubbing a thumb over those two freckles.

"It's not that hard. When I was a kid, I'd help out at my father's mine during the holidays. I got bored pretty quickly and raced around like a hellion. My dad put me to work in the local uniform store on the mine. Instead of buying overalls at exorbitant prices, dad hired a crew to make them onsite. I ended up behind a sewing machine, and the rest is history."

And that explained the grubby rabble-rousing side to Lizzy.

"A mine isn't the safest place for a kid."

Lizzy shrugged. "I liked it. I loved going below ground—descending into the bowels of the earth." She waggled her brows.

Johnny polished off a second muffin. "Your father allowed you to go into the mines?"

"For the men and women who work below on a daily basis, it's a harsh existence. When my father took over the coal mines, he was appalled by the safety conditions and the low labor rates at many of them. Safety and air quality are his biggest concern and he works hard to better the lives of the miners. He pays them well, looks after their families and gets their loyalty in return. It's still not an ideal job, but yes. I've been in platinum mines and coal mines. Platinum mines are incredible—there's this silver dust that floats and sparkles in the air, like moon dust. Of course, it's nice to explore below as a visitor and I've made plenty of friends over the years."

Stepping between her legs and shoving them apart, Johnny said, "You're fascinating and fearless, Lizbug. Every day I learn something new about you."

"You know that's not true. Fear has run my life for the past few years."

He rubbed a thumb over her cheek. "I can help you with that. You're always safe with me." He captured soft lips that tasted of coffee and took his time exploring that delicious mouth.

Johnny slid his hand slowly up her smooth leg to damp panties and nudged them out of the way. She sucked in a breath as he grabbed the back of her head, pulling her in for more. This was the furthest they'd ever gotten. His conscience in Johannesburg had prevented him from stepping over the line. Now, his thumb rested against her folds.

"Can I touch you, Lizbug?" he rasped between kisses.

"Please...yes, please."

Johnny lightly traced her slit before stilling his thumb and applying steady pressure. Then he softly traced again, barely touching her wet heat. Alternating between firm massage and light touches, he started a secondary assault with his mouth, covering hers hungrily. He added a finger to the mix as she slicked up, pressing down with his thumb and stroking around her entrance with his finger. She moaned into his mouth as he slipped the tip inside. "You're so tight. Shit."

When she bit his neck, he thought he'd come. Instead, he eased her back onto the counter and ripped off her silken panties. As he slowly slipped up the skirt, he took in her beautiful pussy—cleanly shaven with a small manicured strip of hair. It called to him, and Johnny answered that call, kissing his way up her thigh to her apex. He clutched the dress material and pulled her down to reposition her against his mouth, his hand bunched as he worked her clit like he was feasting on another muffin. His finger slipped back into her tight entrance just as she came, surging up from the counter and jerking against his mouth.

"Oh, God... Oh, snap!" she yelped.

Johnny smiled into her orgasming heat. He pulled her to him

with her still-fisted dress, cupping her ass and walking them around the counter. Time for the bedroom.

"Careful of Mr. Smithers!" Lizzy said as he plopped her onto the bed.

"Mr. what?"

She pulled a tired-looking stuffed rabbit—missing a fluffy ear and a beady eye—from under her shoulder. God, it was so ugly.

Lizzy laid it gently on the bedside table. "Mr. Smithers has been with me since I was a baby." She turned and wriggled into the covers, grinning back at him. "I didn't know it was like that!"

Johnny frowned as he peeled off his shirt and stripped off his pants, adding to the Lizzy piles of clothes strewn around the room.

"What? Oral?"

"Yes! Everything! That was an orgasm, right?"

He froze halfway through pulling off a sock. "This is inappropriate to ask right at this moment, but you're telling me that your dickbag ex-fiancé never took care of your needs in the bedroom? Did he just rut and roll off? And I don't know why I'm asking you this because I can't think of him touching you."

Lizzy bit her lip. "He didn't get that far. To the rutting stage, or any stage really. Can I just say that you look like you've dropped out of the man-god heavens? That stomach. Son of a nutcracker, whatever is under those briefs... I don't know if this is gonna work, will we even fit?"

He felt shock run through him. "I don't understand."

"This is awkward." She blushed as he teetered and grabbed for the bedpost. "I haven't actually been with a man. Ivan and I were going to wait...for our wedding night. He was a pretty religious guy. That was before he went crazy."

Johnny stood, balanced on one leg, gaping as her virginal

reality slammed in. Silence blew through the room like a grenade. Light shone through filmy curtains, casting the room in muted gold as she shifted awkwardly.

"Say something."

He chose his words carefully. "Lizzy, you're twenty-five years old."

"Gee whiz. I'm the oldest damn virgin you know—thanks for reminding me."

"I'm trying to get my head around—"

"Is it such a big deal?" She looked like she might cry.

He really hoped she wouldn't. "You've sucker punched me, that's all."

"You think I'm a sheltered idiot."

"I don't think that. I need time to get situated. I've never been with a virgin before; it's not my thing."

She winced. The mattress caved under his weight, something dug into his back, and Johnny pulled out a hairbrush from between his ass cheeks and placed it on the bedside table. He settled into a silken pillow, running over the new intel and taking it apart from all angles.

They came from opposite worlds—if she knew what he'd seen. Not on the job, but back when he was a teenager. His mom was a prostitute. There was no easy way to say it. Johnny only started dating when he'd joined the military—still terrified he'd end up like his mom and use sex as a weapon.

Sexually confident women appealed to him; they gave as good as they got. It was a mutually beneficial relationship where he'd always walked away knowing he'd never leave destruction behind. He'd built up a solid persona—a laid-back Johnny who stayed away from drama and coasted through life without a care. Then he'd met Lizzy—and destroyed her—without even touching her. He'd psychologically torn apart an already broken girl before ex-filling out of Johannesburg. That simple act had fucked up his carefully constructed world. And now he wanted to take it a step further? Wanting to imprint himself on her tiny, untouched body with his huge dick? No shitting way.

She was tiny in every way. Johnny stared at her small sandals lying on the floor by the window like they were made for a twelve-year-old. She curled into his side, tracing circles on his chest, and that traitorous dick stirred. Johnny was about to shift her off when she spoke.

"He started out small and worked his way up to the big stuff. First, my wrists were too scrawny; then I was too skinny. Ivan kept joking that I must have an eating disorder. Then I was too loud and silly. I was often told to keep my ditzy comments to myself."

Johnny pulled her in closer, wanting to chase away those newly revealed shadows.

"At first, I ignored the jabs, but eventually I believed them. It was my fault. I wasn't trying hard enough to be the perfect girlfriend. Hell. I was so young, just nineteen when I first met him. Ivan was a tall, rugby-playing engineering student. The star pupil in his field, and he was so charming—at least in the beginning." Lizzy smiled. "He brought me flowers on every date—elaborate dates—with champagne and VIP passes to all the shows and clubs. I felt pretty, and then suddenly I didn't. I felt less than. Less than him, less than the popular cheerleader he flirted with, less than myself."

Brushing a curl from her cheek, Johnny looked down at his beautiful angel with the saddest baby blues. "I want to kill him already."

She kept tracing circles, moving to the center of his chest as she continued. "I've always wondered if, from the start, Ivan knew who my father was. Did he purposely seduce me to marry into a wealthy mining family? Either way, it doesn't matter. My father liked him—initially—and offered Ivan a position at one of his mines. Lining up engineering work that would help him earn his degree."

Her tiny finger traced a figure of eight around Johnny's belly button. Her touch, softly caressing.

"Ivan became a part of the family. We'd been dating for about a year when he proposed. At the time, he seemed perfect. I ignored my instincts and said yes. That's when it all began to change. He grew into a controlling monster. I dreaded the weekends, knowing he'd pull me apart from the way I cooked his food to the way I did my hair."

"What did your parents say?"

"I never told them. They seemed excited about the wedding. I didn't know at the time, but things started disappearing onsite. Mining equipment. First the small stuff, ten pairs of gloves or tools. Then a truck went missing. The local police did nothing, so Daddy hired an investigator. They placed hidden cameras in the hot zones, and the footage pointed to Ivan. Daddy pulled him in for questioning. Ivan admitted to a gambling problem. He cried and begged my father to give him a second chance, said he'd tell me the truth and place himself in rehab. He said he'd pay back the money for the truck and equipment he'd stolen."

"Your father believed him?" Johnny cupped her hand before playing with her fingers.

"He felt uncertain and let Ivan go—delayed pressing charges. He wanted to talk to me first, except I was on an afternoon shift at the Johannesburg General Hospital. Daddy drove over to talk to me, but I'd already left for the night. When I arrived home, I walked into an ambush."

"Shit." Johnny let go and rubbed his hand over his face—not wanting to hear the details he'd craved for so long.

"I'd closed the front door behind me. The lights were off, and I thought I was alone but I wasn't. Ivan sat in the sitting room. The minute I saw him, I knew that something was horribly wrong."

She started to tremble, and Johnny pulled her up, turning her towards him. "You don't need to tell me."

"Yes. I do." Her eyes glazed as she stared past his shoulder. "This was the man I was supposed to marry. My future husband whom I trusted with my life. The first and last person I'd ever be with. The person who suddenly stood before me with dilated pupils—as high as a kite—and a gun in his hand. Ivan called me a whore and accused me of cheating. He called my family pretentious and snobby, and started ranting about my father. As he raved like a madman, I backed into the hallway and pressed a silent alarm. Ivan flipped when he realized what I'd done. I ran for the front door, and he dragged me away and threw me up the stairs, he then tossed me back down, proceeding to beat me with the butt of the gun."

Johnny wanted to barf and sat up, leaning elbows on his knees. She curled away, speaking with a detachment reserved for victims of extreme violence. "The armed response unit entered the home through the back, just as Ivan placed the gun to my head. I saw the certainty in his eyes right before he pulled the trigger."

Johnny inhaled a breath. "He pulled the trigger?"

"Yes, but the gun jammed. Ivan then turned it on himself. Pulled the trigger again and nothing happened. So, he placed the pistol down beside us, before wrapping his hands around my throat and squeezing."

Johnny dragged her into his arms, rocking as she babbled on.

"One of the security guards shot Ivan in the shoulder. They dragged him off of me and called the paramedics. Ivan was hospitalized for a week and eventually sent to prison. He served only three years."

"Yeah, recently released on good behavior. That asshole is now living in Lagos."

"You know where he is?" She curled a hand around his biceps.

"I'll always know where that shithead is hiding. I never knew of the details of that night, but I've kept track of him."

As he laid her back down, Johnny scanned her gorgeous face and traced her delicate brows before whispering. "He pulled the fucking trigger."

"I'm okay."

"I'm not." Johnny crushed her to the bed. Desperately wanting to erase the ghost of another man's fingers around that delicate neck, he kissed that sweet arch. *Ivan Chasov pulled the trigger. He pulled the trigger. He pulled the trigger.* Visions of Lizzy lying broken on the floor, her head blown off was not something he would ever un-see in his jaded brain. There was perhaps a 0.015 % chance of a handgun jamming. Johnny didn't much believe in a higher power, but someone or something watched over his precious princess that day.

That traumatic experience explained Lizzy's existential crisis, why she ran and why she hated guns. Lizzy wasn't just affected by PTSD; this wasn't a case of "He pointed a gun at me." This was "He pointed a gun at my head and pulled the trigger." By some miracle she was alive and warm and writhing under his dedicated mouth. He tugged down her dress and breathed a kiss on a pretty, peaked nipple, before licking and savoring the round bud.

A dainty hand ran over his nape, and Johnny paused to pull it towards his mouth, nipping the delicate skin on that soft palm. Then he guided it down to his thick shaft, enjoying the feel of her eager fingers, tracing his growing heat through his white briefs. "Me—inside you—are you sure this is what you want?"

She looked back up and gave him a wondrous smile. "Since the moment I fell out of that darn tree into your arms." Her hand slipped into the briefs and traced the tip of his cock. It bucked in response, craving her soft touch.

"Baby, you're dangerous."

She smiled. "Dangerous and desperate. Desperate for you to touch me like this."

Looking down between them, he saw her other hand draw up her skirt and slowly circle herself, as she rubbed his cock in time with her ministrations. Fascination and burning arousal had him suspended, eyeing her center like a wolf, narrowing in on its prey. When a finger slipped inside that sweet slit, he growled and flipped her over.

"If we're doing this, we're doing it right. I want you fully naked, and I'll be the one playing." He pulled the zipper and tugged off her dress. She kicked it away as he turned her back over, running a hand over the satin skin.

"Lizbug, you're so damn beautiful. Look at you."

"You've always made me feel pretty."

"I have nothing to do with this." He ran a hand over a pale pink nipple, then slid across her belly and along her thigh. "Or this. It's perfection." Pulling the elastic from her braid, he unwound her hair until it lay in waves on the pillow, then he leaned off the bed and grabbed his pants, pulling a condom out of his wallet. Johnny hesitated.

"Don't," she warned.

"You deserve better than this on your first go-around—you deserve better than me."

"If that's the way you feel, then fine. I'll have monkey sex with the very next guy who comes along."

"Jesus, Lizzy. You know how to piss me off," he growled savagely.

"Well, if you act like a damn fool, man, I'll say damn fool things. I won't wait forever, Jay Jay—make a decision."

In a flash he was on her, fondling her breasts as he kicked off his underwear. Lizzy smiled as she kissed the top of his head. She had the brawny operator wrapped around her finger. It was him, and only him who she wanted in her bed.

She couldn't imagine being with anyone as solid, as sheltering as James Cane. His strength chased away her cowardice, and when he looked at her with those hound-dog eyes, she felt like she could climb Everest.

A future with this handsome soldier still fell somewhere off her radar, but she could enjoy the moment, and what a moment it was. She sensed his thrill of arousal. His expert tongue swirled along her entrance, and her lady parts clenched at the electric touch. She came. Then he made her come again with explosive pleasure. After what seemed like hours of torturous bliss, John pulled back.

He ran a finger up her swollen folds and sat back to sheath himself. "Are you ready, Lizbug?"

She nodded as he raised her knees up to her chest. "Open your legs up… that's it, honey. Just like that." When his finger touched her, she jerked.

"Easy. This is fun, remember? If it hurts, tell me to stop." He slipped a large finger in and used his other hand to massage her clit. As he stroked and rubbed, she began to pulse. He rubbed the tip of his shaft over her entrance, then slipped it inside.

"You're so tight, shit." Pulling out, he worked the tip slowly back in. "You okay, baby? How does it feel?"

"Different. Kind of full. It's not bad."

"Not bad? Guess I'd better try harder." One hand fingered her, and he leaned towards her. "Look at me."

Lizzy stared into his intense gaze.

He pushed a little farther in, then pulled out. "I'm so lucky to be here with you, feeling your hot little flower clenching around me. You're amazing." He pulled out. "Can you feel me fucking you, baby?"

His dirty words turned her on, and Lizzy groaned as he pushed slowly back in. "You like that? My cock likes it, likes it way too much." John paused, allowing her to get used to his size, and she relaxed. Her muscles twitched, craving release, begging him to move. He bent and kissed her slowly, gathering her in his arms as he pulled out and drove himself all the way home.

No pain. Her body slowly adjusted, and she wrapped her legs around his waist.

His arms shook as he held onto his control. "Lizbug. Holy hell."

"I've waited so long for this. Please."

Hard muscles caged her in. The slow rhythmic pumping of his powerful hips held her captive as his cock drilled her into the mattress. Passion rippled through her. This was what it was like to be with a man. Sweaty, messy, warm and oh, so good.

Too soon, muscles tensed under her fierce grip, and John shouted his release into her neck. She knew he'd held back, controlling his frantic pumping action, stilling too quickly and growling into her shoulder.

He'd barely come down before rolling her to the side.

"Are you okay, honey?"

She nodded. "That was good."

John groaned. "So, we've graduated from 'not bad' to 'good,' and you didn't come."

"It was my first time. I didn't feel any of the pain that girls talk about."

"It doesn't have to be painful."

"I liked it, can we go again?"

"Easy, tigress, give me at least thirty minutes."

Lizzy gave him half that. By lunch, she'd come twice, with him inside her. The feel of his hard thighs slamming against her hips was intoxicating. His male strength, driving her towards shuddering ecstasy. She loved the way he'd slow his pace back down, before taking time to roll his hips, grinding his pelvis against hers. It felt so intimate, a large sweaty male buried fully inside her. Then he'd pause to roll his thumb between them before gradually building back up to thrusting wildly.

Trying out different positions was fun—the poor man looked sated by the time they climbed in the small shower. That didn't stop her from falling to her knees and wrapping her mouth around his delicious man bits.

"Oh, shit!"

"Strike first, strike hard, no mercy." She winked and applied herself with gusto as he groped for the shower wall, almost sliding on his butt.

◊ ◊ ◊

Johnny woke to a guitar strumming in the next room. Shadows darkened the bedroom as dusk fell. Was his cock still attached? He reached down—awakened from its nine-month dormancy with the most thorough workout of its existence. He adjusted himself cautiously as he rose, pulling on his briefs.

Maybe if he hid his dick from the budding nympho down the hall, she'd forget it was there. Who was he kidding? Johnny loved every minute of having her eager hands and mouth wrapped around his dick. No woman had ever matched energetic Lizzy in the bedroom, and this was only her first day. The notion that she was a petite and delicate flower was blown to all hell. His phone beeped, and he checked the incoming message.

Walking down the hall, Johnny poked his head cautiously around the corner and spotted Lizzy sitting cross-legged in a furry white bean bag chair. He'd noticed the monstrosity that first day in her apartment. It looked like a stuffed yak.

Lizzy wore his oversized T-shirt and a pair of fluffy gray socks. God, she was small enough to fit into his go-bag. An unfamiliar melody filled the air, and she hummed along, slipping in the occasional word while perfecting the tune.

He lay down on the floor and leaned his head against the yak bag. A warm breeze slipping in from the open balcony door stirred the lace curtains. When she finally paused to tune a guitar string, he asked what she was playing.

"It's 'Leave a Trace.' By Chvrches, a Scottish band. Chvrches is spelled with a V, not a U."

"Nice, it has an eighties vibe to it."

"That's why I'm totally obsessed. They're a synth-pop band with an electric dance feel." Lizzy pulled out her phone and played the original.

He didn't say anything, but Lizzy's voice was just as phenomenal. He handed back the phone. "Lizbug, you kind of sound like Avril Lavigne. Kind of look like her too."

Judging by the haunted look passing over her sweet face, that was apparently the wrong thing to say.

Johnny twisted to look up. "What did I say? What's wrong?"

"Nothing." She glanced away.

"Talk to me."

"Don't get me wrong, I think Avril Lavigne is amazing, but so did Ivan. For months, he'd insist that I play only her songs for him. Over and over. He pushed me to apply to one of those singing talent shows and would critique my performance for hours, telling me how Avril sang it better. After I recovered from his assault, I packed my guitar away."

"That son of a bitch."

"One day in therapy, the counselor encouraged me to start playing again. It was over a year before I played in front of anyone. Abigail was the first person. Then months later, that night at her house was my second go-around—the night that I played for you and for Max. Don't ask me to play Avril. It reminds me of Ivan. I'll get there eventually, just not today."

Johnny didn't trust himself to speak, wanting to punch holes through walls. Instead, he pulled her down and feathered a kiss over her temple.

"You sing like a goddamn angel. That pretentious, talentless ass-tard knew what an asshole loser he was and tried to bring you down to his level by breaking you down."

"I know. That's what my therapist said."

"That one time you sang for me, I recorded it—without your consent—and I'm not sorry. I've listened to that grainy recording at least a thousand times. It's my lifeline in the field."

"John…" She stroked his scruffy cheek.

He waded back out of the touchy-feely quicksand that threatened to sink his toughened heart and rolled to his back on the bean bag, wanting to broach what had happened in Johannesburg.

While chasing an elusive terrorist, he'd befriended Lizzy, intent on using her to get close to Abby. Except he'd fallen hard and fast. He'd wanted to tell her so many times who he really was, even though saying something might have compromised the mission. The last night he'd spent with her, they'd had dinner at an Italian bistro. He'd played with her hand, marveling at her delicate fingers nestled in his large palm. He'd closed his fingers tightly around hers and opened his mouth to ask her to go for a walk—suddenly ready to confess his subterfuge—when Kris Muller joined their group. Abby introduced Muller as her childhood friend. Johnny despised Muller for the way he'd treated Abby and for the way he'd targeted Lizzy that night. When Johnny's control finally snapped, it was too late. Lizzy panicked and left. The next time he saw her, she'd almost died in a shootout.

Johnny shifted on the squishy bag. "I'm sorry I let you down in South Africa, that I almost got you killed. I didn't protect the one person who mattered most to me and I've hated myself ever since."

She didn't say anything and for a moment he wondered if she'd heard.

Finally, she spoke. "You put me at risk, but you also protected me, and you did the same in Peshawar. I'm still learning to trust and I can't promise that this affair will change anything."

"So, for now, I'm a friend who scratches your itch?"

She ran a hand along his shoulder. "More like a friend that strokes my itch… long, delectable, pounding strokes."

He pulled her down for an upside-down kiss, she toppled sideways and giggled.

As she rolled upright, Johnny remembered his earlier text.

"I have news. Brianna and Suzie were sentenced today."

"Oh, God."

"They've both been fortunate and will serve only two months. My agency negotiated a transfer to an all-women's minimum-security facility, with decent dormitory accommodation in Karachi. It's not ideal, but physically they should be safe."

"Two months though."

"Prosecution pushed for a twelve-month sentence. And there are at least twenty thousand pending cases for the Peshawar High Court. The girls were handled quickly, instead of waiting months for their trial."

"I want to see them."

"No. It's too dangerous. Ryker will visit them next week."

"I can—"

"No, Lizzy. We went through a great deal of trouble to extract you. You've been flagged, you can't go back."

She fiddled with the yakky fake fur of the bean bag, twisting it in her fingers before saying, "Thank you for caring and please thank your superiors. I've had nightmares—imagining stonings or dirty cells with piles of hay in the corner."

"They'll both have a bed; the facility is well run."

Lizzy hugged him hard. He stood and pulled her to her feet. "It's my last night to chill before I'm back in the middle of bum-shitting nowhere weighed down by fuck loads of battle rattle. Pull on that cute dress and let's roll—I could eat an entire cow at that bistro down the road, the one with the German beer."

Johnny didn't want to think about leaving her. Their fragile new relationship—whatever it was—may not withstand a lengthy amount of time apart. Switching the relationship from casual to concrete would take time. Uncertain deployment schedules ate into that opportunity and Johnny prayed he'd be back with Lizzy within the week.

Chapter Five

Embrace the suck, Johnny thought as he walked gingerly into the maintenance shelter and laid out the plate carriers next to the holsters and radio equipment. Thanks to a sex-crazed little blonde, and the baking heat in the warehouse, his joystick didn't feel all that joyful.

Velcro crackled as Slater pulled apart a plate carrier. "You okay there, bro? You're embracing that Wyoming cowboy swagger."

"Fell in the shower," Johnny muttered.

"Damn shame. My grandma can lend you a non-slip shower mat if you need it—"

"Screw you." Another hour with Lizzy's luscious mouth and body and he would've been wheelchair bound. He'd forgotten how tough she was; it stood to reason that she'd take to bonking with the same amount of enthusiasm as she climbed trees.

Johnny didn't mind her climbing all over him like he was a giant oak, already counting the days until he could see her again.

Honeyed hair trailing, tits bouncing as she rode him hard before he rolled her over and slammed her into the mattress. His overused junk loved every moment of that early morning session, and now he was here, as Lizzy—five clicks away—prepped for her flight to Egypt. He missed her already. He grabbed another bag of radio equipment from the lockers.

"What's with you?' Max said to Johnny, walking up to the table.

"Says he got some accidental shower action—I'm guessing more along the lines of too much golden-haired shower action."

"Slater," Johnny growled.

"Glad you enjoyed a little R & R, but playtime is over." Max turned. "I've just received a WARNO from Bragg. New warning orders mean a briefing. Grab Donnie and meet me in the briefing room in five."

Johnny went in search of his teammate before heading inside. The MIT2 base consisted of lodgings, a general-purpose warehouse, briefing room, the maintenance shelter, fuel and potable water storage, and a recently upgraded private runway strip.

The forward operating site was a step up from the usual bare-bones facilities, set up as temporary sites by the US Military in Africa. The air conditioning in the briefing room was a bonus, and Johnny resituated himself in a cushioned chair.

Max launched into the new orders. "Naval Special Warfare Unit 12 will be taking over our training orders at the Somalian border. They'll arrive in the morning. Updated intel indicates that the Scythian has been spotted in Ethiopia, near Jimma."

"Hell, that's just a tactical hop and skip away," Donnie said.

"Yes, MIT2 are closest to the elusive target. We're moving out within the hour."

Johnny itched to pull the trigger on the man who called himself the Scythian. The terrorist mastermind used fear to run terror campaigns throughout Central and East Africa. Appearing in extremist videos wearing a hooded red leather mask, he executed so-called enemies online.

They'd learned that the Scythian—also known by locals as the Horse Lord—named himself after ancient warriors called the Scythians, horse-riding nomadic warriors who dominated Asia from the eighth to the third centuries BC. After a battle, Scythian warriors drank the blood of the enemies they'd killed, and scalped them. The scalps were sewn into their cloaks.

The narcissistic terrorist echoed the gruesome ancient rituals, killing his victims on live feeds before scalping them, thus gaining global infamy. He also moved through remote villages, spreading terror and wiping out anyone who got in the way.

The man was elusive and dangerous, avoiding affiliation with any one religion or extremist group. He lent his services to the highest bidder—appearing in ISIL, al-Shabaab, Boko Haram, al-Qaeda and IRA videos.

The Scythian had been on MIT2's radar for over three years. For the past nine months the extremist had gone quiet and disappeared into thin air. Thanks to his spidery network, the Horse Lord was one elusive bastard, and they still didn't have a bead on the man's identity. The second identifier—aside from his leather mask—was his prized horse.

According to intel, the Scythian owned an Akhal-Teke, an ancient breed of horse known to thrive in desert environments. Sensitive, intelligent and a one-master horse.

MIT2 devoted reconnaissance efforts to finding the stallion, and their hard work was paying off. According to Max, the horse was identified in a trailer near the Ethiopian border.

Later, as the plane took off, Johnny glanced at his watch. Lizzy was already in the air. He smiled, thinking of their time together before switching into operator mode. It was time to work.

Nairobi, Kenya
One week later

Valentino was almost back to his bright self, and Lizzy had raced over after landing back in Kenya, spending most of her morning playing with him. Buying a toy dump truck and a fire engine for the playroom was worth it when seeing the dimpled joy on his tiny face. Those trucks rolled over every inconceivable surface, including walls, sofas, other kids and her face. She eventually rocked him to sleep, before heading over to the lunchroom for a quick break.

"Package came for you." Esther handed over the padded envelope, and Lizzy slipped it into her satchel. She'd open it when she got home.

Lizzy paused, reconsidering the rash online purchase burning a hole in her knapsack. So what if she felt green and felt the need to educate herself. The *Kama Sutra* book seemed like a wise purchase a week ago.

Despite her inexperience, John had still seemed pleased when he'd left on his training mission. He'd kissed her goodbye with a goofy grin, even though she thought she might have broken the poor man with her inept gymnastics in the bedroom. They'd both been tender the following morning, and Lizzy had regretted her fervor as she'd waddled to the shower.

It was evident that John was an accomplished lover. She needed to up her game to keep him satisfied—at least until they got tired of each other, or one of them relocated to a new country.

It wasn't like they'd stay in the same city forever. John's home was in Wyoming, and Lizzy wasn't ready to settle for anything more than the nomadic life she now lived. She loved the travel and enjoyed the idea of not knowing where she'd end up next. Being a grown-up and settling on a specific path made her feel ill. She didn't want to be tied down, but she could still have some fun along the way.

When John would return from shadowy war games was anyone's guess. Lizzy would be ready. She already missed him. He could be gone for weeks, maybe even months. Grabbing a glass of lemonade, she sank onto a bench in the lunchroom, thinking of ways to seduce Mr. James Johnny when he landed back on Nairobi soil.

"Lizette Steyn?"

Jerked out of her musings, Lizzy knocked over her glass.

"Bollocks." The tall stranger swore as she swept the sticky liquid off her jeans. "I'm awfully sorry. I gave you a fright—here—take these."

He thrust a wad of napkins towards her, and she swiped at the spillage, all while inspecting the newcomer.

His well-articulated accent indicated he was British. Efficient hands added more paper towels to her growing bundle.

Lizzy raised her hands. "I have plenty, thanks."

Dark hair fell artfully over a finely hewed brow, as his lean form bent to wipe the table. "I've heard great things about you, Miss Steyn. The students are doing well under your part-time tutelage."

"And you are?"

"Dr. Garrison Bankes. I'd shake your hand, but I suspect it would be a sticky mess—the handshake, I mean, not your hand. I'm covered in this stuff."

Lizzy couldn't help but laugh, and she also gaped a little. They didn't make doctors like that where she came from. He looked like he'd walked off a movie set.

"Esther tells me you're a nurse?"

"I wish that was the case. I dropped out in my last year of college, but I'd love to complete my degree."

Where did that come from? Lizzy still had no clue on her direction in life, and working as a qualified nurse held average appeal in her long list of potential careers.

"Not to worry, we'll get you there. Now, are you going to help me with a new patient or return to staring at the wall? Although it is a lovely wall—in all its austerity."

Lizzy glanced at the plain gray wall, chuckling as she picked up her backpack and chased him down the hall. She had a feeling that the attractive doctor would keep her on her toes. Lizzy spared a quick thought for John, wondering how he fared with his team and trusting he'd keep safe.

Chapter Six

"I'm still pissed that we left without the Scythian all wrapped up for HQ in a neat little camo bow," Slater said.

Donnie agreed. "At least we've made progress and trained up a generous contingent of indigenous forces. If the phantom Horse Lord steps back onto Ethiopian soil, the welcome committee is ready."

Johnny glanced at his two weary comrades as he drove. He'd been away from Lizzy for a month and it felt good to be back in Nairobi. He couldn't wait to surprise her—he couldn't wait to catch up on sleep. Four weeks of hunting, then training the local military took its toll. The Scythian had slipped out of their grasp, rumored to be back over the border in Somalia. MIT2 wouldn't give up and awaited more intel. In the meantime, Max had taken the red-eye out of Addis Ababa to Fort Bragg in California, with meetings lined up with MIT's base of operations. Then he'd be flying into Salt Lake City to check on Abby, who'd been placed on bedrest after unusual spotting and cramps. In six days' time, Max would be back with his unit and they'd all be flying back to arid-ass Somalia.

"Well, I'm pissed. Sorry I can't be as laid back as you and Johnny when it comes to Lord Fuckwat." Slater yawned. "I want to liberate that roaming sicko from his precious scalp collection with one smooth pull on the trigger."

Johnny thrummed his fingers on the steering wheel. "Screw laid back. I'm with you, bud."

They drove in silence, frustration and exhaustion warring for space among the three operators.

"How long until we arrive?" Donnie asked, staring out at the passing savannah.

"Ten minutes. It's down the sand road up ahead, two clicks out."

Slater and Donnie had jumped at the chance of helping out at the orphanage and were eager to meet the kids.

Johnny's eagerness was all twisted up in Lizzy. He hadn't seen her in a whole month. As soon as they'd landed back in Kenya, the men had showered and packed the truck with supplies, before cruising westwards towards Teens & Tots.

"Excited to see your girl?"

"Hell, yeah. I missed the shit out of her. Now I can formally introduce you guys."

That concept felt weird. Donnie and Slater probably knew Lizzy better than she knew herself—through the hours of surveillance they'd performed in South Africa.

"Is she still as excitable as she was back in Johannesburg?" Donnie asked.

"As in 'happy' excitable? No. She's matured some since living in Kenya. But she's still restless and wanders through life in a dreamy haze. It's sweet but hella frustrating at times."

Eight minutes later they pulled into the dusty lot. "I'll show you around before we get started." Johnny led them up a side path and paused.

100

Donnie immediately picked up on his tension. "What's wrong?"

"It's too quiet. It's supposed to be the morning tea break. The children are usually racing around—playing soccer."

"Maybe they've changed the schedule?"

"No. Something feels off."

"Let's split up. Talk us through the layout."

His buddies trusted him, and Johnny felt a spurt of gratitude. The three men had worked together for so many years in the field that their finely-honed instincts were in sync. Urgency screamed for Johnny to assess the surroundings and figure out what felt off-kilter.

They were all armed with pistols but were short of radio comms. Sign language would have to do. After a quick huddle, Slater circled round, as the thick bush to the left absorbed Donnie's agile form.

Easing forward, Johnny strained—listening for sound. Sweat dampened his brow as he sidled around a roughened wall.

Noting the empty classrooms, he crept to the courtyard at the far end where he'd heard raised voices. It housed a smaller playground with a couple of swings.

A glance around the corner revealed an armed man waving a long knife in the air. Another comrade stood next to him, shouting in Swahili. Resituating himself, Johnny surveyed the threat. Lizzy stood trapped—centered before the two men—with rusty swings and a wall at her back. She sheltered a small boy who clutched the back of her shirt. Esther corralled the rest of the children, shuffling them towards the canteen.

Sidestepping, Lizzy tried to escape the enclosed space, and the armed target stepped closer.

Johnny swore as Donnie sidled up from the opposite end of the courtyard. The soldiers communicated silently. Donnie would take on the unarmed perp and Johnny would deal with the armed asshole. He sized up the target. Judging by the frantic wielding of the butcher's knife and his stance, the local man was untrained and only weighed perhaps 140 pounds. Lizzy spoke to him quietly, and he pointed at the young child with the knife. She shook her head, shielding the youngster.

Johnny readied himself as the man screamed in fury. Three...two... A third man ran onto the playground, his arms waving frantically. The stethoscope dangling around his neck indicated this was the clinic's doctor. *Shit.* That's all they needed—more civilians in the mix.

The doctor foolishly strutted towards the perp, and the knife snaked out and barely missed the idiot's carotid artery.

He stumbled back but still stood his ground, stepping between Lizzy and the angry men. Johnny was already moving. The MIT team slid in from all sides like raptors. Johnny's entire focus was on that knife, and he grabbed the skinny arm, quickly twisting the blade out of its desperate trajectory. A painful shout to the right meant that Donnie had done his job well. Red dust clouded as Johnny slammed the bastard into the ground. The guttural *whoosh* indicated a severe winding. The perp gasped as Johnny rolled him over, restraining his wrists with the plastic cuffs stuffed in his pocket.

Rage at the threat to his woman had Johnny craving a beatdown. He could easily pound the man to mince, but the look on Lizzy's face stopped him. Slater stepped up beside her, checking for injury. They were safe. Esther came running and Lizzy told her to take the scared kid inside.

The bastard whined beneath Johnny's knee and then began wailing. Completing a pat-down, Johnny dragged him to his knees.

"Please don't hurt him," Lizzy said, stepping forward.

"Restraining the son of a bitch isn't hurting him. He just tried to kill you."

"He was desperate—with good reason."

"What the hell?" Slater stared at her with as much astonishment as Johnny felt.

Astonishment morphed into hot jealousy as the doctor put his arm around her. "Are you okay, sweetheart? You're trembling."

"That was brave of you—leaping in like that. Thank you."

"Anytime. I was wrapping up surgery when I heard the shouts. I came as fast as I could."

The three operators watched, fascinated by the friendly interaction, and not knowing how to take it.

When the perp groaned, Johnny eased up, choosing to ignore the British doctor. "Slater, call the local police."

"No, don't," Lizzy said, talking quickly. "His name's Alfred; he came looking for his nephew. Omondi the only family he has, but Alfred was refused custody. He wants to put Omondi to work in his factory, but the child is way too young, only seven years old. Alfred's grown confused and frustrated with the court system, so he came for the child. He doesn't understand how it all works."

"Threatening the staff with a knife? I think he understands well enough that what he's doing is unlawful," Donnie said quietly.

"Did you break his arm?" The English quack knelt.

"It's just a sprain," Johnny said.

"Well, it looked like you almost bloody twisted it off."

"I could've let him gut you instead. I haven't seen you before—at the clinic."

"This is Doctor Garrison Bankes." Lizzy tried to smooth

things over. "He works with Amity Aidcor. Teens & Tots is lucky to have him on loan for three months."

Amity Aidcor was a famine response program that did good work in drought-stricken regions across the globe. MIT2 had crossed paths with a couple of their aid camps in the past. Their medical teams were solid.

Garrison Bankes stood and glared at Johnny. "Bring him to the clinic. I want to look at that wrist, and I could ask you the same question. Who the hell are you people?"

Again, Lizzy jumped in. "They're upgrading security on the property."

She'd just introduced him as a security guard…and hadn't yet touched him, not even a hello kiss. *Fan-fucking-tastic.*

Johnny handed the restrained package over to Slater, planning to walk to the truck and calm the hell down. A swanky English accent cut through his funk, first directing Slater and Donnie to the clinic with their prisoners and then addressing Lizzy's statement.

"We don't need an upgrade. Esther's husband will be returning shortly, and I stay on the property at night."

Johnny couldn't resist engaging. "Yeah? What happens in a couple of months when you've moved on, or what if a gang of militants enters the property with AK-47s?"

"That's an exaggeration." The doctor dusted off his knees.

"Why would they want to target an out-of-the-way orphanage?" Lizzy asked.

"Seems like a ripe target to me. The past five years mall attacks, roadside bombings and beheadings have become commonplace occurrences in East Africa."

Bankes stood with his hands on his hips. "What is a fence and some cameras going to do."

Johnny's response held impatience. "They'll give you some warning. A delayed entry gives a team like mine—or the police—a heads-up."

"And if you're out of country bullying some other poor locals?"

This little twit was going to be a cramp in his side. Folding his arms, Johnny glared. "What exactly is the problem here? How does this setup offend you? Are you anti-violence? Anti-gun? Anti-military? Or all of the above?"

"Violence doesn't solve problems."

"It solved this one."

"All this additional security and posturing is not good for the children's psyche. They've seen enough terror in their young lives, and don't need to live in an armed prison. My role is to ensure that the youngsters are healthy and happy—"

"And safe," Johnny added.

Esther stood to the side and looked uncertain. Johnny turned to her. "This is your property, no one else's. What do you want us to do?"

"Maybe install a couple of cameras to start? And if you could look at the back fence."

Johnny nodded. "I'll send Donnie over to the office to start on the security equipment."

After an awkward walk to the clinic and the arrival of two police officers, Lizzy turned to leave. "I'm taking the older children for a walk. I need air."

On closer inspection, she looked tired. That made two of them, in addition to his green-eyed annoyance at her budding relationship with the damn doctor.

"I'll come along," Johnny volunteered.

She lifted her chin. "We'll do just fine on our own."

"Well, I'm coming." Slater pushed off the wall. "I want to meet the kids, plus the more, the merrier, right?"

Lizzy grumbled to herself as Slater trailed along, and after a moment's hesitation, Johnny fell in behind.

◊ ◊ ◊

Lizzy concentrated on the rocky path ahead, ignoring the unyielding brute trailing at her back. John chatted easily with some of the older kids, yet she knew from his stiff gait that he was angry with her. Slater walked up ahead and slowed, turning back to shoot her a lazy grin.

Drat, she wasn't much up for conversation. She stared up the path at a fellow volunteer pointing out a random bird to the children, who gathered up ahead. The guy was a bird-watching guru. He yammered on for hours about weavers and hornbills. It bored the bejeezus out of her. Plus, she needed to pee for like the twentieth time that day; her bladder felt like it was about to burst. She glanced sideways at the demigod ambling beside her. Slater was a lethal Lamborghini as opposed to John—an imposing Ford F650 truck.

"We haven't officially been introduced. I'm guessing you know who I am."

"Ditto," Lizzy muttered.

"Let me guess, you met Dr. Garrison Bankes on Pinterest? You followed his board 'Hug a terrorist for a day.'"

"I've heard you're the funny one—in your tough little rat pack."

"You mean wolfpack, sweetheart, and Johnny is just looking out for the little tykes. His heart is in the right place."

"I know." Lizzy tugged a leaf off a passing tree.

"Then why are you so hard on the friendly giant? He saved

your cute derrière back there, and that's not the first time. Third time if I'm not mistaken."

She tore the leaf into pieces. "He makes me mad, that's all."

"Teens & Tots is well run, but it's not secure. Trust us to protect the little ankle biters."

"Please don't make the place look like a Nazi camp. Garrison has a valid point. There needs to be a balance—"

"It's Garrison now?"

"He's just a friend. Is that why John's so mad? He's jealous?"

Slater swiped at a fly. "Sweetheart, we've had a long month and a long-ass day. We were up at one in the damn morning and traveled through hostile territory, and rough terrain for three hours before arriving at the airport. Then it was a four-hour flight to Kenya. As soon as the wheels touched down, all Johnny could think of was seeing you. The man is beyond exhausted, and then he runs into a psychotic asshole threatening to stick you with a knife."

"Is that your way of telling me to apologize?" They edged down a narrow path.

"Hug the barbarian, that's all I'm saying. He missed you."

"I missed him too." Lizzy grinned sideways. "Thanks for the ass kicking." She nudged Slater, and he elbowed her back. She flew into a thorny bush.

Slater swore as he lunged to pull her out. "Shit, you're a light little thing. God, I'm so sorry."

John shoved him out the way. "What the hell, man!"

Aside from landing on her pride, Lizzy felt okay, a couple of scratches never hurt anyone. The teenagers giggled, and Lizzy chuckled back as John pulled her to her feet. Continuing the momentum, she fell into his strapping arms and looked up.

"Hi." She smiled, before balancing on his boots on her tippy-toes.

"Hi back. Are you all right?" He pulled a twig from her hair.

"Never better. Thank you for rescuing my ungrateful ass today. I've missed you."

The kids whistled as he lifted her and crushed her mouth to his.

"Break it up. This is a PG-rated walk—canoodling around rug rats is not allowed." Slater obviously never quit and Lizzy grinned into John's mouth. Only once the rabble had moved on—and after a thorough hello kiss—did he lower her to the ground. "Up for some more bird watching?"

"Gosh darn it, shoot me now. Nope, I need to pee. Jay Jay, find me a quiet bush and guard my bare ass."

◊ ◊ ◊

Two days of hard grafting and the fence was up with cameras installed. They'd even set up a basic alarm system that alerted the staff to intruders on the property.

Lizzy invited the men back to her place for dinner and left the orphanage early to dash home to cook a delicious roast. As the food simmered away, she slipped into the shower. Soaping up, she let out a loud shriek when firm hands wrapped around her waist.

"James Johnny Cane! Do you want me to keel over from fright?"

Already naked, he twisted her around and shoved her against the tiles. "That's what happens when you give your 'friend' a key to your apartment. Now don't move. I need to get clean and then please my woman." He wrenched the soap bar from her hand. He'd already sheathed himself in a condom and she ran her eyes over the very male picture he made.

"I'm not your woman."

"At this moment, you're my very wet and slippery woman."

She stepped up and he gently shoved her back, then raised her arms. "Against the wall—like that. I told you not to move." He went back to rinsing the remaining suds off his chest.

His firm command had her obeying. She liked this rough side to him. That first time, he'd been so cautious. Too gentle. Now, he seemed more himself, eager to climb onboard her adventure train.

After washing, he rubbed up against her. His hard body slid along hers and Lizzy reached out.

"I said no touching."

He caged her in, as callused hands explored her wet flesh. Her nipples hardened, and he growled, sucking one into his warm mouth. Steam rose around them, and her back felt cool against the wall. He cupped her breast as he sucked and Lizzy arched back. His other hand ran over her hip before tracing her entrance. Her moans had him raising her into position and sliding his erect shaft home. Strong fingers tightened on her ass, lifting her and slamming her back down. The sudden desperate tempo had her screaming as his hard length surged in and out.

Rocking, she desperately craved a release. John swore as she latched on, digging nails into taut muscle. Shoving her against the wall and propping her up with one hand, John used his other hand to tweak, then twist her nipple. Pleasure verging on pain had her shattering into a million shards. She writhed, spasming uncontrollably. With deep thrusts he came, jerking and slapping her against the tiles with violent enthusiasm.

Lizzy panted in his arms, then buried her head in his neck. The raw emotion at that moment had her questioning everything. She'd never felt so in sync with a man and wanted to yield to the sweet emotion. Was it like this for everyone?

Too soon, he moved, gently lowering her and placing a kiss on her forehead. "Hell, baby. I don't wanna get out, but we'd better get dressed. The team will be here any minute."

She didn't want to get out either. This moment they were cocooned in a misty world where nothing else existed. She wanted to explore every inch of him or even just lie beneath the warm spray in his arms. Her roast sat in the oven and she needed to put her hostess hat on. She ran a hand over his firm ass, then gave it a hard slap before leaping for a towel.

They sat around the table, stuffed to the gills, listening to Lizzy tune her guitar. She sat next to Johnny as he traced lazy fingers over the back of her neck.

"Why do you refer to Ryker's team as the 'threes'?" Lizzy asked.

Donnie looked for confirmation from Johnny before answering. "We can't give you any specifics, but there are six teams situated around the world. We all work for a task force that identifies key militant leaders and topples them from their infamous perches. Leaders who have gained momentum and power and are a direct threat to US assets and facilities. Men who are protected by money or power. Our team is called MIT2."

Lizzy leaned forward. "So, it goes, MIT1, MIT2, MIT3…."

"Yes. All the way up to MIT6."

"So MIT2—your team—covers East Africa and MIT3 are situated in the Middle East?"

"Correct, and MIT1 covers West Africa—"

"Like Mali and Nigeria?" Lizzy asked.

"Yes, the 'Ones' are based out of Lagos—in Nigeria."

Lizzy tweaked another guitar string. "I've been to Lagos a

couple of times—wasn't much fun, we had an armed escort stationed outside of our hotel rooms. The airline insisted it was unsafe, which was frustrating. I wanted to visit the Lekki Conservation Center in Lagos. What about the rest of the teams?"

Slater handed them all a beer from the fridge. "MIT4 are in Europe. MIT5 are based in Southern Asia—Sri Lanka, the Philippines. MIT6 cover mainly Russia and China."

"That's a lot of area to cover for one small four-man team."

"We focus on specific individuals and not their whole army of extremists. We utilize allies, informants or the resources available in various regions—like the local police and military."

"So, who are you currently chasing down?"

"That, sweet thing, is where classified lines get drawn in the sand." Slater winked at her.

Lizzy grinned. "So, out of all the MIT teams, who's considered the best, if you went head-to-head in a training exercise?"

"Who do you think?" Johnny winked. "No contest—MIT2 has Tank aka Jay Jay on their team."

She laughed. "Well then, a toast to MIT2."

The men smiled and raised their beers.

Lizzy clinked her bottle with Johnny's. "Here's to sexy Jay Jay making my day, cause baby, the twos are here to freaking stay!"

Johnny laughed at her silly toast. Her phone jingled on the kitchen counter and she ran over, sifting through piles of pans, oven gloves and leftovers. Johnny shook his head at the chaotic scatterbrain that was so Lizzy.

"Why does that sound so familiar?" Slater asked when she discovered the device under a dish towel.

"It's the soundtrack from ER," Lizzy replied before placing the phone to her ear. "Everything okay?"

Johnny frowned and got up to clear the plates.

"When, now? I have guests…" She paced the kitchen. "Okay….no, I understand…I fly in two days…sure…if you need me…I can get a taxi." The men paused. "I'll be there in thirty." Lizzy hung up.

"Was that JetHaven?"

"Um…no. It was Garri—Dr. Bankes. He needs my help at the clinic."

"Lizbug, it's ten-thirty at night."

"I know. A family just came in—throwing up with raging fevers and diarrhea. He's understaffed. Our nurse worked a double shift, and she's only just left the orphanage."

"You're a volunteer, right?" Donnie said.

"Yes, but—"

"It's not your job; you're putting yourself at risk. If they're throwing up and running a temperature, it could be contagious. There's a risk of them having cholera, Ebola or hepatitis A. Treating them in a low-level clinic with tiny kids sleeping in the next room isn't exactly wise, Bankes should ideally be transferring them out."

Lizzy looked torn, and Johnny's lid flipped.

"If you decide to go, I'm taking you. I don't understand why that arse-biscuit is calling you out this late. You're not a nurse." That earned him a glare. "You're a lone woman traveling through Nairobi late at night; it's irresponsible for him to ask you to do that."

"I can't not go, and don't be mean. He's a good man and a good friend."

"Call him back and tell him to transfer the family to the general hospital."

"I feel responsible—"

"For what?" Johnny raised his voice in frustration.

Slater stood. "We're gonna head out and let you guys sort this out."

"I'm sorry, I'm a bad hostess."

"Are you kidding? For the first time in five months, I've eaten a home-cooked meal. Thanks, sweetie, for the incredible food. We'll see ya when we see ya."

She hugged the guys and they headed out the door. This conversation was past due, and Johnny needed to have his say, barely giving her a chance to close the door.

"What do you want, Lizzy? Do you want to be a nurse?"

"Garrison thinks I'll be a great nurse. He's encouraging me to finish my degree, and wants me to help him on his next assignment in Peru."

Johnny clenched his fists. Over his dead body—the ass-hat wanted to run his surgical hands all over her sweet-smelling skin. "Is that what you want? To run to South America, to be a nurse. Does that excite you?"

"I don't kn—"

"Because, the way I see it, you're racing in a hundred different directions. Now you're a flight attendant, before that, you were a masseur, and a beautician, a possible nurse, a fashion designer, a singer…"

"Thanks for the shitty feedback. I know I'm directionless. I know I'm screwed up."

He drew in a patient breath. "Lizbug. If you want to be a nurse—to go back to what you were doing before Ivan—I'll support you. That quick brain of yours can do anything. You're incredibly talented, but I hate seeing you like this."

"Like what!"

"Wearing a hundred different masks to cover the pain."

"Screw you." Tiny hands shoved at his chest.

"I won't pussyfoot around you. That's not who I am—all flowery words. If you're looking for a man who'll be less than honest, then you've chosen the wrong guy."

"I haven't chosen you! This was supposed to be a fun reset."

"Yeah, I know." Hurt balled in his chest.

Folding her arms, Lizzy turned to the door. "Can we shelve this for now? I need to get changed."

"If you're going, I'm driving you to the orphanage. I'll wait for you downstairs in the truck."

◊ ◊ ◊

The sofa wasn't large enough for the mighty chaperone spread across its awkward cushions. Lizzy sat down wearily on an armrest and watched John sleep.

When they'd first arrived, he'd offered his help. As a medic, he was more than qualified, but Garrison refused the offer. John didn't argue, instead situating himself in the front room.

At three in the darn morning, they were finally done. It looked like the family had viral stomach flu—a norovirus—and after a round of IVs and anti-nausea meds, they all slept like babes.

All that time, John waited patiently, the diligent soldier always guarding her back. Why her? She didn't deserve his loyalty, still kicking him in the nuts when she should be thanking him.

She'd worried that if John ever found out about her past with Ivan, he'd treat her as carefully as her family did. But nope. He never tiptoed around her. John attacked life like a sledgehammer. He never stopped pushing her buttons and encouraging her to find direction. Lizzy needed a nudge. Hell, she needed to be shoved off the damn cliff.

Like John, all his teammates were weaponized warriors and she was getting used to having them around. If John was a sledgehammer, Max was the knife, slicing through enemy falsehoods, revealing the truth beneath. Slater's honest humor was like a bullet to the brain. Donnie used his economic hands to track and defend.

When the three fierce men gathered earlier for dinner in her apartment, she'd been struck by the imposing energy dominating her usually peaceful space. Exposure to perpetual violence sharpened them into jaded weapons. The intimidation factor had eventually worn off as the evening wore on.

Donnie had watched as she'd floundered around the kitchen in organized chaos. He'd calmly stepped up to load the dishwasher as she worked. The steady man held her attention with thoughtful conversation and shadowed eyes. Slater hid his sooty darkness under humor. She wore the same cheerful mask as the snarky operator—deflect the masses, and they won't get too close.

Except it hadn't worked. The savage sleeping beauty before her had slid beneath all her defenses. She sighed and ran the back of her hand along John's stubbled jaw.

"Thanks for your help," Garrison said from behind.

She turned to face the handsome doctor who—on paper—should be her type. Nonthreatening, intellectually charming, a tree hugger like her. But her heart didn't pound when he walked into a room, or flutter when he brushed past, or beat sluggishly when he looked into her eyes. That control belonged to John, and the thought terrified her.

"No problem." She stood. "Next time I won't be available. I love and care about this place and its people, but I'm a volunteer. I'll help out as much as possible, but I also have a full-time job and a personal life, and putting myself at risk is not worth it." The couch groaned behind her as John swung to his feet.

"Your brawny boyfriend fills your head with sinister scenarios."

"His name is John, and he cares about my welfare."

Garrison regarded her with thoughtful eyes. "Have a good night, Miss Steyn. I'll see you around."

Lizzy rolled her eyes at his disappearing and disapproving back. A huge hand engulfed hers, and Lizzy's heart did a little skip. With a couple of days left before her next flight and John's next mission, that *Kama Sutra* book needed to be put to good use. She turned to the sleepy giant. "Hey, Tank, time to go home. Let's hit the dusty road and get some shut-eye."

◊ ◊ ◊

They made love once, then fell back asleep until lunch, before flipping through cooking shows. John enjoyed a beer as they watched the sun inch below the horizon, and that was when the first round of her queasiness hit.

It was bad, so mortifyingly bad. The romance was out the window as he held her hair back over the toilet, while running a soothing hand along her back.

"I'm not going anywhere. My IFAK kit is back at base. Where're your supplies? Do you have a thermometer? You're burning up."

"Of course, I have a thermometer. Oh, God. Round two." She threw up until there was nothing left. "Make a bed for me, next to the loo. I'll sleep here forever. Crikey fish paste, I feel rough. Oh, gosh. I can't think about fish. That's not good." She dry-heaved again into the toilet.

John wiped an icy towel over her brow. "Lizbug, let me carry you to bed."

116

"I don't want to think about moving. Just leave me here to die."

Ignoring her shivering protest, he gently cradled her fevered body and laid her on the soft mattress. Racing to the kitchen, he brought back a plastic bucket and stood it next to the bed.

Her mind drifted, as roiling nausea swept over her in waves. John took her temperature.

"Shit, babes, it's already 104. I'm taking you to the hospital."

"No, we'll wait for hours at the ER. Call Garrison. I may need a shot to stop the vomiting—if it's the same virus that family had."

"It's obviously the same thing."

Lizzy groaned and reached for the bucket.

◊ ◊ ◊

Johnny dumped more ice cubes in the bowl and topped it up with water. Stripping her down to a tank top and underwear, he wiped down her flushed skin with the cool cloth.

"That feels good." She sighed as tremors racked her small frame. This was an aggressive strain, suddenly slamming into her like a freight train. Her current condition worried him. Putting aside his pride, Johnny picked up her phone. Bankes could get here sooner than a team member with Johnny's kit—besides, his bag only carried Zofran for vomiting.

"What's your passcode?"

"Why w-would you need that?" Her teeth chattered.

"I need Garrison's number."

"I j-just changed the password." Lizzy reluctantly glanced his way. "Oh, shoot. Fine. It's Jay Jay."

He grinned. "Cute, babes."

Johnny dialed the pompous dick's number as she retched.

After the third ring, he answered.

"Lizzy's ill." Johnny described the symptoms.

"It could be something she ate."

"No asshole, it's the same thing those patients had."

"Talk to me in a civilized manner. And I can't make assumptions without seeing her first."

"Then get here—"

"I'm helping out at a colleague's clinic in the city tonight. I'll see what I can do."

Johnny paced the room. "Don't fucking bother. I'll take her to the ER."

"No, I'll be there, just give me fifteen."

Johnny hung up and, as an afterthought, he sent the doctor's number to his phone.

Twenty-one minutes later, there was a knock at the door. He let Dr. Highfaluting in and led him to Lizzy. The doctor paused in the doorway and gave Johnny's Glock on the bedside table a disapproving glare before walking to the bed.

"Her temp is still sitting at 104. She's delirious as all hell."

Bankes sat down and took her vitals. "Yeah. That's a little high. I'll give her a cocktail for nausea and fever. All we can do is manage the symptoms."

"If this is a stomach flu then why doesn't she have any diarrhea? That doesn't make sense."

"There are many strains, but I'll draw blood and send it for testing."

Bankes spoke soothingly to her as he injected the meds. Lizzy grabbed his wrist and squeezed. Johnny watched the interaction from a distance, feeling like a clumsy voyeur, watching the gentle exchange between the refined doctor and his delicate patient.

Compared to Bankes, what kind of life did Johnny have to

offer her? A job where he'd be gone most of the time? A lonely existence on a remote farm in Wyoming? His bright Lizzy needed warmth, social interaction and family. Johnny didn't know much about family.

His childhood was a dirty secret that not even his MIT2 brothers knew about. He envisioned Lizzy's future with Dr. Garrison Bankes. Traveling across the globe, setting up clinics together, spending time in his fancy British home. Judging from his accent, he came from a posh estate.

Johnny folded his arms. "Where are you from?"

Bankes looked down his noble nose. "You mean, where is my home? England."

"Whereabouts?"

"I have a home in Weybridge."

"Where did you study medicine?"

"Oxford University."

And that about summed it up. Bankes stroked her brow once before standing. "I need to be in surgery within the hour, and I'll be unreachable for the next six hours. The cocktail will make her sleep."

"Thank you. I know I've been a dick."

"I'm not exactly proud of my behavior either. It's clear that we both care for her." Bankes patted Johnny on the shoulder. "How about a truce. Call me if you need anything."

Johnny walked him to the door, then headed back to her side. Eyelashes fluttered against pale cheeks.

He stood by the bed, taking in every detail. Her slightly bowed top lip, that stubborn chin and the damp tendril clinging to a delicate brow. He pushed the hair off her face and crawled up beside her, hoping for her sake it wouldn't be a rough night.

"Hey, sleepyhead."

John's scruffy face swam in her bleary vision. "What time is it?"

"Just after ten in the morning. Easy, don't tug at that arm, I've attached a line."

Lizzy eyed her taped up hand and the bag of saline. "Why? When?"

"Around five in the a.m. You couldn't stop puking, even after Bankes shot you up. Donnie came over with my kit; you're on your second bag."

"I don't remember any of that."

"You were pretty out of it. How do you feel?"

"Like I've been run over by a dump truck. The nausea is gone, but my back and stomach still hurt."

"Do you think you could eat something?"

"Maybe."

The room looked like a nuke had gone off. Face cloths and towels strewn across the floor. Her clothes, lying in heaps. A light throw covered her, as the heavier duvet lay crumpled next to her dresser. Five minutes later she gingerly ate a piece of dry toast and sipped on Coke. John looked as worn out as she felt as he repacked his kit.

"I may be okay to fly in the morning."

He shook his head. "You're not working the Johannesburg trip, you won't be well enough."

"I'll be just fine if I rest up today, besides I get to see my parents. I'm not sure how long the layover is, but any time with family is a bonus."

He looked out the window, and she couldn't decipher the look on his grim face. "What's up?"

"I have to get back to base. We're rolling out in the morning.

I called Bankes from my phone, he's on his way, he'll remove the IV and stay with you."

Okay, then. She noted his set face and fixed eyes on an imaginary horizon. He barely blinked.

"I didn't realize you're leaving so soon."

"It's for the best," he said carefully. That had her placing the plate down. She stared wordlessly at John and he never stirred, not even to look her way. It took a moment to find her voice.

"Are you breaking it off with me?"

"We'd have to be together for that statement to be true. You made it clear that we weren't."

"Wow. Okay." She swallowed down the heart-shredding hurt. "Is it something I've done? Is it because you saw me puking?"

"Don't be crazy; I'm a damn medic. Babes, I need space to get my head on straight. I'm not sure if I can give you what you need, and I need to work out our game plan."

"What does that mean?"

"It means we've had a long night and I'm tired. It means you deserve better. Are we even moving in the same direction?"

She took a sharp breath.

He tidied the side of the bed where he'd lain, straightening the sheets. "Look, we'll keep in touch and see what happens when I get back."

"Is that the 'let's be friend' speech?"

"No. It's the 'give me some time' speech."

She felt her chin tremble. "Well, here's the 'Signore, it's been nice knowing you' speech."

"Jeez. It's all or nothing with you. Why do you have to take it to the extreme?"

There was a knock on the door. As far as she was concerned,

this conversation was over. Screw him and all the men on the damn planet with their sanctimonious bullshit. "Have a safe trip."

"Don't shut me out, Lizbug."

"I'm not the one doing the shutting." She closed her eyes against the pain.

A firm kiss lingered on her forehead. Eyes still squeezed shut, Lizzy turned away.

"I'll text you to see how you're feeling. Keep your phone nearby."

Lizzy didn't answer. A war of emotions raged, and her chest felt like it would burst from the heartache. This only supposed to be fun. She knew this moment would come, but she'd thought they had more time. She'd also thought that she'd be the one doing the walking away. When she opened her eyes, John was gone, and Garrison stood in his place.

"Hello, sweetheart, I believe you've had a rough night. Let's get you situated."

Chapter Seven

She had a bladder the size of a peanut. Lizzy slammed out of the aircraft lavatory. Her phone buzzed again for the fifth time and she slipped it out of the apron pocket to glance at the screen. John had sure meant it when he'd said to keep her phone nearby. Two missed calls and five texts from the man. She should just switch it off and place it in her damn carry-on.

He seemed concerned over her insistence on working the flight. She knew he was right to be worried. She felt like dog poop. As soon as she landed in Johannesburg, she'd see the family doctor.

Talking to John was out of the question. He wanted space, well now he had it, and it would probably be a long time until she saw him again. With her packed flight schedule ahead and his covert work, they probably wouldn't see each other for months.

It was better that way. It gave her time to mourn the loss of their budding relationship and to get back to earning a living. She'd bid for more flights, trade in her allocated time off with other attendants and fill up her schedule. The orphanage and Valentino also needed her attention.

Wiping her clammy forehead and ignoring her miserable

heartache, Lizzy pocketed the phone and got back to work. Jane—the fellow flight attendant slash interior designer wannabe—gave Lizzy a sideways glance. "No offense, girl, but you look like shit. Go home before we close those doors."

Jane, as always, looked impeccable. Her thick brown hair was swept into a twisty concoction, and her red lips looked flawless.

"That's not fair, I'm running the galley and then you'd be one down in the cabin. I signed up for the flight and I'll work it."

Jane shrugged. "Have it your way, but don't give me your skanky virus. Five-foot perimeter, sweetness."

Lizzy restrained from rolling her eyes. That was so Jane. The VIP family and their small entourage boarded. It was the American ambassador to Kenya's wife and son, dashing to Johannesburg for an extended shopping spree. All in celebration of his high school graduation.

The elegant woman seemed friendly; her spoiled son, not so much. So far, he'd returned two Virgin Marys, insisting Lizzy had added too much pepper, then too much lemon. Third time lucky, Lizzy presented him with the tomato cocktail and swept back to the galley.

Next came the captain's coffee. Shit, the captain—of all her luck, Captain Stuart was at the helm of the Airbus. Lizzy supposed she couldn't avoid the creepy windbag forever.

She chose to serve the first officer first. He was a new flight member she'd never flown with before, and she'd already forgotten his name. He seemed like a nice guy.

When Lizzy next sidled into the cockpit to hand the captain his hot drink, Stuart gave her the cold shoulder, obviously still sore over the Peshawar incident. She'd bet he'd got into deep trouble over the whorehouse. She waited for him to hand her a dirty napkin and stared at his crotch area, wondering what crawled beneath his briefs. Just thinking about it made her itch, and she scratched hard at her arm, then stretched out her achy back.

"What in the blazes!" The first officer leaned forward.

Captain Stuart scrambled to grab his mic. "Oh my God! Oh shit. Close the cockpit door. Now!"

Lizzy stared in horror at the gang of black-clad men waving guns and surrounding the plane. Another contingent flooded the small hangar and outbuildings of the private airstrip. Gunshots echoed in the distance.

"The door now, Lizette!"

"But the other girls—"

"It's too late!"

Lizzy shouted into the passage. "Jane, close the front galley door, quick!"

Captain Stuart guessed right—it was too late. As Jane tried to close the door, a shot rang out, blowing Jane off her feet. Lizzy screamed and slammed shut the cockpit door, panic bringing her to her knees. The brutal gang now had access to the plane and the only thing separating her from them, was the cockpit door.

Think Lizzy. Think. She ripped her phone from her apron pocket. Nearly dropping it, she pressed redial. "Oh, God, please answer, oh, God, please answer."

He didn't. More shots rang out as she redialed with shaking hands. It rang and rang. She'd leave a message. The last one she'd ever leave…then his deep voice came over the line and she sobbed. "John. Oh, God, John."

◊ ◊ ◊

Johnny contemplated not answering the second call. He couldn't speak to her, afraid if he heard her sweet voice, he'd cave. Instead, he sat on the locker room bench, half dressed in his bug-out gear while staring at the ringing phone. He'd called her earlier, wanting to take back the hurtful things he'd said. Exhaustion screwed with his logic. Now, if she cried on the phone, Johnny would cave, move heaven and earth to be with her. He loved her so damn much.

Let it go to voicemail. You've gotta get mission ready.

Nope, Johnny's thumb had a mind of its own.

"Lizbug, I hope you stayed home—"

"John. Oh, God, John." She was losing her shit and he stood, his thoughts tumbling.

"Baby, what's wrong?"

"They killed her. They're shooting everyone. I'm next. Oh shit, shit, shit, I'm next."

For the first time in his career, he nearly pissed himself. "Where are you? On the crew bus?"

"No, in…in the plane, at the private strip, we sometimes use—the Jet…JetHaven one—we're locked in the cockpit. They have guns."

Johnny ran for help. "I need you to take a deep breath. Tell me what you see, I need a description of the men."

"Wearing all black, they have…have…masks on."

"How many?" Ignoring the hot asphalt biting into his bare feet with every pounding step, he sprinted around the last corner.

She paused, then said, "Eight of them—wait—nine. The leader is circling around to the stairs. I think it's their leader, he…he looks different from the rest."

Johnny barreled into the hangar, shirtless, barefoot, and with pants half-buttoned. "JetHaven's private airstrip. Now. Nine armed militants," he yelled at the team then continued talking to her.

"Different how?"

"He's wearing an actual mask. It's leather and all pointy."

Johnny staggered to a stop as terror rooted him to the spot. "What color, baby? Tell me the color."

"Red."

The room swung and his ears buzzed. Max grabbed his shoulders, getting up in his face. "SITREP."

Johnny blew out a shaky breath, wanting to puke. "The Scythian—moving in on Lizzy's plane." Distantly he heard Donnie alerting the local authorities.

The Scythian Horse Lord and his mercenaries moved through entire villages like locusts, wiping out anything that got in their way. Leaving scalped bodies to rot in the African sun. Anyone who crossed the Horse Lord's path never escaped, and Lizzy sat directly in that path.

Shots rang out, clipping through the phone and she screamed.

"Lizzy! Talk to me. Lizzy! Fuck! No!"

Slater tossed gear in the truck like a terminator. Max shoved Johnny towards the vehicle, thrusting a go-bag in his hands, then Max grabbed a couple of M4s, before running to the driver's side.

"They're shooting at the cockpit door. I don't want to die. John, please don't let me die."

"It's okay, honey. Get down as low as you can. Make yourself as small a target as possible." MIT2 wouldn't arrive in time; instead they'd hear her die. He punched the ceiling, leaving a dent, then reassured her. "Listen to my voice; I love you. Just concentrate on my voice. You're my everything. I love you so damn much. You hear me, baby? I'm so fucking lucky to have you. It's going to be okay. I'm never gonna leave you. I'll be there soon, Lizbug. I'm coming."

John switched the call to handsfree mode, running through the vehicle's speakers.

"Be here now. John," she begged. "Please, help me. Oh, my God, the first officer is dea—" More gunshots and crashing noises drowned out her screams.

Arabic shouts peppered the air. All of the MIT2 men spoke Arabic. Max was most fluent, but Johnny got the gist of what the bastards were saying. Johnny guessed that the one who wore a voice modulator was The Scythian.

"Pull the bitch out, put her with the others."

"What about the captain? Do we shoot him?"

"I want some fun with this little whore," another voice added as Lizzy moaned.

"I'll shoot you myself if you don't follow orders. Take her."

Lizzy yelped in pain. Pleading shouts echoed as they pulled her away. Five seconds later a distant gunshot.

"NO!" Johnny shouted. "Lizzy! Lizzy! No! Baby. Please!"

Rustling, then heavy breathing registered over the airways. Johnny knew who now held that phone. Hatred like he'd never known before bled from his brain. "You fucker. I will spend the rest of my days hunting you. And fuck removing a scalp— instead, I'll be removing your red leathered head."

The disembodied reply slid over his skin like hot embers, with words he'd never forget: "Then the hunt begins."

◊ ◊ ◊

As Max pulled up, Johnny jerked open the door and surged out. He ran for the already cordoned entrance. Slater and Donnie dragged him back as Max dug in from the front. Johnny was living a nightmare.

"Don't touch me. Don't. I was just with her. Yesterday, I held her. She was alive, and I just spoke with her, a few minutes ago. I heard her voice."

"I know, bro. Stay with the vehicle; Slater will hang with you. You hear me, bud?"

Johnny struggled and stared at the pathetic array of flashing lights lining the entrance. With no integrated emergency services and a lack of resources, many incidents in Kenya had poor response times. Lack of specific training of emergency personnel, poor coordination, and a lack of standard operating procedures were invariable challenges when it came to militant attacks. They'd all arrived too late.

"I need to see her."

"I can't let that happen."

That was Max's way of saying he expected a plane-full of deceased flight crew and passengers... no survivors.

Johnny swiped at a damp cheek, then studied the moisture on his fingers. He'd never cried before, not even when his uncle died. Especially not when his mom died. He didn't care if he begged. He had to hold her one last time. "Sir, I need to see her. Let me see her."

"Shit, man. You don't want to do this. I'll take care of it." Max pulled in a rough breath. "I'll take care of her."

"No." Johnny pushed back unsteady legs.

Slater stepped alongside. "I've got Johnny's back. He'll get his shit together. He has to; it's a crime scene, right, big man? They ain't gonna let a raving lunatic in, and you'll get your ass thrown in jail if you ram your way through those Kenyan officers. Here's a shirt. You left your giant-ass boots behind, so watch for thorns." Slater passed him a T-shirt, and Johnny pulled it on with shaking hands.

"If we're doing this, put your game face on and zip up your

pants. I ain't gonna help out with that situation."

"Screw you." Johnny forced out the words as the team stepped up to the cordon. The lone officer glanced at his bare feet.

"He's with us." Max flashed credentials, and they were through. A police inspector approached. Johnny recognized him. He'd attended a terrorism response class that MIT2 ran four months before in Garissa, a city east of Nairobi.

"Inspector Kamathi." Max shook his hand and exchanged pleasantries.

The inspector led them to the hangars. "We've only just arrived. Figured we missed the bastards by five minutes."

The first wave of carnage littered the private terminal, and they skirted the bloody trails. Exposed skulls indicated the Scythian's scalping path.

"Survivors?" Max asked.

"In here? None so far. Seven dead. We're shutting down all the freeways and exit points. We've barely cleared the aircraft; we haven't yet assessed casualties onboard."

Then they were back in the sunlight, exiting onto the airport apron. The Airbus sat centered in the shining commotion. A body lay under a tarp at the bottom of the stairs. The panted legs and shoes indicated a male. Johnny's heart pounded in a sticky rhythm. *Not Lizzy.*

The inspector gestured to the dead man and the discarded handgun lying beside him. "This was the only guard on the property. Looks like he tried to stop them from boarding the aircraft. Poor bugger didn't stand a chance."

That was all they'd had. One lone man with a Ruger pistol standing between them and death. *Walk up the stairs. One foot in front of the other.*

Lizzy was in there—waiting for him—he owed her that. He owed her family that. Johnny clutched at the rail, then climbed the steps towards hell.

Butchery and bullet holes. The carnage that was the front galley had him pausing to suck in a breath. Bloodshed and gore were part of the job. Seeing it, living it, stopping it, causing it—wiping out terrorist cells. Death was a familiar friend. But this was different. Personal. Surreal. A brunette lay mangled on the floor, her pooled blood drying in the sticky heat. Someone's daughter. His eyes ran over the sightless expression of terror, the smudged cherry-painted lips frozen in yawning death. The portion of her scalp above her left eye was hacked off.

Johnny's head turned on its own volition, drawn to the place he'd last spoken to Lizbug. He stepped left, towards the peppered cockpit door hanging off its hinges. The first officer lay over the controls. Blood was strewn across the right side of the cockpit. The captain's seat looked untouched. Johnny's eyes drifted to the floor, imagining where Lizzy had tried to hide—where she'd curled up in terror.

He stepped back out. After a cursory examination of the flight attendant's body, Max stood up from his haunches.

"The captain isn't in the cockpit," Johnny said.

"He's missing," the inspector confirmed.

Johnny nodded towards the cabin. "The others, are they in there?"

Slater placed a hand on his shoulder. "Why don't we head back to the truck?"

Johnny didn't pay him any heed. Max had grown still, spotting something down the aisle. The bulkhead obstructed Johnny's view.

"Stay here," Max commanded. Slater pulled Johnny back as

Max moved deeper into the aircraft. Shoving forward, Johnny launched into the cabin and leaped across the seats. Max knelt before another crew member strewn in the aisle. Bloodstained and golden-haired. Johnny barely registered barreling down the aisle or howling out the pain.

Slater tackled him from behind. Knee buckling, Johnny kept on going.

Max wrestled him away. "It's not Lizzy. It's not her!"

He didn't believe them and kept fighting.

"Look. It's not her." Max let go, and Johnny sank to his knees. The broken woman was taller than his Lizzy. Still so fragile and small. He tucked a remaining bloody strand behind her ear.

Where is she? Where's my girl? Pushing off, he headed towards the luxurious lounge ahead. A female passenger lay dead in her seat. Mid-fifties. Her two-person protection detail lay across the floor. Local police stood nearby. Ignoring the whispers over the woman, Johnny broke into the rear cabin—laid out as an economy cabin capable of seating twenty-five passengers. He counted five bodies, the paid entourage for the female VIP seated in the front area. The back galley sat empty. What was left to search? Lavatories. Showers. Rest areas. With Slater's help, Johnny systematically searched the plane. By the time they'd worked their way up to the front, the newly acquired manifest listed a full count of who was supposedly onboard—Max ran through the list with the inspector, and they both swore.

"The deceased female VIP is the US Ambassador to Kenya's wife, Mrs. Jenna Clark."

"Oh, shit," Slater said.

"His son, Mason Clark, was also onboard and is now missing, along with Captain Stuart Williams and Miss Lizette Steyn."

Walking out onto the stairs, Johnny sucked in gulps of air. Was she still alive? That also meant that the Horse Lord had her.

Not for long. If the Scythian wanted a hunt, he'd be tracked, captured and gutted—James Cane style.

Chapter Eight

"Thanks for my boots, bro." Johnny pulled on clean socks and grabbed a scuffed Magnum boot.

Donnie placed a heavy duffel bag down carefully. "No problem. I had to swing by to grab our equipment. We're now fully prepped, the rest is in the truck." Donnie glanced around the workroom. "How many of these amigos have bigger egos than MIT2? What do you reckon? Think we're still top dog?"

There was a mother-load of brass and bluster sandwiched in the walls of the newly set up base of operations. That was what happened when the most infamous terrorist on the planet kidnapped an American diplomat's son.

The British contingent was gathered around a laptop in the far corner. SBS boys and possibly Scotland Yard. The majority of the Americans worked for the United States Special Operations Command. The CIA made their presence known, and Task Force Green—known to civilians as Delta Force—stood near the back. All the Green boys were good buddies of MIT2, as they often worked the same missions together.

The Kenyan bigwigs tried to keep up with the Western contingent, shouting orders in Swahili to their men. Johnny had little faith in their abilities. Minimal amounts were allocated to training anti-terror police units in Nairobi. An allocated budget as low as seven hundred dollars per month for operations, while the police officers were paid peanuts.

At least there was a handful of Kenyan military in the room. MIT2 worked with Kenyan Special Forces on occasion, and Johnny had confidence in their training. The Kenyan soldiers were well trained and reliable in the field.

Aside from MIT2, Johnny didn't trust any other agency enough to rely on their resources to track Lizzy. That's where Donnie came in. He'd already hacked into security cameras around the city, tracking where they'd dumped the initial vehicle. Now that they were fully operational, it was just a matter of time until they had their first leads.

Johnny said as much to his team. "If any of these grandstanders have solid intel, then I'll be kissing their muscled asses for all time, even though all they care about is finding the boy. All I care about is finding Lizzy."

Slater pulled up a chair. "That's what JSOC wants. The delivery of the kid with solid vitals, and the Scythian's head on a MIT2 plate."

"Let's get all three hostages home," Donnie replied, hooking up an additional laptop to his station.

Johnny studied a map of the area. They'd guessed the general direction that the Scythian would take—he'd head north-east, back into Somalia. That made the most sense. The porous border helped Somalian extremists to target Kenya.

Though the Kenyan government announced plans to build a wall along parts of the 424-mile-long border with Somalia, the wall was still nonexistent. Since the attack, emergency checkpoints had hastily been set up, but there was no way to cover such an extensive territory.

Johnny itched to be out there, hunting. Without intel, it was like searching for a needle in the haystack. MIT2 needed to burn down the haystack by gathering all evidence and information. All that would be left was that red-hot poker, lying in the ashes with nowhere to run.

His phone buzzed, and Johnny glanced down. Doctor Bankes. Had he heard the news already? Johnny didn't have time for small talk and shoved the phone at Slater. "It's Bankes, deal with him."

Taking the mobile, Slater mock saluted. "Yes, sturdy sire. Your wish is my command."

"You're sitting there scratching your balls—answer it."

"I'm waiting for Donnie and Max to set up the tech shit."

"Answer it."

Slater did as he was told. "Hello…Johnny's unavailable. I'm a workmate, we met at the orphanage when I helped to save your ass…" He stood and wandered away.

Donnie leaned forward, and Johnny huddled closer. "I think I have a possible ID on a suspicious vehicle." Johnny shifted to focus on the screen as Donnie continued. "I've run images from ATM cameras, a compound camera and a traffic cam on the route. This road leads to the A104 freeway. A black van with tinted windows flashed amongst traffic on three different occasions. If I've calculated correctly, it's going way too fast. A secondary vehicle following close behind is also tinted."

"How long?"

"Thirty minutes."

Johnny called the other teams over. Slater walked up and pulled him aside.

"Not now, Slater, we have a lead."

"It's important." The grim look made Johnny pause. Slater

filled him in. "Lizzy's bloodwork came back. It's not a norovirus."

"Wait, I don't follow."

"Garrison Bankes didn't know anything about the JetHaven hijacking. He called because he wants to admit Lizzy to hospital. Her white cell count is through the roof."

"Shit." Johnny ran a hand over his mouth. "What about that other family?"

"They're fine. Their bloodwork looks normal; they're fully recovered."

And Lizzy was as ill as all hell…out there. Alone.

Someone yelled from outside the entrance. Johnny glanced over and caught a glimpse of a sunglassed prick. He knew that profile and zeroed in on his prey.

"I'm cooperating as best I can. Don't question me like some criminal. Do you have any idea how this affects my business? Jesus!" Ethan Matthews shrugged off one of the spook's hands.

The CIA agent didn't move fast enough to prevent Johnny from shoving Matthews against the wall.

"What the fuck!" The JetHaven blowhard sputtered as his glasses fell to the floor.

"Where was your security? One brave security guard against nine extremist fuckers! That's how you protect your staff?"

"I'm not a damn mind reader! Nairobi is one of our more secure bases!"

Shoving him higher against the wall, Johnny growled, "Bullshit! Al-Shabaab stated—last month—that they were targeting wealthy Americans and Kenyans. You've had weeks to sort out your shit!"

Max pushed into Johnny's space. "He's not worth your job. Step away."

Obey the order.

Johnny wasn't entirely done. "If they die because of you—if they harm Lizette Steyn in any way, I'm coming for you. You're a greedy, penny-saving ass swipe. I have to call her parents next, to tell them that their daughter might not be coming home." Johnny released the pale man. "I'm guessing Ambassador Clark wants your head on a platter, for not protecting his family. Good luck with that, asshole."

Pushing past the silent audience, Johnny wiped his hands on his pants and walked away, despising himself for not preventing Lizzy from working the Johannesburg flight and hating that he'd walked away when she'd needed him most.

◊ ◊ ◊

The nausea was back, and so was the fever. Lizzy shifted on the metal floor of the van, trying to get comfortable. Her side and back ached, over and above the throbbing muscles in her shoulders from the brutal angle of her arms, restrained with electrical tape. Try as she might, she couldn't stay awake, instead drifting in and out of a delirious fog.

"Do you think they'll leave us here to bake? How long has it been?" the kid asked with a raspy voice. He'd cried over his mother's death for most of the journey.

"Hell, if I know. It has to be at least a hundred degrees in this metal box," Captain Stuart said, before banging his feet against the panel door. "Hey! We're cooking in here!"

Was it hot? Lizzy couldn't stop shivering. The captain yelled in frustration, and she studied his profile. They'd beaten him pretty badly when he'd kicked out at one of the mercenaries who'd groped at her chest. *Go, Stuart.* Her estimation of him rose a teensy bit.

This was the fifth vehicle they were dumped into, handled

like carcasses of meat. Where was the man with the red hood? Lizzy guessed the terrorists had split up. She now counted six men including the driver. Six men who'd removed their masks. That couldn't be good, apparently not caring if the hostages saw their faces.

A humming sound intruded on her rambling thoughts, increasing in strength. The vehicle vibrated briefly as the sound moved overhead—it was a plane. The van door slammed open.

"Out now. Move."

They yanked the Clark kid out first. He tried to hop with taped-up ankles and fell in the dirt. The bastards laughed and kicked him, Lizzy yelled for them to stop. Instead, they dragged her out by her hair. Rolling to her knees, Lizzy swayed, falling sideways as pain spiked in her side. She should've called in sick and stayed home, in her quaint apartment. Snuggled up in a soft duvet.

Tears ran down dusty cheeks as she sobbed, then vomited. That earned her a kick to the head, before being hoisted over a shoulder and carried to a light aircraft that look like it had seen better days. One last desperate glance at the thick foliage encroaching on the makeshift runway scrubbed away hope, as the thug carried her through the door. Was John nearby? Did he think she was dead? Was he still in the country, or searching for her elsewhere? Wouldn't matter if he was, Lizzy had a feeling they were flying far away. Far enough away for her to be a distant memory in a life she'd taken for granted.

Tanzania
Outskirts of the Serengeti Reserve

They'd expected the Horse Lord to have fled northwards to Somalia, Ethiopia or South Sudan—all safe havens for extremists intent on disappearing. Instead, they'd tracked his men into Tanzania. The Scythian had slipped over Kenya's southern border five hours ago, and MIT2 had spent the past hours seeking clues in surrounding villages and towns and offering a reward for any information.

Now they were stationed at a new Tanzanian base, an old schoolhouse, running over developing intel and waiting on the appearance of Ambassador Clark. Delta Force took over in the field, knocking on—and down—doors.

The lagging pace and endless waiting had Johnny desperately wanting to go rogue. Max knew his friend needed to be out there, not sitting around with his thumb up his ass as big dicks wrapped in wads of red tape argued over whose mission this was.

Without MIT2's resources and expertise, Johnny was just a fart—a lethal fart, but still a fart in the wind. Max rubbed his brow. Watching his friend coming undone was torture. This would break him.

Lizzy's chances of survival were below the five percent mark. Locating a wealthy terrorist's stronghold on the vast continent of Africa was virtually impossible without solid leads to work with, and that took months, or sometimes years. Hell, they'd been tracking the Scythian for months. He was a true nomad, making him more difficult to pin down. If they lost Lizette Steyn, they'd lose Johnny too.

"Hey, bud. How are you holding up?" Max squeezed Johnny's shoulder before sitting down beside him.

"I just got off the phone with Lizzy's father. Daniel Steyn and his wife will be flying into Nairobi. They'll stay at Lizzy's place while waiting on news." Johnny pinched the bridge of his nose. "He's legitimately lost his shit. Guess that's what happens when you receive a call saying that violent extremists kidnapped your daughter."

Max leaned his elbows on knees and stared at the floor.

Johnny continued, "I told him I'd get her back no matter how long it took. No matter what state—" He couldn't finish.

"I haven't said anything to Abby; she's too fragile at the moment."

"How is she?"

"Still the same—on bedrest, staying with my parents on their farm in Colorado."

"If you need to go—"

"I need to be here, finding this fucker. Abby will be fine, providing she listens to the doc and rests up for the next month. Once we have Lizzy back—safe and sound—and once we've exterminated the Scythian, I'll take some personal time with my family."

"Thanks, bro. I spoke to Garrison earlier—Doctor Bankes—her blood results are a shitting mess. Our girl has to be in a bad way."

"Does Bankes know what's wrong with her?"

"No. He'd need to run more tests. It could be anything—malaria, yellow fever, dengue fever. There's extreme shit in Africa that makes you bleed from your damn orifices." Johnny stood and grabbed his pack.

"Where are you going?"

"Tagging along with the SBS boys in the field. They're checking out the private game reserve, two clicks to the west of the Serengeti."

"That's a negative. Rather you bug out with your own team in an hour. In the meantime, let Donnie and I work with what we have. Get some rest—you look like shit and won't be any use to Lizzy if you can't function. Besides, this place will be a circus when Ambassador Clark arrives."

Johnny looked torn. Max hoped the big man took his advice.

Johnny stood in the center of the sand road. Sweltering heat shimmered in waves above the baking earth. The bush hummed in a rhythm, surrounding him with the constant buzz of African survival. He turned and walked down the road—alone in his pursuit. He'd outpaced the other teams, drawn to this place that almost called his name. A twig snapped, and he searched the thick foliage, eyeing a sleek predator keeping pace. His long mane gleamed in the afternoon light. Johnny slowed and scanned the thick foliage for signs of more lions; not seeing any, he turned to face the male cat.

"You may be bigger than me, but not by much."

Golden eyes met golden eyes for a long heartbeat. He lowered his rifle. With a bow of the head, the beast slinked back into the shaded grass. Movement down the path had Johnny raising and swiveling his aim. A man. The target slipped back into vegetation—the hooded shape galvanized Johnny into action.

He gave chase, locating the spot, and tracking the son of a bitch through the trampled grass. When a clearing came into view, he slowed. Cautiously keeping to the edge, Johnny circled the space—shaded by a large flame tree.

The man hid behind the trunk. "Step out now or I'll blow your head off." Johnny's entire focus was on the cloaked figure appearing beneath the twisted branches. The Scythian. Sliding into the clearing, Johnny tamped down the hatred and aimed at the scarred leathered hood. "Hands up, you son of a bitch. Where is she?"

The red bastard just stood there.

"Tell me where she is!"

Still no answer.

"Down on your fucking knees. Now!"

The Horse Lord laughed before lunging back behind the trunk. Johnny pulled the trigger. Nothing. He glanced down at the M4, but instead he held a large wooden stick streaked in blood. Where was his weapon?

Johnny dropped the branch and stumbled back. His boots slipped on a blanket of coral blossoms. Thickly spread blooms radiated outwards, hundreds of bruised scarlet flowers covering the earth.

The smell of ripe peaches drifted on the warm breeze and he looked up. Lizzy now stood in the Scythian's place, wearing a bright blue sundress. Her smile took his breath away, ruby-painted lips with one sweet freckle at the corner.

"Hand me a flower, Jay Jay."

As if in slow motion, he obeyed, bending to pick one off the ground. She stepped in and plucked it from his shocked hands, before placing it behind her ear.

Johnny pointed at her suddenly smudged lips, the cherry lipstick now smeared across her pretty cheek. Lizzy put a hand to her mouth, and it came away bloody.

"What's happening, John?" Crimson tears bled from her eyes and tracked down her cheeks.

"It's okay, baby, I've got you." But Johnny didn't. He couldn't move. His boots sank into the red-stained sludge, as he shouted her name.

Blood trickled from her nose, and she cupped her hands to catch the flow.

Falling to his knees, he held out a hand. "Come to me, Lizbug. Come to me."

Her hands opened, and blood-coated blossoms fell to the earth. "Lizzy!" he screamed as she fell. Red quicksand slowly pulled her under as he called to her bleached face, cleared of all expression.

Johnny jerked awake and staggered to his feet. *Fuck. Fuck. Just a dream. It was just a dream.* He swiped his sweaty brow, gasping for breath.

"I've been having those too."

Johnny swung around. Ambassador Clark pushed away from the door. He looked as rough as Johnny felt. "The nightmares. I heard they have your friend, Lizette Steyn?"

Johnny nodded. "Yes, sir. She's more than just a friend."

"You love her. They have my son." The ambassador's voice broke on the last word.

"We'll get them back."

"Or die trying, right?" Ambassador Clark pulled up a chair and sat. Johnny stood at attention, despite having met the ambassador a couple of times on deployments.

"This is a good hidey hole. I'm guessing you ducked out of the pomp and ceremony that comes with me and my entourage." Clark looked around the small classroom tucked at the back end of the corridor. "It's quiet here."

Johnny agreed. "I came here to get away for a minute. I didn't intend to fall asleep."

"You're running on fumes—like all of us—but let me guess, every time you close your eyes, you see her face." Clark patted the seat next to him. "Sit. I have no one to talk to, no one who understands the agony of knowing who has my son."

He sat. "Sir, I'm sorry about your wife."

Clark clenched his jaw and turned away. Johnny had a tremendous amount of respect for the man, a former Air Force pilot who'd served his country well. Clark still served with bravery and integrity.

"Where's your detail, sir?"

"Squatting outside the door. They've stuck to me like leeches since the attack."

"They care about your safety."

"True. So, I believe you MIT boys stir hot coals with your dicks."

"Uh. Sir?"

"Heard that MIT2 is the best covert team on this continent. MIT1 is a close second, but don't tell them that. I'm trusting you to find my son, alive. I don't trust easily. Knowing that you're in the same boat I am means you're it. Don't come back without them."

Johnny nodded, unable to answer.

"I've screwed up so many times when it comes to that boy. Raising kids is hard enough. Throw in an absentee father...I have amends to make."

"I'm sure you're a great father."

"A stubborn one. I've been pushing for Mason to go to a military academy. The boy wants to be a damn fashion designer. Jesus."

Johnny didn't know how to reply. Family dynamics weren't his thing. He blurted the first thing that came to mind. "I'm guessing if that's his dream, then he'd apply himself and be pretty successful."

"If I get Mason back, he can be whatever he wants to be. I

can't lose him, not after losing—" Clark choked on a sob.

A knock at the door and Slater slipped in. The ambassador swiped at his eyes. "Sorry to interrupt, sir. We've found a viable witness. Delta just brought him in."

◊ ◊ ◊

A key turned in a lock, and Lizzy surfaced from her demented dreams. She lay on a filthy pile of hay in the corner of a caged cellar—still a hostage.

The other two prisoners huddled in their respective corners. She needed to check on them but could barely roll over. And she needed to pee. The makeshift latrine in the corner was a rusty cistern that sat low to the ground. She'd been avoiding the foul vessel and decided to lie back and avoid it a while longer.

Her ill health drowned out most of the gut-swilling fear. Two monsters stalked her; one was a fiery hooded villain, and the other, a fiery fever running through her body. Both craved her demise. Lizzy ignored those rabid beasts chewing at her weak defenses, instead her mind flitted back to a sacred moment shared with John, the night before her life had literally gone down the toilet.

Returning from the orphanage after she'd treated the sick family, they'd stripped down for a quick shower. Using a sudsy sponge, John had squeezed foam over her breasts, watching them bud up under his ministrations. He brushed the sponge between her legs, making her quiver.

His large hands rinsed off the soap, stroking her peaked nipples, tracing down her belly, skimming along her folds. As they stumbled onto the bed—still damp—Lizzy grabbed the *Kama Sutra* book. John put it aside, sheathed himself and pulled her onto his lap. They sat face to face, staring into each other's eyes. It was a slow assault that made her gasp. First his fingers played, making her toes curl as he lazily fondled. Then he situated her over his erect cock and eased inside, taking his time to drill down into her tight passage.

When fully settled, he just sat there, tracing the contours of her face and playing with her hair. "I love how thick it is. It's grown so long since I last saw you."

The gentle lines in the warrior's face made her heart pound. She shifted her hips, and he stilled her.

"Look at me, baby. Don't look away." His thumb stroked her nub, and she immediately clenched around him.

"Shit," he growled, stroking again, making her shudder. "Rock slowly. Look at me and don't look away."

Lizzy did as he asked. As minutes ticked by, she traced his brow, then touched the small scar at the corner of his eye. His scorching gaze never strayed from hers. Those banked flames stared into her soul, craving the chance to burn down her walls.

His sensual lips framed perfectly by stubble had her licking her lips. John's jaw clenched as he swelled and her wet heat anchored him. Tracing her collarbone, he ran a hand over her breasts before gripping her waist and suddenly raising her up, grinding her back down.

She took over, riding and bucking, feeling him ramming into her. His nostrils flared as she moaned. Leaning down, she placed elbows on his hard chest. Her hair swayed as she ground up against him, digging nails into his muscled shoulders.

"Come for me, Lizbug." He slipped a hand between them and rolled a finger over their joined flesh, and she shattered. John roared his release, grasping her hips and pounding into her.

Afterward, he'd tucked her into his large body, becoming the big spoon to her little one. She'd fallen asleep with strong fingers stroking through her hair—it had felt like heaven.

And this was hell. Lagos hell. Once they'd landed, Lizzy had recognized glimpses of the city from her work trips. They were in Nigeria. So many miles away from John that she'd given up hope of rescue.

Groaning against the thumping pain, she clenched fingers around the cell bars, then braced herself for the crawl to the latrine. And a grimy crawl it was in the dimly lit dirt. When she finally got situated, she cried out in agony—not able to urinate.

And it dawned—nausea, fever, back pain, vomiting, the urge to urinate… Lizzy had pyelonephritis, a kidney infection—it wasn't a stomach flu. How had she not realized? She was virtually a trained nurse and knew the signs. She'd once had it as a teenager. Not this severely—this was some bad shit.

"Son of a mother trucker," Lizzy mumbled.

"What's wrong with you?" the Clark kid asked. What was his name again? Dixon? Brixon? No, it was Mason.

Stuart stirred. "If it's something contagious, a heads-up would be appreciated."

She glared. "What will you do, request an upgrade to better accommodation?"

"You've always been a sarcastic bitch."

"That's a sexist thing to say."

"Enough," Mason broke in. "You look super ill. Can I help you get back to that pile of shitty straw in the corner?"

Lizzy gasped out thanks. "It's a kidney infection, by the way. It's not contagious."

"It's okay." The teenager tried to reassure her as he pulled her arm over his shoulder. "How do they fix it?"

"Antibiotics, but it's too far gone for a prescription. I'd need to be hospitalized."

Mason settled her back down. "Well, that ain't gonna happen—unless my dad finds us. He used to be in the Air Force. He's a powerful guy."

She smiled wanly. "Thanks for your help, Mason. Your dad would be proud."

His face darkened. "I'm such a loser. I don't deserve him—or my mom either. Oh, God. They killed her. They killed my mommy." His face was bleak with pain and she studied him through her sorrow; he couldn't be more than seventeen.

"How old are you Mason?"

"Sixteen." His voice choked on the word.

"Sit with me. It's going to be okay. Your father will find you. He needs you just as much as you need him."

The boy sank down, and she grabbed his hand. Deep sobs racked his body. The only way she knew how to comfort was with her voice, so she hummed and then sang.

She wasn't profoundly religious and didn't know any comforting hymns. She sang what she knew. The song that came to mind was "Angel" by Sarah McLachlan. Lizzy sang her heart out, imagining she was back on her cheerful balcony with John by her side, a beer in his hand as they watched a Kenyan sunset. Mason rested his head on her lap, weeping out the pain.

The door opened, and Lizzy covered her eyes against the searing light. The man with the crimson hood stood silhouetted, pausing to make what she assumed was a dramatic statement before descending the stairs.

Mason whimpered, scrambling into a shadowed corner, and her pulse leaped erratically. Black terror surrounded the monster, Lizzy imagined it curling through the bars and snaking around her ankles. She pulled her legs beneath her. He was just a man. A human made of flesh and blood. She breathed in shallow breaths as he paused, only the bars separating her from his foul regard. He knelt, and she tried to keep hold of fragile control.

"You have a beautiful voice. You will sing when I demand it." His voice sounded weirdly alien-like, and Lizzy realized he still wore a voice modulator. Was that part of his evil-persona getup?

She turned away, feeling like the dogs in those YouTube videos, hiding from the new kitten in the house by burying their faces in sofa cushions. Out of sight, out of mind, right?

"Do you know who I am?" He asked the question to all his captives, and they warily shook their heads.

"They call me the Scythian. An ancient warrior, returning from the past to wreak terror on the capitalists who run this fucked-up world. I'll soon have an army of Scythians. Like me, my soldiers will be experts at killing, and taking the scalps of their enemies."

Sounded horrific and pretty fucked-up. Lizzy guessed this guy had a super long list of mental issues—of the psychotic and serial killer variety.

"The show will start soon and you're my guests for today. It's a marketing gig that helps to promote my brand." He stood. "You all get to star in my reality show and play a game. As there's three of you, you'll decide who dies today. It's a two to one ratio. If you cannot decide, I'll do the choosing."

As his heavily booted feet walked back up the stairs, two pairs of desperate eyes swung her way.

Lizzy stared back, too stunned to cry. *Oh, snap.*

◊ ◊ ◊

Johnny didn't take his eyes off the local Tanzanian kid and his grandfather, who Max was questioning in Swahili. They sat in a quiet corner as the rest of the task force watched surreptitiously from a distance.

If this didn't go anywhere, Johnny would lose it. With no other leads to rely on, this little boy was their only hope. The child answered with firm replies as the grandfather patted his shoulder.

Max finally stood and walked over.

"It looks like a legit lead. There's a derelict airstrip, five clicks west of here. They live nearby; even though his grandfather has warned him against it, the kid likes to play in the abandoned hangars on occasion. He stopped by on his way home from the store and saw a light aircraft landing on the runway. He also saw five men loading the plane with their human cargo." Max turned to the ambassador and Johnny. "Two males and one female hostage. The child remembers Lizette Steyn's hair. Said she looked like a bright sunflower, shining in the sun."

That didn't bode well; they could've flown anywhere. The search had gone FUBAR. The thought tore at Johnny's insides.

"Did he mention their physical condition? The hostages?" Clark asked urgently. Max's jaw ticked, and Johnny braced himself.

"Your son took a beating—after they pulled him from the vehicle. The same went for Lizette when she tried to protect Mason." Johnny swore, and Max continued, "The kid says by the time they were done, she looked pretty out of it."

The ambassador ran a shaking hand over his brow. Gray lines bracketed his pale mouth.

A commotion at Donnie's desk drew their attention.

"Holy shit. Max. We have a situation." Donnie tapped away at multiple keyboards as the men gathered. He shot Max a harried glance. "Shit. Fuck. Get Johnny and Clark out of here now!"

"The hell you say." Johnny planted his feet as a handful of

CIA spooks joined in on Donnie's tech frenzy.

Donnie paused. "Johnny, bud. Please, man, go for a walk."

The ferocity of those words had Johnny's heart clenching. "What the hell is going on?"

"The Scythian is online and live—on the dark web. We're trying to hack into the feed. The son of a bitch has the best hackers working for him." Donnie swung a large screen around, and with a few more taps, they were in.

The walled room could be anywhere; it looked derelict. Three fold-out chairs sat on one side. A scuffed table presented an array of weapons, and a rectangular mat sat centered onscreen. Black terror swept through Johnny. They'd seen this setup before. This was a Scythian execution video.

"Get them out of here."

"Touch me and you die," Johnny said to the first SBS lad who dared to lay a hand on his arm. He focused back on the screen.

They led the pilot in first. Badly beaten but conscious. When Stuart saw the weapons, he pissed himself. The wet stain spread across the front of his trousers and seeped down his legs.

Next came Mason Clark, trembling like a newborn foal. The ambassador keened. The DSS agents on watch took that as a sign and hustled Clark from the room.

Knowing who was next, Johnny forced his eyes back to the screen, to the last empty seat. They carried Lizzy in and threw her on the chair. It toppled, and after righting it, they roughly dragged her back up.

Without realizing, Johnny surged forward as rage and helplessness fought for control. Teammates pulled him back; he stilled when the Scythian entered the room. Johnny's gaze swung between the marked scarlet enemy and his sickly angel at the corner of the screen.

Jesus, she looked bad. Limp hair clung to a sweat-soaked brow. A vicious bruise marred the right side of her face. Her uniform—torn and filthy—exposed torn-up knees and elbows. Shivers racked her tiny frame, and fear glittered in her dazed blue eyes.

The Scythian ranted in Arabic. As usual, he wore a shitty throat mic—a voice modulator—that made it hard to follow. It was the Scythian's go-to speech, and from analysis of previous videos, Johnny knew the evil-ass words by heart.

"I will eat your harvest and bread, I will eat your sons and daughters, I will eat your sheep and oxen, I will eat your grapes and figs. The Horse Lord is coming."

Then he went off on a tangent about the evils of the West. Johnny jerked his gaze back to Lizzy. Like the rest of the hostages, she stared in fear at the heinous fucker pacing the room.

Her eyes suddenly darted to the left, and she sat up. A shadow fell on screen in the left corner. Her stare remained on whoever had entered the room. Who would distract her from the scariest ass-wipe on the planet? Max also frowned at her actions, he'd noticed it too.

The mercenary standing behind her stepped up and held a blade to her throat before whispering in her ear. She quickly looked down.

The Scythian paused and turned to his captives, switching to English. "None of you will walk away unscathed this night. One will lose a life. Two will lose a limb. Who have you chosen?"

Panic spurted through the feed as all three victims huddled in their chairs. The briefing room fell into chilled silence. They'd effectively lost all three hostages. He'd kill one and maim the others. An amputation without medical interference was just a slower way to die, depending on the limb. Lizzy couldn't survive that, not in her current state. Johnny's heart hammered with impotent rage, as a roaring din filled his head.

Stuart Williams spoke up first. "Lizette Steyn."

"Coward bastard!" Johnny yelled at the pilot, before Mason Clark begged for Lizzy's forgiveness. "I'm sorry, I want to live. I want us both to live. I don't want this, but you're the sickest, and you won't survive."

"Well, I guess that's two against one, and I still need your answer, Miss Steyn."

Lizzy licked cracked lips. "Not *one* of us. I won't play your sick game."

The Scythian casually chose a machete and rested it on her shoulder. "It's awfully sharp. Tell me who you choose."

"You'll kill me anyway."

Her brave words had Johnny's heart skipping a beat, barely hearing anything through the buzzing in his ears.

The blade pressed down, and Lizzy cried out.

"Talk."

"Fine, you piece of dick cheese. Mason is my *one* passenger, and as a crew member, I've vowed always to protect my passengers. Stuart and I don't see eye to eye—he's *one* large piece of dang poop—but he has *one* adorable kid and a wife who adores him. God knows why." Lizzy sucked in a shuddering breath. "When have I ever done anything noble with my life, how often have I given freely for others."

"Hundreds of times," Johnny whispered.

She straightened with resolve. "I'm the *one*. I choose me."

"The motley crew has spoken." The Scythian pulled her onto the mat. "Then kneel."

Johnny's bowels turned to ice.

"You have two minutes to say goodbye." The psycho

scumbag loved to draw out the drama, reveling in all the pain he caused. "Oh, and you will sing for us."

Fear singed the remaining corners of Johnny's control.

◊ ◊ ◊

Max braced himself for the impending implosion. The moment when his teammate would disintegrate. Lizzy swayed. Her bloodless face made her look ghostly in the harsh camera lights.

"To whoever's watching. Don't show my parents this video. Tell my daddy and mom that I love them and that I died a peaceful death."

"Baby. No." Johnny shook with emotion.

"And tell Jay Jay he's always been the *ones*. This song is for him. The *one* I've chosen for him."

"Who is Jay Jay?" Max asked.

"Me," Johnny growled through gritted teeth.

A voice so pure hummed through the screen as Lizzy began to sing a familiar tune. A lonely one. Avril Lavigne, "I'm with you."

Max watched his buddy. Confusion marred Johnny's face for a split second, instantly replaced by soul-wrenching torment. Max turned back to the screen. The Scythian walked over to the table and picked up a sword.

Max gave the signal and operatives converged. He shut himself off from Johnny's hoarse shouts as men dragged him out the door into the night air.

Johnny could not see her die; Max would never allow it. As team leader, he had no choice but to watch, and owed it to Lizzy to seek revenge and to find justice for her brave little soul. Her death would weigh heavily on his wife—who loved her friend. It would weigh on Max, causing nightmares for years to come.

Lizzy was a friend, and he cared for her like a big brother.

He blocked out the impending violence and focused on the subtle nuances he'd picked up in the earlier footage. Watching her body language and listening closely in her last few seconds.

Donnie turned away, unable to watch.

The brutality hit like a tidal wave—interrupting her mid-song. Max stood frozen as the barbarous drama played out and Lizzy's screams filled the air. Not even his analytical brain could block out the savagery rolling across the screen.

"Fuck me." Someone whispered from behind.

Chapter Nine

Huge fists clutched handfuls of sand as Johnny howled. Hearing her sudden screams, which followed him down the path as they'd carried him away, had Johnny fighting every one of the assholes. He'd tried to punch, kick and bite his way back to her. Now he lay curled on the ground. The pain was suffocating in its intensity as his brothers-in-arms sheltered him in a wary circle. Johnny's heart felt like a flayed—yet still beating—pulp in his aching chest.

Slater's blurry boots registered in his peripheral vision. A sentinel standing guard over his broken teammate. Fuck broken; *pulverized* was the word. Johnny couldn't imagine physically getting to his feet, never mind finding the strength to call her family. To tell them she was gone.

His Lizbug was gone. He'd failed her. Johnny rocked against the white-hot pain. Hands squeezed his shoulder. His numb brain focused instead on the night, groping for sanity. The wind whispered through crisp leaves. A hyena barked in the distance. The sand felt cool beneath his hands. Johnny released his fists and clutched fresh handfuls, his mind drifting back to that first day in the sandpit, the day she'd fallen into his arms and into his heart. *What do you call a woodpecker without a beak? A headbanger.*

Johnny laughed, then sobbed and sobbed. A second pair of boots appeared. Someone crouched beside him. *Max.*

"He killed the pilot."

It took a second for Johnny to register the words.

Max continued. "At the last second, the Scythian swung out and attacked Stuart Williams."

"Lizzy's alive?" Johnny glanced up.

Max's mouth tightened a fraction. "He kept to his promise. After killing the pilot, he dropped the sword and picked up a cleaver. His mercenaries dragged Lizzy off camera. Judging from her screams, the Scythian injured her badly. He did the same to the kid, and then he asked for ransom money." Max didn't wait for a reaction. "I need your help. I think Lizzy was trying to tell us something. We've picked up some subtle clues, but I'm not sure what they could mean."

Analysis of body language and human behavior was Max's strength, and Johnny took a shuddering breath, before rolling to his feet.

Max stepped closer. "This won't be easy for you to watch. If you can't handle—"

"Back off. If she's bleeding out, and there's a sliver of a chance we can find them, then what are we waiting for?" Johnny stepped past, then froze. "She was sending a message…" He swiveled around. "She'd never sing me an Avril Lavigne song. It reminds her of her ex. He bullied Lizzy into singing Lavigne over and over again."

"Then why sing it?" Slater asked. "Why bring the dickbag ex-fiancé into this?"

"Exactly. Shit, Slater—you're a genius!" Johnny ran trembling hands through his hair.

"Hell, yes, I am. Wait, why am I a rocket scientist?"

"Ivan Chasov is already involved. What did Lizzy say—'And tell Jay Jay, this song is for him? It's the one I've chosen for him.' She knows that I'll figure it out."

"Whoa, slow down," Max said.

"You saw her face when someone entered the room. Who else would Lizzy fear more than the goddamn Scythian? It has to be him. Ivan Chasov was there."

"We don't know that."

"Yes, we do. I've kept tabs on Ivan, the douche-nozzle. He's in Nigeria. Shit…Lizzy's in goddamn Nigeria!"

Max shot Johnny a skeptical glance as they walked up to Donnie's station. "Let's take this crappy footage apart, one millisecond at a time. If you say she's in Nigeria, then let's prove it. Donnie, I need everything we have on Ivan Chasov. Sniff out the slimy rock he's slithered under."

◊ ◊ ◊

Lizzy knelt on the fancy marble floor in front of the man she'd once trusted with her life. She stared down at the blood-soaked bandage wrapped around her right hand. Shock ran the show. Mind-numbing, brain-melting shock.

Images flashed through her mind like a view-master slideshow. The Scythian stabbing Captain Stuart through the chest, then almost decapitating him. Dropping the sword and picking up a cleaver as his thugs pulled her to the side before splaying out her hand on a block of wood. Her weak struggles were ineffective against the three large men. The blade came down with a *thunk*.

They'd shoved her aside and turned their attention to Mason. Too worn out to move, Lizzy watched them do almost the same thing to him—they'd taken a couple of his toes. For her, it was her right index finger. In medical terms they'd amputated the distal and middle phalanges—chopped half of it off. She'd stared at the tiny finger lying on the block, while clutching her injured hand to her chest.

Her first instinct was to save it, beg them for a cup of ice, but who would reattach it? When blood poured from her hand, down her chest, and spread across the dirty tiles beneath her, Lizzy reached down and drew a shape in the rose-colored liquid, then she'd slid sideways into oblivion.

She'd awoken in this bedroom, on a soft mattress, with a large pressure bandage wrapped tightly around her hand. That would do nothing except fractionally slow the bleed. She needed surgery, needed a lot of things. Needed John. She wanted to cry, but the tears never came. Dehydration and delirium saw to that.

Ivan stalked into the room, demanding that she kneel before him. Instead, Lizzy gave him the international fuck-you sign. That earned her a vicious hair pulling as he threw her off the bed. And here they were. Her left kidney throbbed in time with her sluggish pulse as she knelt before him. There were hard edges to Ivan now; the man she'd met in college was barely recognizable. The indications of heavy drug use over the years scared her. She sat before a stranger.

"How long have I been here?" she rasped.

"Fucking hours. I've left you to recover. Who's Jay Jay?"

Lizzy refused to answer. Ivan crouched before her. What did she ever see in the man? He reminded her of a Komodo dragon. His flat lizard eyes were black orbs in his cruel face. Ivan's angular jaw and harsh brow loomed in her blurred vision. He licked his lips and traced her collarbone through her torn shirt with a damp hand. "When you sang my song—"

"It's not your song, not anymore. It's Jay Jay's song."

She meant that. Avril might still save her life. It was a stab in the dark, but if John saw that feed, there was a slim chance of a rescue. When she'd sang to that soulless camera, she thought she'd die, and hoped her secret code would perhaps save the others or possibly lead John to the Scythian.

At the very least, justice for her death and those who'd come before her. Now it might be her salvation. Oh, it was now John's song, and if she miraculously got out of this, she'd sing it every day for the rest of her life. That song was her talisman, even though she had no way of knowing when John would see that video. It could be months from now after they'd scattered her bones across the plains of Nigeria.

"While I was doing time, you were cheating on me."

"You seriously think we're together? I'm sorry, am I getting mixed signals? When someone holds a gun to my head and pulls the trigger, I take that as a break-up sign."

Ivan stood and unlatched his belt, sliding it off smoothly. "Always had a smart mouth, spoiled bitch. I won't ask you again. Who is Jay Jay?"

"A better man than you'll ever be."

"You act like you're so much better than me. You and your snotty parents ruined my life."

The first blow stung as the belt flew across her arm. "You need to be taught a lesson in obedience."

Lizzy cowered against the base of the bed. Ivan tore off her blouse and rolled her over, leather slaps burning across her back. The sporadic contact of the buckle bruised her skin in its voracity.

When he finally let up, Ivan slid down beside her, panting from exertion. "You'll learn to obey me, Lizette. Otherwise this will be a daily occurrence, and our journey is just beginning."

"Yours, maybe," Lizzy said weakly. "Mine is ending unless you take me to the nearest hospital."

"What are you talking about?"

"My kidney is about to collapse."

That earned her a punch to an already bruised temple. "Lying bitch."

She moaned in pain.

"Is that why you've seemed a little under the weather, my Lizzy Liz?" The Scythian stood at the foot of the bed, his mask still in place.

She gasped at the sound of the nickname. The scary voice changer was gone. She knew that voice—that accent—and looked up as recognition dawned.

Ivan rolled to his feet. "What the hell are you doing here? We had a deal. I get the girl, and you get the kid."

The Scythian rolled his shoulders. "As usual, the Horse Lord flies in like a lumbering fucking superhero to the rescue." He flapped his robe manically, then reached into his robe pocket and pulled out a gun. "I would never leave little Lizzy Liz with a nut job."

He shot Ivan in the balls. Lizzy laughed hysterically as she wedged herself between the nightstand and the bed. Ivan collapsed, groaning in shock.

"The nut job no longer has his nuts! Poor baby." The masked man cackled at his own joke before shooting Ivan—again—this time in the leg. "That's a bleeder. You'd better clamp that sucker." He turned to Lizzy as she tried to hide under the bed base. "You're tiny, but not that tiny."

Only a thin white bra covered her breasts. She crossed her arms protectively as she cowered. "I know who you are."

"Of course, you do. The hunt has been fun, but now I have

my prize. If you'll wiggle that cute ass out from under there, there's a lovely IV full of drugs waiting at my lush digs."

"It's too late for that."

"Don't be so dramatic; I have my very own doctor on call. An international man of mystery like me needs his own medical team. Now get up. You look like kuk, and it's almost dawn, we need to move."

Lizzy glanced at Ivan.

"Don't look at the fucker; he'll bleed out slowly and painfully. You owe me, sweet thing."

Gunfire echoed through the walls. Lizzy's eyes darted to the window.

"Don't get your hopes up, that's my cleanup crew—can't have any witnesses."

"Where's Mason?"

The Scythian sighed dramatically. "Languishing in my dungeon. I have an honest to God, super cool dungeon. You've been in it. It's pretty authentic, right? We have so much to catch up on."

He was off-the-planet, certifiably insane. Maybe if Lizzy played along, she could rescue Mason and herself. First, she needed meds—a truckload of meds. "Will I have to go back to your 'super cool' dungeon?"

"If you're a good girl, you get to stay upstairs with me. Even have a shower. No offense, baby-cakes, but you're pretty damn stinky. Now get moving, before I shoot you in your cute fanny."

◊ ◊ ◊

MIT fucking *one*. Hidden in Lizzy's message to the team.

Aside from selecting Ivan's song, Johnny picked up on her constant emphasis and subtle play on the word *one* in her

163

goodbye speech. Lizzy changed up the words to send her message and Donnie was the one to fit the pieces together.

"Listen to what Lizzy's saying—'I'm the *one*. I choose me.... And tell Jay Jay, he's always been the *ones*. This song is for him. The *one* I've chosen for him.' The word *one* is emphasized everywhere in her speech." Donnie leaned forward. "Johnny, remember, we spoke about the teams with her, at dinner that night. We called them the 'Ones,' and mentioned that MIT1 works out of Lagos. Lizzy has visited Nigeria. She knows where she is."

Slater played devil's advocate. "What if Lizzy was just really out of it and confused her words? She seemed pretty far gone."

Johnny reran the footage, slowing every time Lizzy said "one," which was often. Every single time her gaze drilled into the camera.

Max sat back and crossed his arms, he looked at Johnny who gave him a nod before issuing orders. "Donnie, we need the quickest bird out of here, and the exact location of the ex-dirtbag in Lagos. Let's go get our little Lizzy."

Lizzy's quick thinking had gotten them on a plane to Lagos. Johnny forced himself to sleep on the flight, not knowing what they'd face on the other side. Six hours later and they rolled into the city, MIT1 met them at the airstrip. As they drove deeper into Lagos in the MIT1 bus, Johnny tucked hands into pockets to hide the tremble. He'd always been a machine in the field, never flinching in the face of violence. That was before—before he'd thought her dead, before he'd watched the footage thirty times over to pick up on clues. Johnny ignored the camaraderie catch-up with their West African Contingent; instead he sat in the back corner, staring at the passing shantytown. He didn't have the energy to make small talk, even though he knew the

MIT1 team well. They'd worked closely together in the past whenever extremists crossed over into West African territory and vice versa.

His brain ran over every scenario, and Lizbug's current state. How severely was she injured, was she still burning with fever? Had any of the evil assholes touched her? The last thought made him feel ill.

Johnny knew when the time came, he'd go all He-man on their targets—forget He-man, he'd morph into some scary-ass Skeletor shit. Johnny pictured getting the Scythian alone in a room. Unmasked and cowering like a baby chick—as Johnny used a cleaver to exact his revenge. Doubtful that would happen, most likely it would be a quick kill-shot to the head.

Slater nudged him. "How are you coping, bro?"

"How do you think?"

"I think if things don't go well, I could lose my best friend."

Johnny shrugged and shoved his hands deeper into his pockets.

"Once she's home—wherever that is—that's when the hard shit starts. This will change you both on a primal level."

"Like the Nasari bombing has changed you?"

Slater swore. "Don't go there. No, you're right. It did change me and not for the better. I'm an ass-hole dick that's destroyed all his relationships back home."

One of the MIT1 boys glanced back.

Johnny lowered his voice. "Slater—"

"My parents—my sister won't talk to me after I ruined her engagement party by getting smashed and punching her fiancé in the face. And then there's Kat. The love of my life. I threw her away like garbage."

"Jeez bud—"

"What? Shocked that I finally confronted the hefty PTSD elephant in the room?"

"Uh. Yeah, I'm pretty shocked."

"I've hit rock bottom. I've signed up with a private therapist—Stateside. I want to get Kat back. I want her and my damn life back."

"I'm here, whenever you need me."

"You've always been there for me, loyal fucker. Now you need to be there for Lizzy and yourself. Don't be afraid to get professional help."

"Lizzy might be better off without me."

"That's a tank-load of tripe. She's the sunny yang to your earthy yin. The teeny spark to your big stick of dynamite. The tasty bread wanting your cucumber nestled in her dainty sandwich—"

"Enough!" A grin overtook Johnny's drawn features.

Slater smiled before turning serious. "One step at a time, bro. We'll find her."

◊ ◊ ◊

An hour later, they crouched behind a wall on the perimeter of Ivan Chasov's villa, and the MIT men had all echoed Slater's statement in one way or the other. They had his back.

It had taken too long to get to this point, first stopping by MIT1's base to gear up, then running scenarios before finally getting the green light from JSOC.

With minimal security measures, it would be an easy breach. There was little security on the eight-foot wall perimeter, except for two cameras. The iron gate was secured with a flimsy padlock—a broken lock, which lay beside the open gate.

Infrared imaging was of concern. Only one target radiated a

weak heat signal. According to intel, Chasov's out-of-the-way villa was usually well staffed and adequately protected. This could be a trap if Ivan suspected they were onto him. MIT was ready to breach, and Johnny sent up a silent prayer. Three…two…one.

Three tangos decorated the front courtyard, already deceased and easy to spot in the dawning light. Bullet holes littered all the guards. The same went for the staff.

The MIT teams cleared rooms—first the kitchen, entertainment and living rooms beneath, then they slid upstairs to the bedrooms. Johnny's pulse picked up as they slipped through the doorway to the master.

Blood pooled around Ivan Chasov's still form. Once they'd cleared the room and searched for weapons, Johnny removed his night vision goggles. Max did the same. Someone pulled the curtains and turned on a light.

"He's still alive—but barely. Doubt we'll save him." The MIT1 medic—Tyler "Oscar" Jenkins—got to work on Ivan.

Blood spattered up the bed covers and the rug. A torn-up rag crumpled on the floor drew Johnny's attention.

He lifted it slowly, his voice cold. "This is her shirt." The front was soaked in blood, and the back, torn to shreds.

Max swore. Johnny's attention turned to the discarded belt lying next to the blouse. The dying man moaned. Johnny walked over to Ivan's bloodied form. No belt. Top button, undone. Johnny drew his knife.

"Stand down, Johnny, or I'll ship you back to Wyoming… tonight," Max said carefully.

Oscar tore open Ivan's pant leg. "If you mean to slice off his dick, it's too late. It's a mangled mess, and so are the testicles. A painful way to go."

"Good." Johnny exhaled. "Timeframe?"

Oscar worked to tie off the bleeding. "I'd say shot about twenty minutes ago."

Twenty minutes. Lizzy was here twenty minutes ago.

Max turned to talk to Oscar.

"I've got something," Slater called pointing beneath the bed before scooting the bed frame sideways. Johnny replaced his knife and pulled a torch; muscles froze as the light passed over the letters drawn in still wet blood.

First the figure of eight—Lizzy's infinity sign—then scrawly letters *K* and then *RIS*, written across the floor.

"Max!" he called out. "Holy shit. Holy damn shit."

◊ ◊ ◊

It felt surreal. After so long, he had her all to himself. The Scythian carried an unconscious Lizzy over the threshold and into the bathroom. He laid her in the bath, then stripped off her soiled skirt and underwear.

She looked like a limp porcelain doll. Dried blood and bruises marked her skin and he traced a hand over the damage. He'd caused that. The thought thrilled him, and he felt himself stir. In their future together, he'd be the only one marking her, for however long that may be. He injected her with another sedative, wanting time to admire his new acquisition.

Then he stood and stretched his back before turning to the mirror. He looked like a scary-as-shit mother. Who knew this was what he'd become. His childish dreams as a kid never amounted to anything this spectacular. The scariest human on the planet.

Getting to this point hadn't been easy. It was hard work, developing such a terrifying brand. People walked around every day like sheep, having no idea of how to market themselves. All wrapped up in their small lives. All their insignificant actions and thoughts stamping them as inferior.

If humans applied themselves to developing a personal infamous identity, this world would be a far more interesting place. Restlessness still ate at the Scythian's world because there was no one to challenge him. No superhero to step in his way, nothing to oppose the terror.

With a resigned breath, he removed the mask and stared at the face he was born with.

Kris Muller. The easygoing game ranger from Botswana. And, he was a handsome fokker. He was also a determined bastard who'd beaten the odds. He knew what shitty luck was at the age of eight when his parents died in a vehicle accident. Except that wasn't luck, that was his stupid mother who chose to get in the truck with her alcoholic husband.

Kris ran tepid water in the bath, taking care not to scald Lizzy. He wiped hair from her eyes as he thought back to his harrowing childhood.

Thank God for his Aunt Kerry, who took him in. A nice lady. Not too bright, but she provided for him and left him to his own devices. His Uncle Frank was a different story. He'd watched Kris furtively. Sexually. Kris wasn't an idiot, he knew the bastard would eventually try something. The fateful day occurred in the barn, a year later, sealing his uncle's fate. He'd caught Kris skinning a stray cat. Literally, with a carving knife. When he'd threatened to tell his wife, Kris elected to play the sick bugger's game.

He allowed the bastard to touch him in exchange for silence. It wasn't all bad. Frank taught him to hunt, shoot and kill effectively. When it was time to move on, one day after a particularly bad storm, Kris ran to the house, shouting that he'd seen a leopard.

The Scythian used the sprayer to wet Lizzy's hair, then picked up the rosemary shampoo he'd chosen for her as he thought back to his first kill.

Once he'd lured his uncle to the river, he waited for the old man to wander closer to the bank, then over and over, he'd stabbed him. Rolling Frank down the hill into the river took work, but the raging waters swept him away, battering the body and covering up Kris's first human kill. It was such a thrill and ultimately led to more hunts. A kid walking home from school one year, a lazy worker on the farm, the next. But as he grew, so did his ambitions. It was only when he was at ranger school in his twenties, skimming through a biology book on equestrian's breeds, that he'd read of the Akhal-Teke horse. His first introduction to the ancient tribes of Scythian warriors. He'd finally found his calling. And his horse.

Kris admired horses, just like he admired a well-made female. He traced a thumb over Lizzy's brow before leaning in for a wet kiss. She smelled like herbs and woman. It had been too long since he'd been with a girl. He blamed it on his stupid childhood crush for Abigail Evans. He'd gallantly tried to save her in Johannesburg and she'd spat in his face. But he'd also met Lizette Steyn that night, and for the first time, he felt excitement stir for someone else. At first, he'd ignored the attraction, and the dark-haired giant at her side.

He'd waited in the parking lot and trailed her home. The next day, as he continued watching her, he still wasn't sure what he was feeling. Abigail Evans was supposed to be his wife. Back then, he'd been determined to fulfill that misguided dream. But when poaching work called him away, when things had fallen apart, and he'd ended up getting shot, Kris knew his life was somehow entwined with this blonde beauty lying in his arms.

Scrolling through her Facebook history and her posts, he'd uncovered her past before discovering she'd moved closer to him…moving to East Africa. It was as if the Scythian gods brought her to him.

The water had turned cold and it was time to call in the doctor. Kris wrapped her up and laid her on his bed before pulling his mask back on. Lizette Steyn was the antidote for his numb soul, the true light in his darkness. And no testosterone-driven soldier would ever take her away.

◊ ◊ ◊

A low purr rippled through restless dreams. Warm puffs of air slid over her face, and Lizzy surfaced from her lethargy, cracking open an eye. She sucked in a breath to scream.

"No sudden movements, Saber doesn't like that." The Scythian stroked the wild creature behind the ear. Lizzy sized up the cheetah staring her dead in the eye. Copper orbs glistened—unblinking. Sooty tear tracks matched the moist black nose, twitching as it sized her up. The large cat lowered its head and snuffled at her wrapped hand.

"Saber, no. You've already eaten. Miss Steyn is off-limits…for now."

Lizzy gulped and pulled her hand to her chest. The Scythian tugged the big predator off the mattress by an ornate leather collar in a shade that matched his red mask perfectly.

She almost giggled at the surreal moment—if her mind could take a quick snapshot of the lunacy before her. Clamping down on hysteria, she attempted to shift her heavy limbs. The drugs hadn't helped much. Her side and hand still ached, and she still ran a fever.

Running her good hand over her clammy neck, Lizzy

suddenly realized she wore new clothes. A man's navy T-shirt and no underwear.

The Scythian spoke as he handed the wild cat off to a guard. "Saber's been with me for the past two years. I miss working with wildlife and wanted a felinae as a pet. I rescued him from a traveling circus—if you could call it that. I think he likes you."

Lizzy shuddered. "Where are my clothes. How long have I been out for?"

"All afternoon. My doctor says you're fine; you need a little rest. He hooked up a round of antibiotics, just in case. Can we both agree that you may be a bit of a drama queen."

She ignored the tripe falling from his stupid mouth. "Where are my clothes?"

"I threw them away. Couldn't have you soiling up my pricey bedcovers. I washed you down myself."

No, please. No.

"Now you smell all pretty. Your hair is now clean, skin is so soft—so smooth." He reached out to stroke her cheek. "Don't cower like that. I won't hurt you."

He grabbed her wrist and pulled her roughly towards him, and she bit down a scream. Her only hope was playing his sick game.

"It's the mask. Please, Kris. Take off the mask."

He stilled.

"Do you now have a horribly deformed face under there? I don't get the Berber—slash—Darth Vader vibe."

He pulled her close. "You're the first person who's ever openly challenged the Scythian. We're alone, but if you talk to me that way in front of others, I'll take my time cutting out that smart tongue." He adjusted his grip over her wounded hand and slowly squeezed.

"I'm sorry. Oh, my God. Please. Stop." Lizzy screamed out the agony. He studied her teary face for a heartbeat before letting go.

"Who's your master?"

"You are. You are." The room swung, Lizzy curled into a fetal position, willing away the horror of her new world. *I can save myself, just til John comes for me—he'll find me. Please find me.*

He swore in Afrikaans, "Fokking hell, fine. I'll take it off. Besides, it's too damn hot to wear. Try wearing this sucker in hundred-degree heat." The Scythian stood and turned away, tugging off the worn leather monstrosity.

"Lizette Steyn, meet Kris Muller for the second time." He turned back, bowed and walked over to the mirror. "This fucker makes me break out. Goddammit," he said, picking at a blemish on his chin. "It has made me a wealthy man. People kuk themselves when I walk into a room. Literally poop their pants, like babies. Terrorists pay top dollar for my over-the-top executions. It's an art form. A well-rehearsed Broadway show, pulling the right degree of terror from my victims and their respective families."

Lizzy tried to flex her hand and moaned against the screaming pain. Kris ignored her as he continued preening in the mirror.

"When you sang for me—thinking you'd die—it was a pinnacle moment on the dark web. My audience ate it up, increasing my fan base tenfold. They want to see you die, demanding that as the next act. How does that feel? Knowing the only thing that stands between you and death is me." He grinned manically.

Lizzy ignored him, staring at the wall.

Kris chuckled. "I might offer up the ambassador's kid instead—he's not faring that well, besides, I like having you around. Abby wasn't wrong in trying to set us up all those months ago. What did she say back then? 'Wouldn't it be wild if the two people I adore most eventually got together?' But she didn't know about the crush I had when I met you that night." Kris walked over to the bed and gazed down at her. "Love at first sight. I wanted to mount you—right then. But that giant fuck-tard slobbered all over you." He stroked her hair, and Lizzy closed her eyes, willing him to disappear. "I always loved Abigail. But after her rejection, I followed you home. Then followed you on social media for months as I lay in bed recovering from that dick-bag's Yankee bullet. You should check your privacy settings, anyone can hack your account."

"What bullet?"

"You don't know? Probably classified shit that your boyfriend never bothered to mention. Back in South Africa, Max shot me from a distance…like a coward. Minding my own business, escaping armed terrorists, and I get blasted in the shoulder. Thank God it missed the socket but caused a fuck load of muscle and nerve damage."

Lizzy didn't dare say anything as his face contorted in rage. She couldn't imagine Max shooting at an unarmed or defenseless man; she suspected that Kris Muller was neither.

Abby had grown up with Kris Muller, a game ranger, and stayed on his aunt's farm in Botswana. Abby had hero-worshiped Kris, never seeing the darkness seeping from his black soul. Lizzy had recognized the evil on some level when she finally met him. He'd been a nasty drunk, and his flat eyes and biting remarks had reminded her of Ivan. Two psychotic peas in a pod.

"I brought you to Ivan on purpose."

"What…what do you mean?"

"When I discovered how he'd betrayed you in South Africa… I saw the police reports."

"How?"

"I pay my IT team well. I own the web. I thought I'd gift you with revenge—wasn't it thrilling to see him bleeding out for almost killing you? He nearly took you from me before I ever knew you existed."

This was all a sick game. Kris Muller had her brought here because of Ivan?

"So now that you've had your revenge, it's my turn. Where is Abigail Evans?"

"I don't know," Lizzy answered honestly.

"Lizzy Liz. Don't fok with me." He growled in his rough accent.

"I'm serious. We had a falling out, something to do with me getting shot at and her not giving me a decent heads-up."

"The slut betrayed us both. Is she still with the American spook?"

"I have no idea."

"Where is your soldier—that big strapping bugger? Is he hung like a dinosaur, or is it a small side of beef?"

"We broke up—in Johannesburg."

"Now that's a lie. That was his voice on the other end of the line—in the aircraft. I've seen him with you in Nairobi. Do you think it was just a coincidence—you being on that plane? Sure, the Clark boy is fun to play with but he's just an appetizer. You're my dessert, my bright little cupcake. I did this all for you. And to piss off Abby—the bitch—but mainly I just wanted to get to know you."

She stared, wordlessly. Kris was deranged, like from another galaxy, shooting through the milky way on a pink-unicorn level of derangement. He bent and placed a kiss to the corner of her mouth. She clenched her good hand, feeling her nails biting into her palm.

175

He turned back to pull his mask back on, then he adjusted the voice modulator at his throat. "It's time for your surprise. I have a whole afternoon planned, so shift that lazy ass and meet me in the stables. One of my men will show you the way."

Meet him in the stables? Lizzy thought numbly. She could barely stand and hadn't peed in over forty-eight hours—she had no urge to either. Her kidney screamed in constant agony, but terror smothered her body's distress. She swung her limp body off the bed.

◊ ◊ ◊

"The SOB is alive." Max took a photo with his phone, looking as grim as Johnny felt.

"It says 'Kris,' right?" Johnny confirmed.

"That's the only word that makes sense." Max studied the markings.

Slater crossed his arms. "If Kris Muller is alive and Lizzy tagged him, how does he play into this?"

"This is the location of the message; I'm guessing he was in the room, and he sure as hell ain't here now," Johnny said.

"Stands to reason then that Kris killed Ivan," Max agreed.

"Are we then looking for two crazy jerk-offs? Is he the Scythian's sidekick?"

Johnny answered Slater's question with a shake of his head. "Negative. It's too much of a coincidence."

"Now that we have a possible suspect, I'll use Muller's height and build; we can compare voice prints." Donnie stood after examining the blood patterns. "If the biometrics and gait are the same as the Scythian, then we have our first real lead."

Max stood. "We'll need to look at the timeline of Scythian killings and when Kris Muller was supposedly in Southern Africa or the Middle East. My gut says that he initially built his fortune through poaching, and ran the Horse Lord gig on the side. When he became notoriously famous on the dark web, he transferred all his time to Scythian terror."

Oscar called out, "Chasov didn't make it. He's gone."

No one batted an eye. Diane "Rayne" Santos—the MIT1 sniper—came through the comms. "White Mercedes heading this way—ETA thirty seconds." The teams ghosted and moved into position as the vehicle pulled into the triple garage. Johnny crouched behind the kitchen island, waiting for the target to walk from the mudroom into the kitchen. He didn't wait long. Two steps in, the suspect barely had time to throw keys on the counter before seven men ambushed him.

"Hands up. Hands where we can see them."

"On the ground now!"

In no time, they had him subdued and cuffed. Looked to be a local Nigerian. This was confirmed when he began babbling in a local dialect. Shit out of luck, buddy, Johnny thought as Oscar chatted back in a language that Johnny assumed was Yoruba. Oscar's mother was Nigerian, born in South West Nigeria. The suspect knew English; he'd obeyed their commands. Most Nigerians spoke English, the preferred language in Lagos. Either way, they'd find out who he was.

It turned out he was Ivan Chasov's driver, who'd escaped death when checking on his ailing mother in the city before starting his day. It took another hour's worth of interrogation to get the slippery bastard to talk. He whined about cleaning the upholstery in the car after picking up Ivan and the sickly American girl, the one who'd stunk up the interior.

They now had a location…and received a biometrics match. Kris Muller and the Scythian were the same beast. If Lizzy's profuse bleeding originated from her right hand, it was likely an amputated finger.

◊ ◊ ◊

Ojuelegba, Lagos

The rotten structure, sandwiched between matching derelict homes, looked like the gateway to hell. Endless seasons layered worn stone walls with gray grime. Hidden horrors called out from the fissured windowpanes, a slaughterhouse that marked the end of the journey for many captured souls. Breaking down doors and moving through the stagnant maze, Johnny prayed he'd find a loitering mercenary waving a weapon. Vengeance for the unsaved—and for Lizzy's suffering—stirred up his bloodlust.

The final furious steps into the execution room revealed no one. Residual terror lingered like a dispersing fog, highlighted by evidence of carnage. The camera stood, erect and proud. The sloppy assholes hadn't bothered to clean up. Johnny's weary eyes traced the violent trail from the previous day. All that remained in Captain Stuart's corner was a scuffed shoe and a mother-load of blood. His body, missing. Turning away from the tragic sight, Johnny cataloged the kid's injuries. Two toes lay in the corner. Then Lizzy's corner. Ignoring the other operators, he hunkered down next to the stained floor, concentrating on the squiggly circles she'd drawn and not the blackened digit lying on a wooden block a foot away. Her bravery stunned him, and her breadcrumb faith that he'd follow her to hell. He would. He had. This was hell, a soul-breaking madness that shredded him to the marrow.

Jerking when Donnie touched his shoulder, he stood and pointed to the decaying joint. "That's her finger." He then pointed to the encrusted circle. "And that's her message to me. Start the prep on the package. I need fucking air."

The RFI package was part of Donnie's deal as an intelligence specialist. After gathering fluids, hair, fingerprints, and any remaining evidence, Donnie would compile and send a digital file off to the Intelligence Collection Director at HQ. Johnny knew the primary objective was rescuing Mason Clark, but the generous resources allocated gave Lizzy a fighting chance.

As a time-sensitive mission, MIT2 rotated shifts for the next twelve hours, catching shut-eye between the relentless hunt for the Horse Lord's West African location. There were no records indicating any property purchased or leased in Kris Muller's name. Money trails led to dead ends.

The locals refused to roll on the Scythian. Fear over the notorious extremist delayed operations, but thanks to intelligence collection, satellite imagery, and MIT1's indigenous network, they narrowed in on a supposed new member of The Scythian's circle.

The target, Mongo Hassan, lived in a newly built container home. Container homes were being built throughout the city, a cheap solution to help with the ever-growing slums. Two shipping containers were stacked and converted into a two-bedroom home, fitted with bathrooms and ventilation. At midnight, MIT and a Nigerian SF team moved in on the small structure at the edge of an abandoned lot.

They took the Hassan family by surprise as they made a loud entry into the small structure. Johnny ignored the screaming women, focusing only on the adult male with a fork frozen halfway to his mouth. Mongo glanced at his weapon lying a few feet away.

"Move towards it in any way, and I'll blow you away. Hands in the air, now!"

Mongo Hassan smiled but didn't lower the fork. He spoke in heavily accented English. "The Western dogs have arrived. Do you enjoy picking on humble Nigerians?"

One of the Nigerian soldiers stepped forward. "You're the one who kills our own people. Murdering innocent civilians in the East!"

Mongo spat as he was thrown off the chair and restrained. "Jealous? I get paid well for what I do."

"Enough!" Max stepped forward.

Johnny's finger twitched but they needed Mongo alive. He'd pay for the lives he'd taken. They cleared the room and shoved him against the steel wall, his wrists and ankles restrained. His family were shuttled outside and kept under guard as MIT prepared to question the soldier for hire.

Max turned to the others. "I'll need time alone with the suspect, guard the perimeter."

Max had just broken protocol and no one blinked. Johnny knew why. Without immediate answers, they'd lose the small window for a rescue.

Johnny shifted to leave, and Max laid a hand on his arm. "You'll stay."

For the first time since Lizzy's disappearance, Johnny smiled wolfishly. "Yes, sir."

Mongo stared at the remaining two men. His chin lifted in defiance. Max ignored Mongo, instead taking his time to shed some of his tactical gear and his jacket, then rolling up his shirt sleeves.

"It's a brand-new shirt. I don't want to get blood on it," Max said by way of explanation.

Mongo swallowed. "Are you going to beat me? Torture me? I will never give up my master's location."

"It's not me you need to worry about. The big soldier behind me…different story. He wants his woman back."

Mongo looked confused. Max elaborated. "We want Lizette Steyn's location."

"The blonde bitch?" He turned to look at Johnny. "She has the prettiest ass. I squeezed it real hard as she lay at my feet in the van."

Johnny erupted, and Max threw himself between Mongo and dumb-ass's certain death. "Easy, brother. Easy!"

Mongo grinned as Johnny panted.

"Why are you smiling? If you don't give me answers, next time I'll let him play."

Looking unsure, Mongo swore. "I don't give up my brothers. I'm not a rat. I'm a Scythian."

"Has your master ever revealed his face to you?"

Max received no answer.

"I'm thinking that's a no. We know who he is. I'm guessing you think he's some invincible-looking nomadic warrior. You'd be wrong. He's a spoiled farmer's son. From a large farm in Southern Africa. He doesn't care about the West African people. He only cares about himself."

"You lie! He's a god! Untouchable—and he's one of us."

"His name is Kris Muller." Max handed over a photograph. A purposely chosen image of Kris Muller at college, looking preppy as he posed with his cricket league outside their clubhouse. Mongo stared in horror. Max pulled a file from his pack and produced more evidence.

"That's your master. Feel free to die for him." Max nodded to Johnny, who produced a knife.

"Which extremity should I slice off first?" Johnny roughly pulled off a sandal. "Two toes for Mason Clark? Or a finger for

Lizette Steyn? How about the whole hand, retribution for daring to touch her?" He grabbed the man's wrist and twisted.

Hassan started screaming. "No! Please! I'll tell you. I'll tell you everything."

Johnny hesitated before roughly shoving him aside. After Hassan stopped sniffling, he began to talk, giving up an address for a structure twenty clicks outside the city. Satellite imagery indicated it could be Kris Muller's West African compound. With only two hours of darkness left, they headed east—joined by Delta, MIT1 and the Nigerian SF contingent.

All units were prepped and loaded for retribution.

Chapter Ten

The rainforest surrounding Kris Muller's fortress posed both an advantage and a logistical challenge, with one road leading in—and twenty-foot walls—causing possible breach delays.

Even with all the security measures providing blockades, the teams slid in undetected. Thanks to past fieldwork, MIT2 worked seamlessly alongside the Delta team and MIT1. The familiarity nudged Johnny into full battle mode. This was what he did best. Lizzy's welfare was now in his hands; they were no longer separated by endless miles or unknown terrors. It was Johnny's game—as brutal as the Scythian's—with a dash of justice on the side.

His woman lay beyond the gate ahead. Behind those mansion walls. Johnny knew in his gut that Lizzy was close. Donnie and Max were the first to infiltrate the compound, slipping over a back wall. They made their way around to the front, took out the guards at the gate, then opened it for the rest of their team.

Johnny moved to the right and snuck up on a target on the west side, quickly slicing the man's throat before heading for the side entrance. According to their informants, there were supposed to be ten armed mercenaries, four additional staff members and two prisoners held in the basement. Two assets below and the rest above ground. MIT2 was assigned as the ground-level clearing team and waited for Delta Force to perform a shotgun breach. The time for stealth was over, now it was all about shock and awe.

"Standby, standby. Go!"

They moved from room to room in a concussive dance of death, perfected through years of training, quickly eliminating three armed assailants who attempted engagement. Comms filtering through indicated two more tangos taken out by MIT1. Still no sign of Muller.

The basement door lay up ahead, Johnny thrummed with an adrenaline spike knowing that Lizzy possibly lay beyond that door. He hung back as Delta Force performed a mechanical breach.

MIT1's team leader came over the comms, saying the words that stopped Johnny in his tracks. "Positive ID on Lizette Steyn."

Johnny stilled. MIT1 had cleared the upper level, which meant they'd found her upstairs. "Oscar One, your location?"

"Top floor. Second room to the left."

"Go," Max said to Johnny. "Take Donnie. Sierra Two, you're with me."

"Copy that, sir," Slater confirmed.

Johnny took off with Donnie covering his ass. He ascended the stairs quickly, heart thumping as he rounded the last corner. He staggered, then paused, taking in the scene. She lay unconscious on crumpled sheets, her wrists and ankles restrained.

Johnny rushed up beside Oscar, who held Lizzy's limp head and checked her vitals. Johnny cut the plastic restraints, refusing to accept the stark reality. He tore open his medical supplies.

Thanks to years in the field, Johnny knew if someone's chances of survival were low. Hers was one of the lowest he'd seen. Lizzy was dying, her breath shallow and labored. Skin so pale, she glowed whiter than the sheets she lay on. Fresh marks layered upon yellowed bruises indicated multiple beatings. The bloodied bandage on her hand had soaked through to the mattress below. Johnny swore as he looked for a vein. "I don't have intravenous access. We're going straight to an IO."

An intraosseous infusion—an IO—was the only way to provide fluids when they couldn't find a vein. The decision to insert a catheter just below the knee joint, injecting directly into the bone marrow made his stomach turn—it was her only hope.

He'd performed five IOs in the past. All of them spelled agony for the patient. The fact that Lizzy was unconscious helped. His hand shook, and he clenched the drill, preparing to drive into her already shattered body. Lizzy groaned as he began the procedure and Donnie stepped forward. "Doesn't she need lidocaine?"

"There's no time; she'll die if we wait." Johnny prepped the saline flush and took a bracing breath before pushing in ten ccs of fluid.

Lizzy screamed, nearly coming off the bed.

"Jesus, stop!" Donnie yelled.

"It'll take a couple more seconds, then it's over."

A second scream had Donnie pacing. Lizzy collapsed back as soon as Johnny completed the task—thankfully, she was out cold again.

He paused to cradle her head and bury his face in her neck. "I've got you. Don't leave me, keep fighting."

Reluctantly he pulled away as Oscar placed a bag-valve mask over her mouth. "Her vitals are thready, let's move."

Johnny helped roll her onto a stretcher, ignoring the torn shirt. The implications had his stomach churning and he wanted to bellow with rage. In three days, she'd lost half her body weight, and he watched her delicate chest rise as she tenuously grasped for breath.

Max stepped aside as they shuffled through the door. "How is she?"

Johnny shook his head, too choked up to answer.

"Will she make it to the safe house?"

They'd set up a facility just outside the city where a Trauma One team waited in the wings.

"That's the only option. Anything out of country will be too late."

If Lizzy had been stable enough, they would've transported both patients directly to Landstuhl—the US military hospital in Germany. Adjusting plans, they'd rush her to the safe house. Then came the trip to Germany.

Max walked down the stairs with his team. "We found Mason Clark in the basement. Delta Force are stabilizing the kid. Lost a lot of blood, and he has an infection from the amputations, but I think he'll be okay."

Johnny knew as much—still keeping track of the comms coming from the cellar.

Stepping onto the landing, he turned to speak. A violent whump shattered the air, and smoke and dust punched through from below. The men crouched, Johnny and Donnie sheltering Lizzy from falling plaster as the blast reverberated through the sprawling mansion.

"Holy crap!"

"Get her out, now!" Max shoved Johnny up as the dust filled the air.

An incendiary device detonated, and the blast zone included Slater and Delta Force.

After breaching the cell door, three soldiers immediately got to work on Mason Clark. Slater moved down the passage to the second cell, with two men at his back.

An old man cowering in the corner raised his hands. "Don't shoot, please, help me. Get me out."

The prisoner sounded like a local.

"Who are you? Identify yourself." Slater's rifle never moved off the possible target.

"I'm from Ibadan. The Horse Lord killed my family, took me. I am just a civil servant; I work for the associate justice in my city. Please do not shoot." His thin arms shook as he shied away from the soldiers.

"Keep your hands where we can see them." Slater nodded, and a Delta operative attached an explosive breach to the door. "Stay where you are. Cover your face."

The skinny captive huddled down. With a small discharge, the door swung open. The breacher stepped back, and Slater stepped in. The asset stood, his long robes falling to the floor.

A steel *thunk* and a rolling echo had Slater freezing for an instant before diving for cover. "Grenade!" he yelled as men scattered. The blast blew him sideways, and then the sky fell down in concussive rain.

◊ ◊ ◊

Relentless pain pounded as Slater cracked open his eyes. He raised a hand to pull off his scratched goggles. Why didn't his hand move? Slater tried again. Screaming agony shot through his arm—his dominant arm. Where was he, under a damn tank? Felt like one was parallel parked on his ass.

Tamping down panic, Slater moved his other arm. Rubble shifted as he brought it to his face. Wait, where were the fucking goggles? Not on his face. Blood and dust clogged up his sight. Shifting his head to wipe his eyes made him want to toss his cookies. *Shit.* His head swam. *Focus, Derek. Where the fuck are you, and why is it so damn hot?* The oppressive heat felt suffocating, and he stretched his good arm, poking around. Distant voices filtered through the mortared wreckage.

"Help!" Slater croaked. "I'm here."

"Don't leave me," he said more to himself.

An icy finger ran across his hand. Another whisper echoed. "Don't leave me."

Slater froze. Kathleen. She lay next to him. Had they been out together? At dinner? A concert? Why couldn't he remember? Gritting his teeth, Slater slowly turned his head towards the voice. He had to get Kat out of there. Dust motes swirled in the dirty light. He now faced a wall. Slater blinked. Kat lay on the floor in a singular ray of light. Her face just a foot away, glowing like an angel.

"Kat?"

Pale lips parted, and her breath misted out. Irish eyes fringed with sooty lashes captivated him. He missed those eyes and that stubborn Celtic chin.

"It's so cold," Kat said.

Frowning, Slater tried to shake his head. "We're baking in here."

Her thumb stroked again; icy tentacles crawled across his skin. "Derry, I'm scared."

"So am I," Slater admitted.

"Then don't leave me." Except he was leaving, floating away. His vision dimmed. Someone yelled. Max?

Then nothing.

Delta checked in, two of theirs were unaccounted for, three including Slater. Men ran towards them with Mason Clark strapped to a stretcher.

"What the hell happened?" Max yelled.

"The second prisoner ambushed us, a planted target. I think he used a grenade. The wall collapsed when we were already out in the hall."

"I'll stay behind to help," Donnie said.

"No," Max said over the chaos. "We have enough men on the ground. I've got this; I need you to help with both the injured assets, get them to the safe house."

Donnie hesitated.

"Go!" Max ordered. "I'll pull Slater out. I have two additional medics and seven men at my back. I'll get our boy."

With one last look at Max racing down the passage, Johnny and Oscar hustled Lizzy out into the open, as Donnie covered their run to the MH6 assault bird.

◊ ◊ ◊

Max scrambled to clear the rubble. They were taking a risk, not knowing the origin of the blast or whether the zone was still booby-trapped. Groans filtered through the dust, and Max ignored his aching back and burning arms, desperate to get to his buried friend. Brave operatives worked alongside him, never tiring as they cleared section by section. They'd pulled three men out and still no sign of Slater.

Max kept calling his name. No answer. *Hold on, buddy, I'm coming. Hold on.*

They'd moved deeper into the passage when someone yelled from the right. Max fought his way over and recognized Slater's boots and legs. Large rocks pinned his torso. Max made his way to Slater's head, praying it hadn't been crushed in the blast. Grime coated his mouth and nose. Max coughed and spat before hunkering down beside his teammate. He felt for a pulse and breathed a sigh of relief. No signs of head injuries although Slater hadn't regained consciousness. Max reassured him, then helped the others to shift rubble.

Concerned over neck injuries, they stabilized Slater's neck and rolled him onto a stretcher. The sniper's arm lay awkwardly, and Max secured the shattered limb to Slater's side.

Slater opened his eyes. "Kat."

"Kat's not here. It's me, Max."

"Help…Kat."

"You're okay. Just relax."

"Kat's hurt. Find her."

He wasn't making any sense. Max tried to calm him. "We're in Nigeria. She's safe in Utah. Let's take care of you."

"Call her. I need to know…"

Slater passed out as they carried him to safety. Max swore, his stomach in knots. Somehow this was his fault. As the team leader, his men fell under his protection. They should never have split up.

Max needed answers—he needed to make this right.

Chapter Eleven

Tinkling wind chimes teased her awake. Lizzy stretched, and her toes stuck out the bottom of the covers—her Lizzie McGuire bed cover. When last had she lain in her childhood bed? Hadn't she outgrown this clunky wooden bed when she was ten? Too tired to care, Lizzy's eyes ran over her bright blue walls. What on earth had motivated her to choose such a crazy color? Kids made no sense.

The smell of pancakes wafted up the stairs. Mom made the best pancakes, with thick British syrup and loads of cream. *Yum.* She wiggled her toes.

Time to get up. Lizzy looked up at her blue ceiling. Wait. Blue? She stared up at the open sky. The endless blue surrounded her tiny bed. Relaxing into the comfy duvet, she watched a single drifting cloud. Playing the shape game, she supposed it looked like a man on a horse. Two birds flew across the sky, their silvery wings capturing her gaze.

Her eyes flitted back to the now pink cloud. No, wait— orange. No. Red. The rider turned on his fuzzy steed, expanding as he drifted towards her.

She tensed, gripping the sheet below. No longer a cloud, the shadow galloped closer, closer, closer. She opened her mouth to scream as the fully formed Scythian leaped from his horse, dropping down onto the bed. Straddling her, he gripped her neck.

Lizzy gulped for air, and the Horse Lord shoved a gloved hand in her mouth. "You're mine. I'll always find you." She flailed, punching out and gasping for air.

"Easy, honey!"

Mom? Her eyes shot open, and all she could see was white. White ceiling. White walls. White sheets.

A masculine voice spoke softly in her ear. "It's a ventilator, baby. Calm down. Let it do the work. Don't fight it."

Another voice filtered through the terror. "You're safe now. You're in Germany. The doctor will be in shortly, sweet girl. They'll wean you off; then you can breathe on your own."

"Daddy." She tried to say the word, and a tube tore at her burning throat. A firm thumb wiped at her tears as a scruffy man moved into her line of sight. A rough-looking giant. She frowned in confusion.

He frowned back. "Do you know who I am?"

She shook her head. Her father appeared, hovering, and the men exchanged a look.

"Is it her low sodium levels?" her father asked.

"Could be," the giant replied. "It causes confusion."

Lizzy swiped at her wet face; a white blob bumped into her cheek, and pain exploded. Was she still dreaming?

"Don't, Lizbug. Keep it still." The Herculean bloke cradled the ridiculous swaddling enveloping her aching hand.

Lizzy wanted out of this place, out of her weak, aching body. She hurt everywhere. Her brain wouldn't work. How did she get here and why did her family look so grim? Her father looked so old all of a sudden—so frail. That devastated look scared her more than the stupid ventilator or her damaged hand. Her brain groped for answers, answers she wasn't sure she wanted.

The ventilator pushed air in as Lizzy tried to breathe out, and panic took over again.

"Stop fighting it," the giant ordered. "You'll hurt yourself."

Could she punch him in the face? Once they yanked this torture device from her very essence, she'd shove it down his brawny throat and see how he liked it. Lizzy had no time to contemplate his demise as the machine kicked back in, pulling air out of angry lungs. Lizzy launched herself up.

"Shit!" He lunged to support her. "She needs a sedative. Where's the damn doctor?" Then he was gone, replaced by her concerned mom.

"I hate this!" She wanted to scream, but all she could do was curl up against unexplainable pain. Men in white coats stepped in. She felt the cool sedative slide into her veins and fell into blissful nothingness.

◊ ◊ ◊

The doctor finally removed the damn ventilator. Lizzy moaned in her sleep and Johnny stroked her brow. Her parents left for the night—first decent sleep they'd get since racing to Germany to their daughter's side. It had been four long days since they'd flown her into the Landstuhl Regional Medical Center. Five counting the twenty-four hours at the safe-house in Nigeria. They'd lost her there and used the paddles.

SOCOM had provided a C-17 cargo plane to transport Lizzy, Slater and the rest of the injured patients from Lagos to Germany. The Landstuhl Regional Medical Center spanned over two kilometers, made up of fourteen buildings. Johnny had never been to the facility. He always thought if he had, he'd be airlifted in with traumatic injuries. Instead, he was the healthy one standing on the sidelines.

This was only the first step. For Lizzy, the hard part would come later, for Johnny it was one never-ending nightmare. First, mentally cataloging evidence of a probable sexual assault as he'd noted her injuries. Then, watching her die. Forced to stand back and trust the doctors to bring her back to him.

Next was the waiting game as they pumped in the first round of antibiotics. That hadn't worked, but thankfully the next cocktail did the job. It was septicemia. The bacteria from a kidney infection spread through her bloodstream.

On top of being beaten, and maimed, it was a miracle she'd survived.

She still needed the surgery on her finger, to file down the bone, clean the site and seal it over with a flap. The doctors were waiting for her to stabilize. Next would be the rehab. Scar massage, nerve therapy, physiotherapy, over and above her mental progress.

The last part terrified him; no one walked away from this ordeal unscathed. Whatever she needed, Johnny would give her. Her health came first. If Lizzy wanted to go back to Johannesburg, that was her choice. She had an actual family there, and Garrison would be arriving any minute. Yes, Johnny had called the blowhard. Bankes cared for her, and if he were what she needed, Johnny wouldn't stand in their way.

"Jay Jay," she rasped.

"You remember me now?" Johnny grabbed her hand in relief, then pressed a kiss to her palm.

Her eyes darkened. "I remember everything."

"Here, drink water." He cradled her head as Lizzy drank greedily. He eased her back down. "How do you feel? Do you need something for the pain?"

"It's manageable." She closed her baby blues, then opened them. "Did you find me? Was it your team?"

"Yes. It was a joint effort."

"Did you kill him?"

"No. Apparently Kris got a tipoff, went to meet an informant and never came back. He even left that fancy horse behind, but MIT will find him."

"He needs to die."

He flinched at the dull pain in those four words. Not knowing what happened to her in those three days tore him up.

She licked her dry lips. "When Kris finally took that hideous mask off, he looked so normal—all that cynical, boyish charm. He saved me from Ivan," she said matter-of-factly. The hairs on Johnny's neck rose. Her choice of words and cold delivery hinted at what came next. "The true monster lies beneath that mask."

That small statement held pain for both of them.

"If you need to talk to someone—"

"I can't think about Kris, not his stables, not the—"

"When were you in the stables?"

Her face went flat. "After Ivan. The Scyth—Kris—insisted on giving me the grand tour."

Something terrible had happened in those stables. Johnny pulled in a careful breath and started to reach out when Garrison announced himself with a quick knock.

Johnny stood. Garrison ran a concerned gaze over Lizzy and stroked her hair. Johnny handed over her chart before stepping back and excusing himself. "I need a shower. You're in good hands, honey. I'll be back later to check on you." He ignored her baffled expression, forcing one foot in front of the other as he walked out the door.

He managed to stay away for a whole nine hours, even shaved and caught some shut-eye, before stepping into a viper's nest. Lizzy was the spitting snake.

Max loomed over her. "Don't try it. One toe even touches that floor!"

"And you'll do what?"

"Lizette Steyn, what the hell are you doing?" Johnny leaped forward as she swung her legs over the side.

"You forgot to mention that Slater got injured trying to rescue my tiny ass!"

Johnny glared. She glared back.

"I didn't want to stress you out."

"I want to see him." She folded her arms.

"He's way over in the next building. When you're feeling stronger, I'll take you."

"What's his condition. Be honest."

"His right arm is shattered. Compound fracture in his right humerus and a distal radius fracture. The surgery went well, but the recovery will be a slow one."

"Did anyone die?"

"One of the Nigerian operatives didn't make it, and the blast injured two Delta men," Max said, "and they were helping exfil Mason Clark. Your tiny ass had nothing to do with that explosion—that's all on Muller's man."

Lizzy slumped back. Fatigue etched her every move. Johnny tucked her legs back beneath the covers, clenching his jaw against the patchwork of bruising running up her thighs. He hated how thin she'd got, a combination of the ordeal and her illness. And he couldn't even feed her—fatten her up—not yet. "You need quality rest; you're scheduled for surgery later today."

She nodded wanly, turning away to stare out the window.

Johnny exchanged a worried look with Max before walking him to the door.

Max pulled him into the passage. "The Agency was just here."

"What did they want?"

"What everyone wants—to find Kris Muller. Lizzy will be debriefed, in case she saw something, knows where Muller might be, but it's too soon for the assholes to be crowding her for answers."

"Wait, the CIA was interrogating her?" Johnny felt rage bubble.

"Two men attempted to interview her. I got wind of it and came straight over. Walked in on some rough questioning, told them she's a vulnerable witness who can only be interviewed by a female and requires support in the form of her mother. They never got Lizzy's consent, just launched into it. They're the ones who told her about Slater."

"Shit. I was gonna tell her; I just wanted her to gain a little strength first."

"Speaking of Slater, MIT2 is standing down until we've been debriefed and know what's happening with him. You're free to return to Wyoming or stick with Lizzy—wherever she ends up. If you require additional leave, give me a heads-up."

"Thank you, sir."

"I'm here if you need anything. Donnie's heading Stateside tonight. I'll follow in a week's time. Slater is my priority."

"After I've helped Lizzy back on her feet, I'm finding Kris Muller and killing him," Johnny said with firm conviction.

"Johnny, he's being hunted by every ally nation and agency of the US, and SOCOM is fully invested in the search. Muller will be tracked down."

"I'll be the one doing the tracking, and I'll take personal time to do it. I may need to disappear for a couple of weeks."

Crossing his arms, Max asked. "And if it takes longer than that?"

"Jesus, it wasn't a coincidence that he chose that aircraft. He was after Lizzy. I know it, and I won't rest until I know she's safe. What if he tries again, or goes after Abby?"

Max's voice hardened. "I've assigned additional security to my family. They're safe in Utah. I'm not sitting on my hands—every spare moment is spent finding Muller."

"I need updates on any information that comes your way. When they have a bead on him, I'll be there."

"You're a stubborn dick, but I'll be by your side. Muller won't walk away from either of us."

The noisy commotion down the passage heralded the arrival of her parents; her father clapped Johnny on the arm as he rolled a large suitcase into the room. Johnny followed.

"We packed up some of your things in Kenya, baby. We even have Mr. Smithers." Daniel Steyn pulled the aged toy from the front pocket and placed it on her pillow.

"Thanks, Dad," Lizzy said colorlessly, gazing instead at the tree outside the window, her mind a million miles away. Lagos, Johnny assumed. Lizzy turned towards the wall, curling into a ball. He rubbed the back of his neck. *Ah, shit, those CIA dicks.*

◊ ◊ ◊

Germany
Two days later

Not too shabby, Lizzy thought. She'd cruised through finger surgery. The doctors were pleased with the injury site.

The next day the shady dudes in suits were back to question

her. This time it was a lady with perfectly coifed hair and artfully applied makeup who made Lizzy feel like a soiled pile of bones, languishing in starched and sterile sheets. Refusing to have any family members present, Lizzy soldiered through the barrage of questions, pleased with her robotic responses. She'd handled it like a boss, all on her own. What was all the fuss about?

Lizzy's gloomy entourage was getting on her damn nerves. John looked like he wanted to start a phonebook-ripping rampage when Lizzy asked them all—including him—to leave the room while the agent questioned her.

John could never know the details of her last day with the Scythian, and Lizzy didn't need to hold her mom's hand during questioning. She didn't need a counselor present, nor did she need to be treated like a fragile butterfly. She felt fine.

Now, a row of watchful attendants hovered around her bed, apparently expecting an implosion. Garrison shuffled at the end of the line. John stood to the side, leaning against the wall.

"Are you okay, dear?" her dad asked.

"Yes, Daddy. Just as okay as I was a minute ago and five minutes before that when you asked the same question."

They all treated her like she was a wounded puppy. Lizzy had had enough of the hospital, enough of the hard mattress, and enough of her scuzzy hair and depleted body. The sponge baths weren't cutting it.

"I want to go home, to Kenya. When can I be released? And I want a shower—like now."

John pushed off the wall. "You can't go back to Kenya. At least not yet."

"Honey, we can discuss the options. You're welcome to come home with us. Your room is just as you left it; I'll make you all your favorite foods. Minestrone, cottage pie, and pancakes and syrup."

Lizzy shuddered. "No pancakes, Mom."

"But they're your favorite, with syrup and—"

"I said no damn pancakes!"

Everyone stared.

Lizzy clapped a hand over her mouth. "Mom. I'm sorry. I don't know why I said that." Her voice shook.

"It's okay, baby. I won't make pancakes. Don't cry. Lizzy, it's okay."

"She's welcome to stay at my place," Garrison volunteered. "I have a fully staffed estate in London. I can hire a full-time nurse when I'm working back in Kenya."

"I'm not an invalid." Lizzy sniffled.

Her father stroked her hand. "There's no rush to decide, sweetie. Wherever you go, we'll all care for you."

Lizzy speared John with an ireful gaze. "So those are my only two options?"

"Come to Wyoming. If that's what you want."

"Gee, thanks. Wouldn't want to put you out."

John's nostrils flared. "Can you all give us a moment?"

The gloom parade shuffled out. Closing the door, John turned—not coming any closer. When had he touched her? Stroked her hand? The past few days, he'd kept his distance.

His withdrawal stung, and Lizzy refrained from rubbing her chest. There could be any number of reasons. He wasn't attracted to her anymore. Who would be? She was a pale, skinny, soiled mess. *Soiled.* That was a good word. Appropriate. Was it because of Slater? Did he secretly blame her for his friend's horrific injury?

"I want you to get better. You need to choose what's best for you. Your well-being comes first."

"And what about yours? Do you still want me?" Lizzy fisted

her good hand. "You left me in Kenya. Left because you needed space. Is that what you want, to never see me again?"

He rubbed at his forehead. "Choose your parents. They're family. They know how to look after you." He said the word *family* like it was a dirty word.

Screw him.

"Where will you be?"

"Wyoming. We're on hold until we know what's happening with the team."

Lizzy studied his exhaustion. Fluorescent lighting emphasized dark circles and harsh lines. She'd done that.

She set her jaw as he opened the door and called them back in. He purposely positioned himself towards the back of the room and glared out the window. Anger over John's remote attitude warred with compassion for the man who almost killed himself trying to rescue her.

When she'd lain in the dungeon that first day, her foolishly naive brain imagined him charging in and carrying her into the sunset like a blazing hero—what a stupid dream. Instead she'd choose whose burden she was to become. Her throat thickened with shame.

Distancing himself even further, John stepped into the far corner. Her brain steamed. Did he think she'd choose Garrison? That choice would sever ties with anything that mattered. Lizzy could very well run to an estate that held no meaning. Revel in an anesthetized state, staring at manicured shrubbery—garden shrubbery—not Garrison's personal shrubbery. Thoughts of any male's man-scaped rocks and shovel revolted her. She had no room for intimacy—intimacy was as alien to her as Garrison's London home. Her mind wandered back to John.

She'd destroyed his team, injured his friend. How could he

stomach having her in his home, and bear to look at her stupid face? Acidic thoughts embedded themselves like barbwire, yet none of those wicked barbs stopped her from making her fateful decision.

She spoke up. "Wyoming. I'm going with John."

He turned and walked out.

◊ ◊ ◊

The men's toilet felt like miles away. Johnny shoved through, slammed into a stall and tossed his cookies. Jesus. He prayed he could help the woman he loved. The way her parents looked at him like he could save their daughter from the soul-crushing nightmares that lay ahead. There was no doubt that he'd stay by her side, even if he knew shit about family—and this touchy-feely crap.

Johnny cruised through life on autopilot. The military provided a physical outlet for anger over his troubled past. He knew how to do his job, and how to run a farm.

Rinsing out his mouth, he heard the bathroom door swing open. Daniel Steyn's shiny loafers appeared in his peripheral vision. *Shit a stick.*

"Are you okay with having my daughter stay with you?"

Johnny nodded.

"She'll need constant support, both personally and professionally."

"Yes, sir. I'm aware of that." Johnny ran his tongue over his teeth.

"If this is not something you're—"

"I love your daughter. I love her very much."

"I know you do." Daniel squeezed soap into his hands. "Don't look so surprised; I knew that the first time I met you.

Back in August last year. You fell hard; I'm betting it was love at first sight. That's our little Lizzy for you."

"When she fell out of that tree. I knew then." Johnny smiled at the memory.

"I don't know what happened in Johannesburg when you left her in pieces. You broke her heart, and I wanted to kill you for it." Daniel pulled a paper towel. "I think she broke yours too."

"It was unavoidable. I acted like an ass."

"This might not be the best time to work out all the emotional baggage with my feisty daughter. All I care about is that she heals."

"That's my priority, sir."

"Good. Expect us to visit—regularly. I'll leave Lizzy to settle for a couple of months and then I'll be knocking at your door." Daniel tugged at the back pocket of his jeans. "The Kenyan police retrieved Lizzy's personal belongings from the…the plane after… Anyway, here's her American passport, one less thing for her to juggle with her injured hand." He handed it over, then pulled out a large wallet and flipped open a checkbook. "How does fifty grand sound?"

Johnny stepped back. "Unacceptable. What is that?"

"An advancement on her medical bills. Physical therapy, the psychologist, hospital follow-ups."

"Whoa. Firstly, I earn enough money to cover any expenses. Secondly, JetHaven's insurance policy should cover all invoices—they've covered her in-hospital medical bills."

"I never meant—I meant on a soldier's salary—"

"I may not be rolling in money, but I've saved over the years, and I earn good pay. As a specialist, I get paid accordingly." Johnny felt his ears warm.

"Hell, boy. I'm screwing this up." Daniel tucked his wallet

away. "I apologize. What you brave men do out there, on a daily basis. You're a thousand times a better man than I'll ever be. I'm proud to know you, and I know my daughter is in safe hands, so I'm putting this out there, now rather than later. Welcome to the family. And if you're done puking out your guts, let's grab a beer at that sports bar near the inn. I don't know about you, but after this suck-ass week, I need a stiff drink."

The door creaked closed behind Lizzy's father. Johnny's mouth snapped shut, and he blinked, then took a bracing breath and caught up with Daniel Steyn's quick strides to the exit.

Someone called his name, and they both paused. Garrison held up a hand and walked towards them. Johnny cursed inwardly.

Daniel patted him on the shoulder. "I'll meet you downstairs, outside the gift shop."

Johnny turned and crossed his arms. "Bankes."

"Calaway."

"Something I can help you with?"

Garrison took his time answering, and Johnny wanted to wipe the privileged look off his smooth face.

"If you break her heart—"

"You'll do what?"

The doctor shook his head, then licked his bottom lip. "I care for her. She's a good person. I can offer her a sanctuary back home."

"Don't jump on your gallant horse. If she'd chosen to go to London, do you think I'd let you whisk her away without me? You would've had an extra guest because I go where she goes."

Garrison folded his arms too. "You love her."

"Hell, yeah. I may not be a fancy doctor—but a basic medic like me can still look after her."

"From what I hear, there's nothing basic about your skills in the field. You saved her life with that IO."

"It wasn't just me."

After a considering look, Garrison visibly relaxed, then smiled. "When Lizzy's healed, I'm inviting you both to London."

"Okay. Sure…"

"So, you can meet my partner." Garrison's grin widened.

"Your…um…partner?"

"Yeah. My boyfriend."

Johnny scratched a shoulder. "You're not interested in Lizzy?"

"Robert isn't into threesomes—or girls. That makes two of us."

"I'm sorry. I'm—"

"Speechless?"

Johnny narrowed his eyes. "Does Lizzy know about Robert?"

"She suspected."

"You didn't think to tell me?"

"Call it a test of sorts. I saw how jealous you were, and I wanted to know if you felt the same way about her as she did for you. As I said, Lizzy is a good friend. I was watching out for her."

Shaking his head, then laughing, Johnny clamped a hand on Garrison's shoulder. "You sneaky asshole. For being such a dick, drinks are on you."

"What drinks?"

"The expensive round you're about to buy with your fancy British pounds." Johnny steered him towards the elevator. "What does Robert do?"

Garrison grinned. "He's an architect."

Pressing the button to close the doors, Johnny turned and smiled. "Get that cash ready; we've got a lot to catch up on."

Something crashed into his bed. *Fucked-up situational awareness,* Slater thought as he cracked open a lid.

Lizzy's curls swayed as she tried to reverse the wheelchair with one hand. "Crikey poop! You'd think they'd have at least one kid's wheelchair in a place this huge. Drat!"

Johnny's voice boomed as he turned the corner. "I turn my back for one second—how the hell did you get in here so fast!"

"It's not my fault you need to stop at every vending machine to find the right muffin; you're the one with the darn tapeworm."

"The muffin was for you, Lizbug! Easy with that thing. Don't you dare use your right hand, keep it elevated!" Johnny grabbed the handles and smoothly parallel parked her alongside the bed.

"No, wheel me to the other side! Line up my good side with Slater's good side."

They were like a bickering old married couple. Slater watched them furtively. "Are you two lovebirds finally done, now that you've woken me up good and proper?"

Once the chair was resituated, Lizzy reached out and gently clasped his hand. "How do you feel?"

"Like a wall fell on me."

She winced, then studied Slater's fully plastered arm. "Are you in much pain?"

Slater lied. "I can handle it."

He studied her, not liking what he saw. "How's the finger, sweetheart?"

She shrugged a shoulder. "MIA."

Slater laughed, then sobered, recognizing the shadows behind those cornflower eyes. "Are you ready to get checked out, to escape this sanitized hell?"

"I wanted to see you first."

Waving his good hand down his leg, Slater said, "Here I am,

baby girl, in all my unwashed glory."

"I feel you. I had my first proper shower this morning. I'll never take feeling clean for granted ever again. I think I'll carry a bar of soap in my handbag in the future."

Johnny chuckled. "I'm sure it'll fit right in, next to your hobbit ring, rabbit's foot and twenty sets of lipsticks."

Lizzy stuck her tongue out and turned back to the bed. "I brought you some magazines and a book to read. I found them in my bedside drawer." She pulled them out from behind her seat and laid them on the bed.

Johnny's sly grin should've warned him. Slater glanced down and recoiled. *Cosmopolitan* and *Vogue* slid aside to reveal a book cover of a shirtless man—in a loincloth—clutching a woman in a torn dress on a beach. His long hair blew in the wind as he gazed into her doe-like eyes.

With a twinkle in her eye, she said. "It's the only English book I could find."

Slater scooted the reading matter to the end of the bed with his foot. "I think I'll survive."

She turned serious. "Thank you for coming for me. I'm sorry you got hurt."

"I could tell you it was just an assignment, but I'd be lying. This mattered, it's personal for MIT2. We would never have given up on you." Slater turned his attention to Johnny. "Bro, this was my last mission. I'm leaving MIT."

Lizzy sucked in a breath. Slater squeezed her hand. "Don't tear up, honey. It has nothing to do with this op. I've been readying myself for a long while. It's time."

Johnny stepped up and clamped his shoulder. "Where will you go?"

"For now, I'll stay with my sister and her husband. After that,

I have no idea."

"You're my brother in every way, and that will never change. If you need any help—"

"I'm not traveling to damn Mars. You'll get sick of my whiny ass when I'm healed and squatting on your porch in Wyoming."

"You're always welcome. I'll keep the beers on ice."

"Yeah? I'll need a fuck ton of those after therapy. That shit is gonna hurt. Have they found Muller yet?"

"Negative. Possibly spotted in London. With Muller's face plastered on every news channel, there aren't many places for him to hide. MIT1 captured more of his mercenaries, found and froze all his bank accounts. Rumors are that al-Shabaab and al-Qaeda have turned their backs on him—he stole funds from them when he went on the run. The Botswanan boy is now a liability."

Slater reached out and squeezed Lizzy's good hand. "You're safe now, sweetheart."

Haunted eyes blinked back. She didn't look convinced.

After soppy hugs, Johnny pointed her towards the door. Slater had to ask his friend. "Did you hear anything yet from Kat?"

"No. I'm sorry, bud."

"When I lay under that rubble, I saw her. A vision—so clear. I need to know if she's okay."

When he'd come around, he'd called Kat 's name, over and over. The team had reached out to her, leaving messages and voicemails. She'd ignored every one of them.

Looking uncomfortable, Johnny replied, "We spoke with your cousin, Casey. She's heading to Germany next week. Casey says that Kat is fine."

Slater's cousin was Kat's best friend. That was how he'd met the Irish beauty in the first place.

"She's probably just busy," Slater said, swallowing down the hurt. It was time to let her go. Kathleen Flynn was a distraction, and if Derek "Slater" Banez didn't get his head on straight, he'd end up blowing it away with his G19X pistol. The door closed behind Johnny. Slater was back to being alone. Not entirely alone. Just him and his screwed-up brain.

Chapter Twelve

They were off to a good start on the ride from the Landstuhl hospital to the Frankfurt airport, chatting as Johnny negotiated the ninety-minute drive. Lizzy was happy to be discharged after twelve days in the hospital. It all went to shit when he pulled into the rental lane, ran around and leaned over to unclip her belt. It could've been the click, or him looming too far into her personal space. She flinched like he'd hit her. Her panic attack slammed in like a tidal wave. This was something new to her, and her terror and confusion slammed through him as she wordlessly begged for help. Johnny crouched on the tarmac for thirty minutes, ignoring angry motorists, instead chatting, asking questions, and gradually pulling her out of the flashback.

His mind raced over his limited choices. Take her back to the clinic or check them into a Frankfurt hotel for the night or board the plane with an emotionally traumatized subject. Once she'd recovered her senses, stubborn Lizzy met his gaze squarely and chose the last option.

Johnny guided her through the airport. Much to her horror, a second anxiety attack hit when she saw the aircraft lined up outside the terminal. Johnny guessed it had everything to do with that fateful day—curled up on the flight deck in terror. He carried her to a quiet corner, her good hand gripping his shirt as she gasped for air.

Sitting down, Johnny tucked her bandaged hand between them. "We're not doing this. I'm taking you to a hotel."

"I…need…to—" she whispered. "Seeing the planes made… me… remember."

"Lizbug, this is too soon. We can stay in Germany for however long you need."

"John." She pierced him with a resolute look. "You're taking me home."

"We'll see. Just breathe, I've got you." He tucked her head into his shoulder, running a hand up and down her shuddering back.

Once her breathing slowed, Lizzy shifted on his lap. "People are staring."

"Yeah? Screw 'em. They would break. Most soldiers I know would splinter—going through what you've gone through."

"Maybe it did break me. I'm splintering as we speak."

Looking down, he ran a thumb along her jaw. It was time for some Wyoming honesty.

"I've gone through some bad shit in my career. You've just gone through horrific shit—being held for days by extremists— not many people on the planet have experienced that, including me." Shifting her on his lap, Johnny allowed her to see his distress. "How do I help you through this? If it does break you, it's not because you're weak, it's because you're human. But I won't let this destroy you, not on my fucking watch. I exist to make you whole again. Your family is there to make you whole again. Do you think we'd let you cope with this on your own? I've already lined up a therapist in the States who'll help to prevent C-PTSD."

"What's that?"

"A form of PTSD. Something that affects many hostage and kidnap victims. Prolonged trauma without a viable means of escape will trigger it, but we're going to kick its ass, and I don't want another apology slipping out of those gorgeous lips. You're entitled to feel the pain and the loss and helplessness and sadness."

Smiling softly, she asked, "Are you giving me permission to cry myself ugly?"

"Ma'am, I'm giving you permission to heal, and right now, I'm looking at the prettiest woman I've ever seen. 'Ugly' doesn't exist when it comes to you."

"Look at that cowboy charm." She stroked his cheek once, then turned away. How did his Lizzy looked wiped out and determined at the same time? Guessing she'd refuse to take no for an answer, Johnny placed her on her feet, helped her back to the gate and handed over their boarding passes.

The business class seats—courtesy of JetHaven—helped somewhat. Thankfully, the flight didn't include another episode. Instead, he sat next to a shell-shocked and listless female who refused to eat a meal. He forced her to nibble on a bread roll and take her meds.

She eventually slept. He didn't and couldn't.

Fifteen hours of travel later, and she'd barely said a word. He gripped the steering wheel as she watched the Wyoming countryside. Only thirty minutes from home. Now he paid the price of not sleeping on the flights—fighting fatigue on the four-hour drive. He glanced over, guessing from her drawn look that her hand was in pain.

"I've never been to Wyoming. It's lovely."

He strained to hear the quiet words, attempting to see the

rural landscape through fresh eyes.

They drove up to Jackson Hole alongside the Snake River, which sparkled in the afternoon light. The surrounding green and black forests blanketing the rugged hills were greening up as summer rolled in. Soon they'd see the jagged peaks of the Tetons.

He wondered if she would fall in love with the ever-present mountains hovering in the background, ever-changing in the valley light. Johnny loved everything about this fifty-mile long valley—the sagebrush, the big sky, the raw freedom. She was a city girl, but the tomboy in her might take to country living. If she asked to leave, he would take her wherever she wished.

"I live pretty close to Jackson, near a town called Wilson. Not that near, about eight miles out. It's a little greener, not as scrubby as the rest of Wyoming. The bonus of this stretch is knowing the Tetons are virtually in your backyard."

Lizzy didn't say anything, just watched the passing landscape with weary eyes. When his ranch house finally came into view, he breathed a sigh of relief. Even under the circumstances, it felt good to be home.

He handed over a pain pill and opened a bottle of water before pointing out the cabin and the outbuildings.

"Who takes care of it when you're away?" she asked between sips.

"My small piece of land is surrounded by the original farm, which is run by Jack and Charlie Quinn. They have a cattle and sheep ranch. I own a handful of sheep, which they absorb into their herd when I'm away. Charlie stops by to feed Hercules and Catapult."

"Hercules and who?"

"Catapult. My cat. Hercules is my parrot."

"I didn't know you owned pets."

"The last time I was home, Catapult decided to own me. The scrawny stray launched herself at my head as I stepped off my front porch. Looked like she went head-to-head with a puma. Poor thing lost an eye."

Lizzy smiled. "Girl knew what she was doing, throwing herself at you…"

"Why do you think I called her Catapult? I'll introduce you to the gang later. First, you'll need to rest."

He came around to her side. Lizzy stepped out of the truck, and her legs collapsed. He hoisted her up and carried her up to the guest room. Although it was natural for her to feel this wiped out, it still worried him. They should have stayed a few nights in Frankfurt.

With a kiss to her cheek, he pulled the curtains.

"Leave a light on," she rasped.

He clicked on the bathroom light and walked back over. Lizbug was already asleep. Dark circles rimmed her eyes. Her lips held a blue tinge offset by her pale skin. As reassurance, he craved crawling in beside her to rest a finger over her pulse. Listen to those soft breaths while she slept. He forced himself to walk away and retrieve their luggage from the truck.

Lizzy slept and slept. Paranoid that she would have a nightmare or wake to a panic attack, he didn't venture far, and hunkered down overnight on the floor next to her bed.

He woke her the next morning and forced her to swallow some oatmeal. Then she slept some more.

Ignoring the endless chores screaming for his attention, he sat in a nearby rocker. His room felt too far away. Curling up beside her seemed like an obvious choice, but she wasn't ready for proximity with any man, even one who adored every hair on her pretty head.

By late afternoon, Johnny prepared a mountainous tray of sandwiches, along with the freshly squeezed juice. Taking the feast upstairs, he paused to hear the shower running.

Gently placing the tray on the dresser, he listened for regular shower movement. Sounded like she was washing her hair. Exhaling a tense breath, he slid out, giving Lizzy her much-needed privacy.

Hercules screamed as he danced up and down the wooden perch. As soon as Johnny's hand touched the bird's claw, Hercules raced up his shoulder and pecked at his neck.

"Yeah, I missed you too, buddy."

The African Grey worked his way over to the other shoulder, then down Johnny's back as Johnny bent to scoop up torn newspaper in the corner of the large aviary. Late one autumn, Hercules had flown onto his porch, hopping up and down and squawking like a baby.

Johnny assumed it was someone's pet, who'd flown the coop. Placing the bird in a crate, he posted dozens of flyers in town, but no one claimed the feisty bird. So, Johnny did what any decent man would do. He built a giant aviary, rigged with heating systems, fancy bird toys and twenty different perches. Hercules loved the perches, but the new toys, not so much. Except for a small fluffy teddy bear that fell victim to bird vomit.

Apparently, Hercules thought the teddy was a mate and regularly regurgitated on the dirty teddy—to demonstrate his undying devotion. Johnny guessed he should perhaps find Hercules a mate of the feathered variety and give Teddy a break from all the love.

As Johnny straightened slowly, Hercules used his beak to swing back up to the regular perch position—beside his right ear.

"Cute bird," Lizzy quipped. "Now all you need is an eye

patch." Afternoon sun danced around her before she stepped into the enclosure. She looked a little more rested. Still as pale as linen but her recovery would take time.

"How's the finger feeling?"

"You mean half-finger. Fine."

"Did you eat? Did you take a pain pill?"

"Stop man-fussing. I'm happy to be on my own two feet. I took a walk around your cabin. It's nice. Welcoming."

Johnny grinned. "It's pretty basic and old-fashioned. I'm not around long enough to renovate the furnishings. There's a lot of wood."

"I like that wooded cabin feel. You could do with some pictures on the wall."

Johnny folded his arms as Hercules nibbled at his ear. "Are you volunteering to add that woman's touch?"

Lizzy raised her brows and changed the subject. "I like your feathered friend."

"This is Hercules. He's the resident stud. No. Don't put your hand out; he doesn't like females."

"You mean 'she' doesn't like females."

"Huh?"

She elaborated. "You'd have to get a blood test to know the sex, but usually female birds bond with male humans and vice versa."

"Are you saying that Hercules is a chick?"

"Yup. That's my guess."

"So…all that bro talk with my feathered teammate about bro stuff…"

Lizzy sniggered. "She doesn't mind; she just likes the sound of your masculine voice."

"Oh, jeez. Stop already."

Lizzy closed the door as the cat wandered past.

"You don't have to do that; Catapult and Hercules are friends."

"That is one fugly cat. Are those bald patches on her back?"

"Yup. The vet can't figure out why her fur won't grow back."

Leaning down, Lizzy examined the whiskered face looking up at her. "She has an honest to God overbite…with a scraggly tooth sticking out."

"That she does," Johnny said as he fiddled with the rusty enclosure latch.

"That has to be the cutest cat I've ever seen." She used her good hand to scratch a scarred ear.

Johnny shrugged, then paused to take in the adorable picture the duo made—two tough-as-nails souls bonding in the dimming light.

◊ ◊ ◊

The night had been a rough one, even with the light on and Johnny back on the floor. The screams that woke him had Johnny trying to calm a spooked Lizzy. The terror reflected in her unseeing gaze broke his heart, but not half as much as the pitiful begging that followed.

Gripped by the nightmares, she pleaded, "Don't hurt him, master. I'll wear it. He's just a kid. It's me you want. No! Let go!" She grabbed at her splinted finger.

"Lizzy, baby. Wake up."

Instead, she went stiff. "Don't let him eat me. Please. No. No!"

Johnny grasped her shoulders and gently shook her. Gulping sobs had him pulling her onto his lap. She screamed and fought, but he held her to him, humming an old country ballad as he rocked her.

She finally settled, whispered thanks and asked him to let her go. She turned her back and curled into a ball. The second attack occurred an hour later and then again in the early morning hours. She eventually gave up on sleep. Johnny's gaze tracked her to the bathroom.

When she emerged and wandered down the stairs in shorts and an oversized cardigan, he followed. They sat in silence on the back porch, sipping on steaming coffee. The first rays of sunrise lit the sky, first gray, then pink and finally orange hues skimming over the fields as the sun rose.

The warm rays weren't enough to erase the bruised look on her bleak face. He studied her drawn lines. "Is your finger hurting?"

"I can handle it." She stood and walked to the fence at the bottom of the yard. Charlie's horses wandered into the field from their stalls. Activity stirred as farm hands started their chores.

As he was already up, Johnny got to work mucking out the pens while keeping an eye on his girl. Two hours later and she hadn't moved—not even twitched a limb—just stood staring across the fence at the horses. He brought out an orange juice and a bacon sandwich. She barely acknowledged him or the food. Next came a chair, which served as a decoration. She still didn't move—at least she stood in the shade of a cottonwood.

"If you've elected to hover in this spot for the day, here's a chair."

"Thank you." She refused to look at him. He'd noticed her reluctant eye contact since arriving in Wyoming. If she had to look his way, she focused on his chin or a shoulder.

Johnny rubbed his forehead. "Please eat something. You need your strength."

Lizzy met his comment with silence.

"I'm patching a wall in the mudroom, if you need anything."
Still nothing.

His skin felt hot and itchy. "Lizbug, let me help you."

"Give me space. I'm sorry, John. Today I'm not a functional human. Let me catch my breath."

He backed off, praying that the Wyoming sunshine and Dr. Greene, the therapist rolling in later, would help her take those first small steps.

◊ ◊ ◊

The nightmare still haunted him. Lizzy under a flame tree, bleeding out. Johnny jerked awake from his awkward prone position on the couch and rubbed a shaking hand over his head before glancing at his watch. Two in the morning.

The last thing he remembered was sitting down to pull off his Salomon boots after locking up for the night. He must've keeled over from exhaustion. The past week had kicked his ass.

Thanks to the nightly lack of sleep, combined with jet lag and the heap-load of chores to catch up on, he was officially a zombie. He hadn't even started his daily PT. Johnny swore. He needed to be mission ready; it was essential to his job. Three weeks of zero physical activity was unacceptable.

Something *thunked* upstairs, putting him on immediate alert. Another body moved through the house. Lizzy probably couldn't sleep, but the hairs on the back of his neck stood to attention. Rising, he pulled his Glock from its holster and crept up the stairs towards the bedrooms down the hall.

He cleared his room. Lizzy's sat empty. His heart rate sped up as he narrowed in on the remaining third bedroom down the hall.

Slipping in, he noted the light shining from the guest

bathroom. The door stood ajar. A metallic clang echoed against the sink, followed by a muffled sob. Pulling in a breath, he eased over to the doorway and froze. His heartbeat flipped into a slippery race as he cataloged the scene before him. He lowered the weapon slowly and re-holstered it.

"Put the scalpel down."

Lizzy flinched as he stepped forward.

"You don't need to do this. Baby, it's going to be okay."

The blade glistened in the fluorescent light. She held it in her good hand, a hand that shook as it hovered over the sink. It was an unsheathed box-cutter blade, one of many he kept in his toolbox. A toolbox she'd stood over earlier in the day as Johnny fixed a blocked pipe beneath the kitchen sink.

Now the lethal weapon lay inches away from the delicate wrist of her injured hand, which rested in the basin. He'd underestimated her mental state. This was all his fault, her parents had left her under his care, and this was the result.

"I can't do it." She sobbed.

"I can help. Just hand it to me." He raised a hand, calculating how much time he needed to lunge before she slashed at a wrist. If he chose to brutally twist the blade from her hand, he'd hurt her. Their relationship would likely never recover from the violence he was about to unleash to save her life.

"I need your help. I need two hands for this."

Momentary confusion at her words almost had Johnny shaking his head. Did she need two hands to cut herself?

Her eyes met his. "I need you to do it for me."

Had she lost it completely? He felt the blood drain from his face. He spoke carefully. "You need me to do what exactly?"

"Cut my hair."

"I don't understand."

Blue teary eyes turned his way. "I'm trying to cut my hair. This damn splint is in the way, and I keep bumping my finger."

"You're not trying to…hurt yourself?"

Lizzy frowned. "No. Why would I do that?"

"That's a scalpel, baby."

"I know what it is. I couldn't find any scissors—in any of your drawers. I need an electric shaver. The scalpel will work just fine to start."

Easing out a breath, he stepped forward and held out a hand. "Promise me you'll help."

"Always, Lizbug, but let's first talk. Okay?"

She handed over the blade—dull side facing him—and turned back to the mirror. After placing it over by the bedside table, Johnny took a second to gather his shit before easing back into the small space behind his tiny woman. He gently pulled her hair over her shoulders, and she froze.

"Don't play with it." Lizzy growled.

He raised his hands and kept them up, watching her in the mirror.

"All I need you to do is cut, then shave it all off." Her nostrils flared with determination.

Her hair sat just below her shoulders. When they'd first met nine months ago, Lizzy wore it just above in a layered cut. Her natural curls had framed her pretty face perfectly. Now it was doubled in length, and the longer weight pulled those curls down into soft waves. Johnny remembered running his hands through those golden locks in Kenya as they'd made love. Gripping silk as he'd repeatedly thrust into her.

"Give me a reason why you want to hack off your pretty hair, and I'll consider it."

"You don't understand."

"Then make me understand."

Lizzy buried her head in his chest as she stumbled over words.

Wrapping gentle arms around fragile shoulders, he said, "Slow down, Lizbug. I'm not getting any of this."

Turning her head to the side, she repeated her words. "In the stables. Kris played with it. Then braided it. Then…"

"Then what?" Johnny growled.

"I want it short enough so it can't be braided. So, it can't be tied up. So, it can't be held."

"What did he do to you…before I found you?"

"I keep dreaming of him touching my hair."

She wouldn't tell Johnny what he craved to know. Bloodlust and the need for vengeance soared through his veins. That he was good at—killing sick fuckers who hurt the innocent. He'd kill for her and not bat an eye. But being a therapist and healing the one person who mattered most, he sucked at that.

"Help me, John. Please help." She looked up at him with such hope in those doe eyes, and he knew he was screwed.

"Why don't I take you to one of those fancy hairdressers in Jackson tomorrow?"

"I don't want strangers touching me. I'm not ready."

"Will you be okay with me touching your hair? While I trim it?"

"I want it all gone."

"I refuse to shave it off."

"Kris loved how long it was. You love it. All men like long hair."

"That's not true," he said carefully, wanting to spit nails at the comparison to Muller. "I loved your hair in Johannesburg. Why do you want to shave your hair off? You say you don't want it braided or tied up. Tell me why?"

She pursed her lips.

"Lizbug, I'm trying to understand."

"Don't make me punch you in the dick!"

He tried not to smile.

"Fine! He braided my hair, then showed me where he'd cut my scalp, to get a clean...clean—"

"Shit. Stop!" Johnny's eye twitched, and he wanted to break something. Muller's bones, he'd smash them into powder. "You're safe. He won't get near you again."

Lizzy set her jaw. She was determined to do this. It was like arguing with a brick wall.

"If it helps you to heal, how about this? I cut it short enough so it can't be braided."

She gnawed on her lip, then nodded. "Deal."

"There's a pair of good scissors with my tools under the stairs. Sit at that dresser." He pointed to the bedroom. "I'll get set up."

After grabbing the right tools, towels, and a sturdy comb, he wet her hair in the sink and sat her back in the chair.

"I'm probably going to screw your hair up. If you end up with a mullet, it's all on you."

A small smile was all he received.

"Don't look away from the mirror, Lizbug. Keep watching me. It's me touching you. No one else."

Johnny began with trepidation. By the time he was done, he felt proud. He went for a bob cut that lined up with her chin. He started out with a blunt cut but noticed how her wispy ends curled up prettily. So, he snipped tiny jagged layers through the bottom, ensuring both sides hung even. To finish, he whipped out his electric shaver and trimmed up her neck. The relief shining in her eyes made him feel fifty feet tall, and he eased down and placed a kiss on her forehead.

"I hope I didn't fuck it up too badly. Bonus that you have a beautiful face, you pretty much can get away with anything."

After running her good hand over her exposed neck and tracing over the choppy cut, she grinned. "I feel clean and pretty. You gave me that. Thank you."

Clean as opposed to…? Johnny swallowed down the rage and smiled back. "Time for bed, Lizbug."

Grabbing his hand, she asked, "Will you lie next to me?"

"Hell, yeah, in a heartbeat."

◊ ◊ ◊

Five days later and her new routine held her cemented in that same spot. Three nights of bloodcurdling night terrors and agonizing pain around her injury. Mornings spent at this fence post. Afternoons with Dr. Greene, who was an okay therapist, Lizzy supposed. She battled to open up to the old biddy. What did that old bird know about being held hostage by extremists?

What did anyone know? It was tempting to reach out to Mason Clark. He was the only other one who lived through the Scythian terror. Was he as broken as she felt? Did he have a stable support system?

John was her rock. Lizzy wasn't sure what a self-entitled, ungrateful and now damaged girl did to deserve such devotion. He'd slept on the freaking floor beside her bed—a fussing warrior watching her every move.

Well, that wasn't fair. Not every move. He kept his distance when there were chores to be done, only pausing to shake her out of the reverie and force her to eat.

Catapult stirred Lizzy from the afternoon trance, curling around her aching legs. Lizzy swayed. Her back burned from standing for hours. How had she not noticed that before? Or the gnats swarming sporadically. Swatting them away, she glanced away from the equestrian beasts grazing in the corner…and blinked.

Her eyes felt dry. Not just her eyes—she touched her cheek. Her skin felt tight. When had she last used face cream? Slathered a rich moisturizer over her sad face? And her hands—she ignored the ugly splint, not ready to address the giant elephant in the room or in her case, the finger stump. She'd start physical therapy soon, remove the stitches, and she'd deal with it then.

The rest of her digits looked awful. Nails chipped and worn down. Her stomach growled for the first time in days, and she looked towards the house.

A rider approached on a pretty brown gelding. Whoever rode knew what they were doing, their seat perfect in the saddle. A wild-haired woman pulled smoothly to a stop and dismounted in a fluid motion before tying up the horse to the side and trotting up the back porch.

"Yo, James! I'm using your kitchen," she yelled.

Lizzy glanced around. With John nowhere in sight, curiosity got the best of her.

Cursing and a generous amount of drawer-slamming drew Lizzy to the small kitchen.

"Why does it have to be a stupid-ass pie," the stranger muttered before throwing open a cabinet door.

"Um. Can I help you?"

The crazy lady jerked and bashed her head on the cupboard. "Holy shit! Talk about giving a gal a freaking heart attack! Mother of a—"

Lizzy yanked open the fridge and gingerly handed a packet of frozen peas to the staggering cowgirl, who clutched the top of her head.

"Thanks. Shit, that hurts. Did I break the skin?"

Lizzy stood on tiptoes and tried in vain to spot a potential injury, but the girl had enough hair to start a wig shop. A frazzled nest of never-ending strawberry-blonde curls engulfed the injury site.

"I think you're okay," Lizzy guessed.

The woman's firm forearm swept the hair back, and Lizzy studied the face staring back.

Full lips that most girls would die for stretched into a wide Colgate smile. A cute turned-up nose and sparkling brown eyes completed the wholesome picture.

She was of average height and weight, yet Lizzy felt dwarfed by her confidence and strength.

"You must be Lizzy. I'm Charlie." She yanked Lizzy up against firm breasts for a bone-crushing hug. Almost as quickly, Charlie let go. "I'm sorry, I do that without thinking. I'm a hugger."

"Wait. You're Charlie?"

"Charlotte Quinn, at your service."

"John never mentioned you were a woman."

"Who's John?"

"I mean James." Shoot, Lizzy forgot that John's birth name was James. He'd asked her to use his real name in front of the Wyoming locals and she'd already forgotten.

"Yeah, well. I think he sometimes forgets that I'm a girl, especially when I out-shear him." Charlie must've picked up on Lizzy's confusion. "You know—sheep shearing. Give me the right trimmer, and I can turn those babies out. Do you know your way around a kitchen?"

They sheared sheep together? Lizzy wondered if that was the only physical exertion they'd performed in the fields. Charlie looked at her expectantly.

"I can cook and bake a little. If that's what you mean?"

"Excellent. I have to make some fancy pie for my dance group tonight. We all take turns, and the last time I got away with buying a box of donuts. Now they insist we bring something homemade. I bought some ingredients. Have 'em over at my place, but I have no fancy baking tools. I need a pie shell tin thing, a mixer of some type and a big-ass spoon."

Lizzy couldn't help chuckling. Charlie was some kind of special, and Lizzy couldn't help liking her.

"Let's make a deal. Bring your supplies over. Give me twenty minutes to take a shower, and I'll help you with the pie."

Lizzy turned her back on the beaming Charlie. That's the kind of girl that John needed, a well-balanced farm girl to work at his side. Simple, uncomplicated, and his equal in every way.

◊ ◊ ◊

Thanks to their joint effort, the banana cream pie turned out okay. Lizzy enjoyed the afternoon with chatty Charlie; she was easy to talk to, and her natural confidence drew Lizzy in. They were sitting on the porch with large glasses of lemonade when John came ambling up.

"Well, it's about time," Charlie said. "I've been hollering for you for the past hour. If it weren't for Lizzy here, I'd be pie-screwed."

"Stop whining. I fixed your fence line to the south, on that bit of marshy land."

"Thanks, Jamie. Always helps to have a bit of swaggering brawn helping with my long list of unpleasant jobs."

John sat on the top step and stretched out his legs. "You need to kick that new farmhand's ass. Where did you find him anyway, pretendcowboys.com?"

"Leave Pete alone. Not everyone can be as capable as your giant butt."

"How's your dad doing?"

Earlier, Charlie had told Lizzy about her ailing father. He suffered from heart failure and needed additional surgeries to add two more stints.

"Not so good, and he refuses to sit his stubborn ass down. He has another surgery scheduled for Wednesday."

"I'll swing by later to visit."

They spoke about livestock, and since their easy familiarity positioned Lizzy on the periphery, she stood to leave.

John pushed to his feet, concern evident in his amber eyes. "Are you okay, Lizbug?"

Yeah, she was just fine and annoyed that he walked on eggshells when it came to her. It contrasted with his laidback mannerisms with Charlie. Was he ever that relaxed with her?

"Sit with your friend. I still need to unpack the rest of my clothes. I'll be upstairs if you need me."

"If you're sure—"

"There's a jug of lemonade sitting out in the kitchen." Lizzy turned and walked inside, refusing to acknowledge Charlie's curious glances or John's ever-anxious state.

Unpacking took forever thanks to her injured hand. She wasn't too fazed by the rumpled stacks on the shelf. At least her clothes had a temporary home. She needed to get back to Nairobi. She missed Valentino and her friends at the orphanage. Except she now didn't have a job. She couldn't bring herself to work on another flight. Her stomach roiled at the thought.

Bending to arrange the shoe rack, Lizzy froze.

You're mine. The last words Kris whispered to her snaked around her like a toxic fog. The Scythian squatted in her brain like a bloody tick, attaching himself to her every move and every thought. "Screw off, you evil dick cheese," she yelled into the silent room.

Forcing herself to continue, she folded the last of her shirts, then paused and picked up her Canon camera lying on the bed. Switching it on, she flipped through the previous photos taken. They weren't half bad. Most were of the Peshawar markets. The compositions highlighted the dusty chaos of the narrow streets.

A close-up of an elderly vendor, two front teeth missing in his broad smile as he held out a flowered wreath. A family shopping, their little girl clutching the hand of her little brother as they skipped down the street. Another of a teenage boy pausing to scratch his donkey behind its ear in a narrow side street.

She flipped to the next. John. An image of him on her balcony, grinning around a sip of beer, his legs propped up as the sun set on the Nairobi skyline. She remembered that day well. They'd made love in the shower…on her sofa…on her bean bag. She chuckled. That had been a challenge. She remembered being draped over it with her ass in the air as John knelt behind. His knees kept sliding off the sinking bag, and they'd giggled as he'd fallen, tangling with her in a sagging heap. When they'd finally got the angle right, he'd made slow love to her, pressing her into the bean bag with long, firm thrusts.

She ran a hand over his rugged profile on the screen. The small scar at the corner of his eye made him look like the toughened warrior he was. She'd never asked him how he got that scar. Come to think of it, she didn't know much about his past. She knew what kind of man he was, knew his soul like it was her own. It felt like she'd known the loyal, kind, brave soldier all her life. In the short time they'd known each other, they'd lived a lifetime's worth of memories.

The small device in her hand could record more memories and she fiddled with the settings before pulling out the lens cleaning brush and readying the Canon for action. With little daylight left, she threw on a pair of jeans and sneakers and raced down the stairs.

◊ ◊ ◊

That night, Johnny lay in bed straining his ears for any sounds of distress. Perhaps it was too soon to tell, but it seemed as if Lizzy had had a good day. By the time dinner rolled around, her usually pale cheeks had been flushed with color. The afternoon walk, with Catapult strolling alongside, had put a smile on her face.

Her fancy camera had clicked away as they'd walked. Across the fields to the small stream running along the fence. Over and up a hiking path, through a couple of gently rolling hills. Two hours later as the sun dipped behind the mountains, Johnny grabbed her hand and led her back home.

"I like it here."

"You do? I thought it might be a little too quiet for you."

"It's nice. Peaceful. I'm sorry I've been distant. You must have the patience of a saint to put up with me."

Johnny swung her around. "Don't you dare go there. You're entitled to heal and take as much time as you need. I won't get in the way of your recovery. If you decide to go home to your family, I'm on board with that. If staying is what you need, I'm not going anywhere."

She stood on her toes, pulled his head down and kissed his cheek.

Never-mind a good day, it had been a damn beautiful day.

"John?" Lizzy stood at his door, pulling him back to the present. The hall light illuminated her from behind. She wore one of his old Ranger shirts, and it hung down to her knees.

"Hey, baby."

In a heartbeat, she was at his side. "Can I lie down with you?"

He pulled the covers back, and she crawled in. He kept his body in a neutral position, not wanting to scare her with any sudden moves. Lizzy snuggled up to his chest, a tremble snaking through her slight frame. "Please hold me."

He cautiously wrapped his arms around her shoulders. Having her back in his arms felt surreal, and he hugged her tight while burying his nose in her hair.

"Mmm. Peaches."

"Apricots," Lizzy corrected. He felt her smile on his naked chest.

His voice turned gruff. "I never thought I'd smell that again or hold you again. Three times. I thought I'd lost you three damn times. Once on the plane. Once on the video feed. Shit, that was bad. And then at the safe house, when you flatlined. We lost you then, for a full minute."

Shifting her head, she looked up. "I died? I didn't know that."

"You did. I had to stand back and trust the trauma team to resuscitate you. You have the constitution of a stubborn bull. Your determination puts most strapping men to shame."

She settled back in. "And now you're stuck with me."

Wouldn't have it any other way. But something still didn't feel right. He knew it had something to do with her captivity and everything to do with Kris Muller. *The red fucker.*

◊ ◊ ◊

Upon waking, the first thing he registered was the smell of bacon and eggs. The night had been a peaceful one. No night terrors or gut-churning screaming. His phone buzzed. MIT. Johnny reached over to take the quick call.

After pulling on a T-shirt, he wandered downstairs. The happy scene made him pause. Lizzy munched on a piece of toast as she laid out some plates. Freshly picked flowers sat in a vase; the bright blooms matched the cheeriness of her teal blue dress. Minimal makeup enhanced her ethereal beauty. He loved her whether she chose to go barefaced or chose to wear makeup, he knew the makeup made her feel girly, and it was nice to see that small sparkle twinkling in her wide blue eyes.

She plated a massive portion and plonked it down in front of him.

"Shit, girl, I'm going to have to double my PT on the course today, to get rid of this mountain of calories."

"What course?"

"I built an out-course. It's a smaller rendition of the Seal obstacle course in San Diego. It still gets the job done."

"I haven't seen it!"

"It's well hidden in the north corner, between a forest of trees."

"Does Charlie know about it?"

"Yip. She watched us build it. Max and Slater helped me lay it out." Johnny grinned. "We told her it's because we want to try out for *Ninja Warrior*. She doesn't know what we do."

"I want to see it. Why build a whole course?"

"We're required to work out—to keep at our peak levels regardless of where we are. The rest of the team has access to a gym in their respective cities—aside from their running regimes. I make do with living on a farm. I use weights, jog seven miles every day and utilize my course."

"I haven't seen you run."

"I'm starting back up today."

"Fudge buckets. I've kept you from your normal routine."

"It happens. I'll catch up quickly."

Surrounded by aspen and pine trees, the out-course stretched out in a meandering circle. John pointed out some of the structures as Lizzy stared in wonder. Parallel bars, low and high walls, Burma Bridge, tires, monkey bars, balance logs… Lizzy lost track and just sat on a log, watching him warm up, then run the course over and over. To say the man was fit was an understatement. He worked the obstacles like a machine, flying over walls, netting and through bars like he was born to it.

After an hour, Lizzy wandered off to snap some photos of wildflowers. When she returned, John stretched out a leg on her log seat. His bare chest shone with perspiration, highlighting his powerful physique. *Holy shiblets.*

She sat at the other end of the log and tried to shove her camera back in its bag, but her stupid splint got in the way.

"That should be coming off today or tomorrow. I'll book you in with a doctor in Jackson," John said between short breaths.

"I can take the stitches out. There's no need to traipse all the way into town. Or you can do it; you've done a great job changing my dressings."

"Lizbug—"

"Please, John. You have a full kit here. I don't want to leave the farm. Not yet." The farm felt safe. She felt unassailable on the peaceful stretch of land. She didn't care if it sounded cowardly, her mental struggle towards normality was one small, shuffling step at a time.

After his shower, they sat at the dining table. He sterilized the surgical scissors and tweezers. Then swabbed her wound site. Lizzy still couldn't examine her hand, and always refused to look with every dressing change. The last time she saw the injury was when the cleaver came down on that dirty wooden block. Now she turned away to stare at the fireplace.

"You're going to have to see it at some point."

Silence greeted his remark.

"It's not half as bad as I'm sure you've pictured in your head. The doc did a good job. That's the prettiest amputation I've ever seen."

"I'm not ready."

"When you start therapy, you'll have to be ready."

She swallowed back the tears.

John paused, then cradled her hand. "This has to be the most heroic hand I've ever held."

"Don't bullshit me."

"This is the story I'm going to tell our kids one day when they ask what happened to mommy's finger."

Kids? Did he consider having kids with her? "What story?"

"There once was a little index finger who had an adventurous life. When it was young, it was well loved and squeezed and kissed by parents who loved its owner. Not all index fingers were that lucky. Some never knew love."

She frowned. Somehow, she knew he referred to his childhood.

"It learned the guitar and played incredible tunes. One day, an obnoxious giant called Jay Jay came into its owner's life, followed her around and acted like a big bossy pants. The finger poked him in the chest...often."

Lizzy smiled, still staring away into the living room.

"Then suddenly, Little Index found itself in Kenya living a busy life. Pushing fabric through sewing machines and saving local girls from a life on the streets. Little Index injected life-giving medicine into sick kids and stroked their brows when they were sad. It traced figure of eights in the sand and made the kids smile."

He traced circles on the palm of her hand as he spoke. When he paused, she braced herself for his next words.

"One sad day, Little Index got ripped from its owner. And although it didn't complete its journey, it had a life filled with kind deeds. It was time for its nine other friends to take over those noble adventures, and so they did. They traced squiggly lines on the ground; those heroic acts led to the rescue of a young boy and their brave owner."

Swiping at her tears, she turned to look at John as he finished the charming story.

"Now these nine little buddies wait for new adventures, determined to live up to the bravery of their lost friend."

Lizzy sniffled trying not to laugh. "You're such a sappy tart."

"Hey! Don't insult me with your South African twang."

"Thank you, John." It was time, and she took courage in his kind words. She closed her damp eyes before bracing herself and looking down. The shock of seeing half a finger slammed into her. At times it still felt like it was there, but it definitely was not.

Looking away, Lizzy willed her chin to stop trembling; then she looked back. Unmoving, John observed her reaction. This time she tried to examine it objectively as a nurse. He was right; the surgeon had done a good job. The horseshoe flap of sewn-over skin looked healthy and had healed well. She would allow time to mourn the loss of a digit, but she had nine others to compensate for that loss.

A determination to train her right hand rose to the surface. If she set small goals and worked hard, in six months she could be fully functional. The most significant challenges were writing and playing her guitar, she'd do both even better than she did before. Screw the Scythian. Nothing would stand in her way. Lizette Steyn was back.

"Well, what are you waiting for, Jay Jay? Yank that ugly black stitching out of my brave little finger, and let's get this party started!"

Chapter Thirteen

Therapy started the next day with massages to the injury site to reduce scar sensitivity. Lack of mobility and stiffness were challenges to be overcome. The occupational therapist limited her activities, and Lizzy could see why. The hand was far from functional and would remain that way for three months. No gripping, twisting tightened objects or using the palm to push out of a chair. The surgery had removed and rerouted tendons and nerves, to aid with functionality, and to overuse the hand would cause damage.

When her first session finally ended, and the therapist left, she shook with pain. John stepped through the back door as she gulped down a couple of pain pills.

"You need to eat something."

"Yes, sir!"

"Don't get snarky," he said, pulling out a loaf of sliced bread. "By the way, I need to run down to Salt Lake tomorrow. I'm meeting the team at Camp Williams. We're looking at a potential replacement for Slater."

Lizzy stilled—her mind racing. "How long will you be gone?"

"I'm not going anywhere if you need me."

"I'll be fine. Charlie is just across the way. Besides, if it's okay with you, I might borrow the Ford and take a drive up to the Grand Teton National Park. I'd love to snap some photos."

John slathered butter on the many slabs of bread he'd laid out. "Is your hand up for that?"

"I think so." She looked down at the light bandage that now replaced the awkward splint. "The truck is an automatic; I'll do just fine. When will you be back?"

"I'm hoping it'll be a day trip but more than likely, we'll run late, and I'll only be back the following morning."

"Take your time." Lizzy snagged the slice of tomato he'd just cut.

"Patience, princess! Sit that cute ass down."

She did as he asked, happy to watch him plate up their lunch.

◊ ◊ ◊

Late the following evening, Johnny drove the last stretch home. Wanting to get back to Lizzy, he'd elected to head back to Wyoming instead of staying overnight in Utah. Thanks to late afternoon traffic, the drive from Camp Williams took longer than Johnny expected.

At almost nine in the evening, waning summer light still lit the dusty farm road. Lizzy wasn't answering her new cell phone or the home line. She'd texted him earlier in the day—around lunch—saying she was heading out of the national park and heading back to the farm.

Another ball of dust rose from behind and Johnny slowed, recognizing the old pickup. Cedric Williams, a neighboring cattle farmer, pulled up alongside.

"Howdy, James."

"Sir, what are you doing rolling into town this late?"

The senior man climbed from the truck. "I'm running

behind. Meeting some old timers at Eileen's diner. It's poetry night."

Johnny smiled; he'd heard about their poetry club. Old cowboys who wrote poems about Wyoming and the cowboy way. Johnny meant to stop by and listen to some readings.

These fine gentlemen were a dying breed, as tough as the sage that peppered the land. Land that was being bought out by greedy estate moguls. Soon the old ways would be gone, driven out by time or drowned out by city folk who wanted a slice of the mountain life.

Cedric handed over a thermos of thick black "cowboy" coffee, and Johnny poured himself a cup.

"Your job take you away again?" Cedric didn't know what Johnny did; he liked to keep it that way. As far as the townsfolk knew, Johnny sold military equipment, a traveling salesman of sorts.

"Sure thing. It was just a day trip."

Cedric nodded. "Congratulations."

"On what?"

"On the pretty little thing staying on your farm."

The news had spread that fast? Johnny had kept Lizzy sheltered; Charlie Quinn was the only person who'd met her.

"Not sure what you mean?"

"Your girl came into town just after sunrise. Drove your pickup right up to the diner, caused quite a stir."

"Wait, that early in the morning?"

"Yup. Then she drove on out of town. If it doesn't work out with that filly, there's a whole line of cowhands to sweep her off her dainty feet."

Johnny knew that. As far as he was concerned, whenever Lizzy was in the room, everything else dimmed in contrast.

239

"Cedric, you tell them townsfolk to stay away. She's going through some hardships and needs space."

"Well, space is what you get in Wyoming. Wide open space that will fix you right up."

There was a whole lot of truth in that. Johnny had returned from many a violent mission, craving the therapy of this open land.

"I've gotta get rolling." Johnny pushed off his door.

"When is she coming back?" Cedric asked.

"What do you mean?"

"The pickup sure ain't back in your driveway; I just passed your place. Maybe she's staying over with friends for the night."

Johnny swore and jumped back in his truck. Tires scrambled for purchase as he raced towards the homestead. Cedric turned and followed. Johnny's mind ran a mile a minute. Eight hours. Eight long hours ago, she had been heading home. They'd closed the effing national park for the night.

Why would she lie? Could she have run out again? He doubted it; there was nothing around for miles. If she left at eight in the morning, that meant she'd been gone for thirteen hours. What if she'd gotten lost or broken down? The roads were potentially hazardous. The truck slid as Johnny's foot came down on the accelerator. He corrected, blocking out thoughts of Lizzy having a breakdown or purposely driving over a cliff. He should never have left her. It was too soon.

He skidded onto his lawn. No Ford truck parked on the front drive. Maybe she'd parked the pickup around back? He ran around back—still nothing. Then he unlocked the front door and barreled into the security room. Cedric followed.

"That's a fancy setup you have there," Cedric said suspiciously.

Ignoring the old man, Johnny checked the camera footage. This was all his fault. Driving on the opposite side of the road than she was used to, she could've had an accident—flipped into a ravine.

"Why would you need all this equipment?" Cedric looked at Johnny with new eyes.

Because I hunt extremist masterminds for a living... Johnny kept the thought to himself.

Pushing past, he snatched the home phone and called the police. After hanging up, he contemplated who to call next. He didn't want to call Max, who had a family and a baby on the way, but his team leader lived close by in Utah. He cursed and dialed the number.

"What's up, big man?"

"Lizzy is missing."

"Do you think Muller's found you?"

"Shit! Why would you say that? Is he in the States?"

"Still rumored to be in Europe. Besides, we're ghosts; he has no idea who or where we are. Talk to me."

"Lizzy left this morning—early—to drive through the Teton National Park. The security footage timestamped her leaving at seven thirty this morning, only thirty minutes after I'd gone. I received a text at 1300 hours saying she was heading home. That was over eight hours ago."

"I'm on my way. I'll be there in four, probably closer to three hours. I'm bringing Abby."

"Don't drag her into this. Abby needs to rest."

"She's feeling fine. The doc cleared her last week—besides, she's worried about Lizzy and wants to see her friend. I'll call when we're on our way."

Once he'd hung up, Johnny considered all the options. If he

went looking for her, where would he start? Night had fallen, and there was a motherland of cliffs, valleys, and ditches between the farm and the park. Johnny called the local hospital, motels and inns in the nearby towns as Cedric hovered. Fifteen minutes later, lights lit up the drive.

Yanking open the door, he spotted two local officers ambling up the path. He knew one of the men, Bill Thompson. This would be a hard sell; she hadn't been missing long enough. They'd be reluctant to send out any search parties, and Johnny couldn't give away mission-sensitive details. Mentioning that she was recently held captive by a notorious terrorist would draw too much attention and raise questions that he or the government couldn't answer.

He was right in guessing it was a lost cause. Not only were they rolling their eyes at his urgency, but they began to view him suspiciously. More officers were called in, questioning the urgency and the agitated muscled boyfriend. Blue lights lit up his front yard like a Christmas tree.

"I'm sure there's a logical explanation," Bill said, pulling him aside. "Maybe she lost track of time and decided to stay overnight in Jackson."

"I've called every place I know," Johnny replied, holding on to his patience.

"She could've headed to Idaho or Utah."

"Why the hell would she do that?"

"Maybe…she's with another man. Perhaps you argued? She decided to leave ya?"

"Listen, you lazy dickw—"

"What's going on?" Lizzy stood on the threshold of the open door, her curls illuminated by strobing lights.

In under a second, she was in his arms. Lifting her and

burying his face in her neck, he allowed a moment of knee-caving relief before anger took over.

"Where the hell have you been!"

"I lost track of time. I stopped in Jackson Hole."

"Nine hours of time?" Johnny studied her face; she was lying. "Answer the question."

She looked away. "I ate dinner before driving back."

"Where exactly?"

"Is this an interrogation? Am I your prisoner, I can't take a day to myself?"

"No, Lizbug. I was worried, because you said you were heading back at lunch."

"Well, I changed my mind, and so you called the cavalry. What do you think happened? Did you think I did something crazy?"

Clenching his jaw, he stepped back. "This conversation is over. We have an audience."

"Did you think I offed myself? Blew my brains out?"

"Stop. Now," Johnny growled.

Bill strolled past with a grin. "No, please continue. This is shaping up to be an interesting domestic. When the only calls on night duty are lost sheep and drunk tourists at the bars in town, us boys will take any entertainment we can get."

Johnny shot him an amused look. "Screw off, Bill. Go find yourself a girly sheep and get out of my house."

With a couple of back slaps and a tad more ribbing, the posse filed out with Cedric at the rear.

"Thanks for your help, Cedric."

"Anytime, James. Glad you're okay, ma'am. You had us all worried. Cedric Williams is the name."

He extended a hand and then pulled a stiff Lizzy in for a hug.

Human contact was still an issue for her, but she hugged him back. After closing the door, he turned to the wall phone, ignoring the distinctly uncomfortable woman standing in the corner.

He dialed the number, then waited. "Hey, buddy. She's safe; you can turn back."

"Thank God. Hold on." Max relayed the information to Abby. After a short, muffled conversation, he was back on the line.

"We're still heading your way, but we'll come over in the morning—pack better supplies."

"You don't need to, I've—"

"We want to. Besides, we have that surprise for Lizzy. We'll be there around lunch."

Johnny hung up.

"Who was that?" Lizzy hugged herself.

"Max…and Abby."

"They were coming here?"

"Of course. They were worried. They're still coming."

"I didn't mean to cause any problems. I thought you were only arriving home in the morning."

Scrubbing a tired hand over his face, he turned to the kitchen. "I need to see to the animals and lock up for the night. Go to bed, Lizbug."

"I'm sorry, John."

"So am I. You're hiding something. Ordinarily, it would be none of my business. But you're staying in my home, sharing my meals, and my life. Whatever it is you're not saying, I hope it's worth it."

He walked out the door into the night, refusing to look back.

When Lizzy woke, she dressed and snuck out of the house, not ready to face John. He was right, her behavior towards him was unfair. Why did she always mess things up? It was as if he fought for their survival and she pulled them to their demise.

She assumed he'd have stayed overnight in Salt Lake. She'd guessed wrong and should've known him better. John would never have left her overnight and her misjudgment had got her in trouble.

Lizzy sidled through the fence and wandered through the outbuildings on Charlie's property. She greeted a couple of cowhands before walking past the barn.

She paused, staring at the open doors. *It's just a barn.* The smell of hay and farmyard animals drifted on the breeze, and her stomach roiled. Would she ever see stables and not think of the Scythian? Charlie's actual stables sat two buildings down from where she stood, and from what Lizzy could see, the barn itself only held machinery and farm implements.

"Hey, cupcake." The whack to her butt had her jumping a foot off the ground. Charlie sprang into view and grinned. "Your timing is excellent. Jamey tells me you're a wizard with car engines. I have a beat-up utility tractor that needs expert help."

Trying to calm her thumping heart, Lizzy took a breath. "I'm good with cars, never worked on a tractor though." Growing up, she'd helped her dad in their garage with his hobby of working on vintage cars. "I can take a look, but I won't be much help physically." She waggled her half finger.

"That's okay. You can diagnose the problem and show me how to fix it."

Charlie dragged her through the open doors towards the vehicle in the corner. Aside from the compact utility tractor, the considerable space sat empty—apart from large piles of straw.

"Um. What lives in here?"

"Nothing as yet. We built it last year. I'm planning to breed alpacas. Also, want to buy a few Great Pyrenees Mountain dogs to guard the pack."

"Wow. That's darn cool." Lizzy turned to admire the space and froze, then pointed. "That, not so much." Weapons and tools lined an entire wall. "Shit, girl. Are you expecting a zombie apocalypse?"

Charlie grinned. "You don't like my weapons?" She stalked over and picked up a rusty but wicked-looking scythe.

Lizzy's neck felt clammy, and she stepped back. *You're in Wyoming. Not in Lagos. Not now. Never again.*

Lizzy stared at a familiar-looking weapon. Charlie followed her gaze. "This is a machete. It's actually an East African panga. I ordered it online."

"Why?" Lizzy said in horror.

"Because it has history. In the Caribbean, a machete is referred to as a cutlass. It's kind of like the modern Scottish dirk. A multi-functional tool used for hunting, fishing…killing." Charlie slashed the air, and Lizzy locked her knees to keep from collapsing.

"It's great at slashing. I'm sorry, did I scare you? I have a passion for weaponry—more for the history of weaponry."

"It's fine" was all Lizzy could manage.

Charlie looked at her oddly, then placed the broad blade back on its hook. "Tractor time. Fix my beast."

Lizzy hoisted herself up to examine the engine as Charlie hovered.

"So, you and Jamie. Is he a Rambo-stud in the bedroom?"

Choking out a laugh, Lizzy turned. "You didn't just ask that!"

"What? He's not my cup of tea, but I've been wondering how you two fit…you know…together?"

"Excuse me?"

"He's so large, and you're so tiny; is it like riding a hard and raging stallion?"

Lizzy giggled so hard that she had to lean against the hood. When she'd recovered, she wiped her eyes. "I needed that. Damn, girl."

"Are you gonna answer my question?"

"Are you gonna tell me why he isn't your type? You're both into farm implements; both find livestock magazines riveting. Are you saying you've never been tempted?"

"Shit no. He's like my cousin. I'm not into muscle and brawn. There are too many swaggering cowboys around these parts. I want me a city man. Tall, dark and dangerous."

Grinning, Lizzy folded her arms. "Careful, those city boys will take advantage of an innocent country girl like yourself."

"Cupcake, there ain't anything innocent about me." Charlie winked, and Lizzy laughed, knowing she'd found a friend.

◊ ◊ ◊

The doorbell rang and Lizzy sat frozen on the sofa.

"Are you ready for this?" John asked.

"Doesn't matter. Either way, you're answering that door."

John squeezed her shoulder before walking across the sitting room and Lizzy relaxed her grip on the throw cushion. She hadn't spoken or contacted Abby since the day she'd been thrown to the floor as bullets flew. So much had changed since that fateful day. Lizzy felt like a different version of that confused yet still idealistic girl. Aside from living through captivity, Kenya had changed her. She'd grown a tougher skin, working with children and families who had nothing, who never knew where their next meal would come from or where they'd sleep. Seeing that harsh existence made Lizzy grateful for all she had, and that included friends who fought to stand at her side. Friends like Abby with hearts of gold whose only crime was protecting her own child. Lizzy's anger had evaporated months ago. Now she just missed her lovely friend.

Lizzy eavesdropped on the conversation as Abby stood at the open door. "How is she?"

"About as nervous as you look. Are you going to come in or hover on my front steps all day?" John replied.

Abby grinned. "I would if you moved your hulking ass out of the way."

"I missed you too, sweet cheeks."

Abby punched his arm before stepping past. Lizzy rose, her eyes glued to Abby's very pregnant belly. Her friend was just as beautiful as before. More so, if that was possible. Lizzy guessed that had something to do with being married to a man who adored her and having her family back. Her naturally tanned skin spoke of her Italian ancestry. Glossy brown hair fell in waves down her back as deep emerald eyes landed on Lizzy. John stepped out into the front yard and closed the door behind him.

"Hi, angel." Abby came to an elegant stop and Lizzy felt an insane urge to rush into her arms.

◊ ◊ ◊

Lizzy seemed tinier than she'd remembered. Choppy curls framed a porcelain face, haunted by desolation and wariness. Her usually cheerful friend was hidden from sight. Abby's heart broke.

"Fudge buckets, you're so pregnant."

Abby laughed. Okay, that was so lil Liz. "Tell me about it. My bladder feels like it's going to explode."

"Do you need to go—"

"I just went…twenty minutes ago, at the last gas station we passed."

"Where's Max? And Gabe?"

"In the car. Max thought it best if we iron out our issues first."

"Bleh. Issues. Are we suddenly on *The Jerry Springer Show*? And what's with you not hugging your friend?"

Abby battled the sudden onslaught of tears as she embraced Lizzy against her burgeoning stomach. After clinging like limpets, they both sat on the sofa and maneuvered awkwardly into comfortable positions. Abby collapsed back with a groan and Lizzy shifted sideways with an injured hand waving in the air.

"Aren't we a right pair." Lizzy giggled.

"How's the finger?"

"Annoying as all hell. I've just discovered while preparing lunch that I'll need to purchase an electric can opener. I doubt I'll be able to handle the manual version, even when it's healed. That's the first challenge I've added to the list."

"This is all my fault."

"That's a bunch of baloney."

"I introduced you to Kris. I swear, Lizzy, if I'd known what a psychopath he is…"

"He hurt the both of us, just in different ways."

Abby shook her head. "I've tangled you up in my life and almost gotten you killed."

"I've been thinking about that a lot lately. I would never have met John, or my friends in Kenya if I'd never known my lovely friend, Abigail—and I've missed you so much."

"You're not mad?" Abby asked while rubbing a palm over her swollen stomach.

"I was, but not anymore. So much has happened since Johannesburg. Good and bad things, but that's life. It's a roller coaster with highs and lows. Just so happens my lows scraped the bottom of life's barrel, and I'll need to fight for more highs."

"Girl, you're speaking my language." Abby thought of her struggles before meeting Max. "We are a right pair. And I wouldn't want any other friend standing by my side. I've missed you too." She reached over and squeezed Lizzy's good hand, before letting out a yelp. "Quick, she's kicking."

"So, it's a girl? Oh gosh, is that a foot?"

They sat together, relishing the sacred moment before falling into another hug.

Abby groaned as she levered herself up. "I have something for you in the car. Stay where you are."

As Johnny unclipped Gabe from his car seat, Max met Abby at the door with a squirmy package. She smiled widely, alleviating the concern in her husband's icy eyes before turning back.

When Johnny had called the previous night, his worry and anguish were evident. They were all worried about Lizzy's mental stability and prayed that this next step would help in her recovery.

Nobody wanted to watch her fall apart, possibly turning to self-harm. Lizzy was like family, and they'd fight until the end for her.

Lizzy was halfway across the living room when Max stepped in and placed the gift on the floor—a gift with a wriggly tail and sweet puppy breath. The black and tan puppy turned in excited circles before spotting Lizzy and running over. She knelt, and the spaniel sat and licked her splayed hand. The tail swished like a happy windscreen wiper.

"Oh, my gosh! What is she? Or he?"

"It's a female, and she's a Cavalier King Charles spaniel."

The silky dog got a solid ear scratch before Lizzy planted a kiss on top of her soft head. "I bet Gabe loves her? What's her name?"

Max stepped forward. "She's not ours, and her name is Ray— we named her that because she's such a happy ball of energy."

"And because that tail never stops wagging!" Abby added.

"Hello, Ray." Lizzy cooed and giggled when Ray rolled to her back, begging for a tummy scratch.

Abby spoke carefully. "She's a service dog. She's six months old."

Lizzy met her words with confusion.

"And she's yours if you want her."

"I don't understand."

"A friend of ours runs a canine school in Idaho that trains assistance dogs. Many of the dogs go to veterans and are specifically trained to deal with PTSD."

"Ray was trained by them?" Lizzy sat on the floor, and the pup crawled into her lap.

"Yes. But Ray failed the program on her last test."

"Why? She's perfect!"

"The foster family she was with took her for a walk one day, and a larger dog attacked her. He bit her pretty badly. She's developed a fear of larger dogs."

Lizzy pulled her close. "That got her kicked out?"

"Yeah. Aside from that, she's fully trained," Max said. "Trained to assist a person in waking from night terrors and nightmares. She'll distract you by nudging, pawing, and licking. Ray can even bring medication to a person on command. She'll stand in front of you in crowded areas to create personal space, or she'll lead you to a building exit when you're experiencing a flashback or anxiety attack. She can even alert Johnny. At some point, you'll have to travel to the training facility to learn all her commands and to get used to each other. Idaho Falls is the location."

The dog nudged Lizzy's hand, and she looked down. Abby waited with bated breath.

Her voice rough with tears, Lizzy spoke. "I can barely take care of myself. How on earth do I take care of Ray? I don't even know where I'll be tomorrow. And what about Catapult? Will they even get along?"

Johnny spoke from the door, holding a sleepy Gabe. His gruff voice had them all turning. "They'll get used to each other. If you decide to move on, Ray can stay. She's your dog and will be yours forever, but if you haven't found your place in this world, then the puppy can live with me."

"John, I can't let you do that—"

"Let me finish." He ran his free hand over his mouth. "I want you here, but I'll never force you to stay. This puppy is ours, and Ray and I will both be here for you, whenever you need us."

Max turned to face the wall, and Abby wiped the wetness from her cheek. Lizzy's eyes sparkled with unshed tears as she stared into the little dog's face. Ray stared back—her chocolate gaze unblinking—connecting in the fragile moment. A little lick had Lizzy first smiling and then sobbing. "She'll never leave my side. I need her. John, I need you both."

John walked over to crouch beside the pair and looked relieved. Abby knew why; this was the first time Lizzy showed any real emotion since arriving in the States, the first time she'd let down her guard. Max placed an arm around her shoulders as they watched their friends get to know the happy puppy with the waggy tail.

He must be around three years old, Lizzy thought as Gabe clambered into her lap. Darn her stubborn nature, she'd left this reunion for too long. The ragamuffin had grown. Lizzy ran a hand over his thick dark curls. She saw so much of Abby in the little man who even had his mother's slightly stubborn looking chin.

"Careful of Aunt Lizzy's hand!" Abby yelled as Gabe tucked in his stubby legs and situated himself.

Max chewed on a gummy worm and handed the kid a sip cup.

The two women sat in the shade of the cottonwood chatting as John warmed up the grill. Lizzy played with Gabe's curls. The last time she'd seen the tyke, he was around eighteen months. Now he was a whole little person with a clear agenda.

Gabe yelled at his dad. Lizzy didn't catch the garbled request. Abby rolled her eyes as Max answered. "I said no, Gabriel. Uncle Johnny doesn't have any and I'm not going into town." Max ignored the responding whine; instead laying on the ground to play with Ray.

"What does he want?" Lizzy whispered to Abby.

"I wanna bayloon!"

"You're not getting one." Max narrowed his eyes before groaning. "Jeez, not even hardened insurgents are as stubborn as that little monster."

"Pwease, daddy. Just one bayloon."

Grunting, Max plonked Ray on his chest.

"What's a bayloon?" Lizzy asked. *Was it a newfangled kid's toy?*

Abby sighed. "He's trying to say 'balloon.' It's pretty sweet. He's obsessed with balloons at the moment, balloons and snails. The trouble is, we forgot to bring a packet of freaking balloons with us, so the nagging continues."

Lizzy laughed. "I thought he loved frogs?"

"So last season." Abby grinned. "He still likes frogs, but now it's snails. He discovered a snail in the front yard one evening, so the new nightly ritual is Max wandering behind an excited kid as he searches for snails."

"I'm sure Max doesn't mind. I bet he's made him a bunch of paper snails." Lizzy admired Max's artistic origami streak. Give him a piece of paper, and he could build the Eiffel Tower.

"He has. We also just bought Gabe a children's book about a snail, it's called *Escargot*. It's pretty funny, about a French snail who slithers up a picnic table. But now I can't kill the little buggers with Gabe trailing my every move—and they're eating my precious garden."

Lizzy poked her in the arm. "Maybe you can do a snail relocation to a nearby hiking spot. Give Gabe a bucket for a mass gathering." That made her friend laugh.

Donnie wandered down from the house and Lizzy waved him over. He'd driven up for the weekend; it was going to be a busy couple of days with all their sudden house guests. Lizzy hoped she didn't embarrass herself with her crazy night terrors.

By early evening, as they gathered around the fire pit, Lizzy felt more relaxed than she'd been in weeks. Abby retired early and put Gabe down for the night.

Ray slept in Lizzy's lap as the men chatted about when their next possible deployment might be. Slater was their primary concern. He was due to arrive back in the States in three weeks; it was on everyone's radar to follow his recovery and to visit. They'd possibly found his replacement, but the men were keeping mum on the details.

"Hey, boys!" Charlie appeared from the shadows, taking

Donnie off guard. He jerked around, sheltering Lizzy.

"Dude! You almost crapped your pants." John laughed. "It's just Charlie."

Donnie glared. "Screw you, Goliath. I knew it was her."

"You knew shit. Didn't know one small woman could scare you so much."

"Yeah? If you weren't over there scratching your balls, I wouldn't need to protect your woman. It could've been anyone."

You're mine. I'm coming for you. Lizzy shifted against the Scythian's voice in her head. A wet muzzle snuffled her hand.

"Paranoid much?" John smirked at his teammate.

Lizzy changed the subject and glanced over at Charlie. "I forgot to ask, how did the banana pie go down the other night?"

"It was damn awesome! They polished it off. You rock." Charlie whipped open a beer before taking a long swig. "What a shitting long day."

Donnie's nostrils flared before he turned away. Interesting. Lizzy wondered what was up. It looked like a hornet had flown up his tight ass.

"Have you met Charlie?" Lizzy asked Donnie.

"They've met," John confirmed.

Donnie's lip curled. "Yeah. A few times."

Charlie's eyes narrowed. "I wouldn't know—he stands in the corner like a damn statue with a wet diaper. Have we actually met?"

Wowzer.

Beer spewed as Max choked down a laugh.

Donnie fired back. "Not sure, I hardly recognize you. Did you use a mud puddle as a mirror this morning?"

So not fair. Lizzy registered the hurt flaring on her friend's face.

Max glared at Donnie. "Don't be a dick. Charlie, do you wanna meet my very pregnant wife and grab some ice cream?"

Lizzy placed Ray on the ground and stood, and Max walked both women back to the house.

She glanced back to the two men standing at the fire pit. John got up in Donnie's face; she was too far off to hear what he said but it was obvious that he was berating his friend. Lizzy turned back. Charlie Quinn obviously pushed all of Donnie's alpha male buttons. Behavior so out of character for the reserved man that it made her wonder.

Chapter Fourteen

Balancing tentatively on the ball of her foot, Lizzy poked her head through the canopy of leaves. Wyoming was truly breathtaking. Silence surrounded her. Not true silence as she could still hear insects buzzing, the leaves rustling in the afternoon breeze and a bleating sheep answered by three more. The distant hills looked so clear in the waning light, the golden rays contrasting with shadowed crevices in the craggy mountainside. She missed climbing trees; she still loved it.

Her head sank back below the branches, and Lizzy looked down. The branch she balanced on bent under her weight, and she transferred her foot to a sturdier limb. The new branch instantly disintegrated, almost melting into thin air. Before she could comprehend her predicament, she fell to the earth, bouncing through and over battering limbs. Just before she slammed into the ground, strong arms caught her and they fell, rolling down a steep hill at a dizzying pace.

A scarlet blur filled her vision as they slammed to a stop. Lizzy opened her eyes, and squinted through the pain, expecting a scolding from a super-mad John.

She sucked in a breath. The Scythian sat over her; his defined thighs straddled hers as she struggled. She tried to scream and he clamped a hand over her mouth—a hand that smelled of leather and sweat and damp soil.

"I'm coming for you," he said as he whipped off the mask.

John's face stared back. She blinked. It morphed back to Kris Muller. He removed his hand from her mouth, and with his other hand, shoved the mask down her throat.

"Wake up, baby. Wake up!"

Something wet licked her cheek and kept licking. It felt oddly comforting. A soft whine and a puff of warm air pulled her out of the dark terror. John sat with her on the floor at the foot of the bed, her head resting on his broad shoulder, as he cradled her sore hand in his lap. Ray pawed her chest gently, staring into Lizzy's face.

Another nightmare. Of course, the worst night terror occurred when guests filled the home.

"Is she okay?" Abby called from the door.

"She's awake," John replied as he resettled them against the bedpost.

Shuffling outside the door indicated more than one body lurked in the hallway, and the distant cry from the guest room meant she'd woken Gabe. Great, she'd terrified a toddler with her poltergeist screaming.

"How loud did I scream?" Her voice sounded raspy.

"No one cares. We've all suffered from PTSD nightmares at one point or the other. Including Abby."

She'd been doing so well. This might be a marathon instead of a race, and the finish line was her sanity. Ray's ears were so soft, and she reached to stroke one. John rubbed her goosey arm. His soft T-shirt smelled like solid male and she wasn't ready to make her way back to bed.

"What if the Scythian finds me?"

"He won't."

"How can you know that?"

"Muller doesn't know our real names. Our backgrounds are locked away—essentially in a motherland of classified MIT tape. Not even senators or White House players can access that information. Plus, Muller is all about saving his ass, there are a shitload of agencies hunting the psycho. He stole money from his extremist buddies—they're also after Muller blood—he's pretty screwed."

"As long as he's out there—"

"He won't be for long. I told you, I plan on joining the search. I can't let it go—what he did to you."

"You're sure?"

"Yes, baby. But I won't leave you yet. Not until I know you're okay."

"I keep dreaming of him...of him finding me."

"You're safe here; he has no way of knowing where you are. Besides, I'd never let anything happen to you."

Lizzy played with the hem of his shirt. "What if he finds you—on social media?"

"Lizbug. Do you think any of the MIT gang are stupid enough to have social media accounts?"

"Your families might."

"Not even families know what we do, except for Abby. Wives are allowed to know. That's about it. Charlie is suspicious, guessing we're more than just ex-military sales associates, but that's because I live on the property. You and Abby are the only people who know my real name—outside of our covert circle."

"What about your parents?"

John stiffened, silent for so long that Lizzy thought he wouldn't answer.

He pulled her close. "My father left when I was six. No great loss—he beat the shit out of me and my mom. Despite the abuse, she adored him. His leaving triggered her alcoholism. A couple of years later, she graduated to hard drugs."

"I'm so sorry."

Ignoring her sympathy, he continued. "We lived in a trailer. Whenever Child Services caught wind of my situation, we'd relocate. My mother pimped herself out. Became a prostitute and screwed anyone waving a twenty-dollar bill."

Lizzy tried to imagine John as a scared kid, too many responsibilities at a young age. Trying to take care of his mom.

"She sent me to school whenever she could. Said it was because I'd take care of her one day and pay my dues. When she entertained clients, I'd stay late at school, or sit in the library until closing time. Anything to avoid the trailer. A dirty curtain separated my sleeping quarters from her 'office' where she serviced customers. On the nights when the weather was too cold or rainy, I was forced to listen."

Lizzy stroked his arm, trying to bring comfort. He shifted awkwardly and stared at the wall.

"The day after my twelfth birthday, as I lay there planning my permanent escape, she let in a particularly vicious bastard who beat her and tried to strangle her. I was a tall kid, but on the skinny side—due to malnourishment. I tried to protect my mother. Climbed on the fucker's back and beat him around the head. He threw me off—like I weighed nothing—then grabbed a pan off the stove and clocked me upside the head."

Lizzy gasped. John ran a finger over the scar running from his temple to his eye. She reached up to trace the path.

"When I woke, the trailer swayed. My head pounded, and I kept slipping in a pool of blood. Terrified that he'd killed my mom, I screamed for her over and over. Apparently, she'd grabbed the gun tucked into his waist, and shot wildly at the bastard. After he drove off, she hooked up the trailer and drove to new pastures. I realized that she was driving the car as I lay in the trailer."

Lizzy kept stroking his temple. How had she never known about his childhood? John came across as so stable, and so in control. She'd assumed his parents helped to create this honorable man. No. It was all down to his own inner strength. Her respect for him grew tenfold.

"When we eventually stopped—hours later in Denver—my lovely mother poked her head in the door and said, 'Goddammit, boy. I thought you mighta been dead. One less mouth to feed. Don't just lie there, make yourself useful and buy me some ciggies.'"

"John—"

"Instead I rode my bike to the nearest police station. Could barely stay upright with a concussion and all. Knew that I had choices, I'd either go to foster care or to my uncle. I prayed the authorities would find him. All my mother told me was that he lived in Wyoming on a fancy-ass farm and that he looked down on her lifestyle choices. That he thought he was better than her."

"Did they find him?"

"Yes, the officers and social workers were incredible. Took me to the hospital to get stitched up, and they looked up Uncle Levi. I spent a week in a foster home before he came. Levi told me later that my mother never mentioned a kid. He had no idea that he had a nephew. When he laid eyes on me, Levi said he knew I was family—made of his blood and his bone. Before we left for Wyoming, Levi stopped by the trailer and gave my mom his address. Said as long as she was trying to get clean, he'd pay for rehab, and she was welcome by anytime to see her kid. She never came."

Lizzy got to her knees. "Never?"

"No loss, baby."

"Not for you, but she lost out on knowing an amazing son."

"My uncle helped with that. The first year was difficult; I had a giant-ass chip on my preteen shoulders. Levi put me to work and thanks to his patience and discipline, I came around. He taught me how to be a good man with solid principles. I caught up and did well in school and a month after I graduated high school, Uncle Levi died. Diagnosed with stomach cancer. They gave him six months; he only lived out three."

"I wish I could've met him."

John smiled and kissed her eyebrow. "He'd have loved you, would've said you had spunk. I've scattered his ashes throughout these hills. That's what he wanted."

"I bet you miss him."

"I do. After Levi died, I saw him everywhere; I had to get away. Charlie's dad said he'd look after the place, so I traveled across the States. When I found myself back in Denver, I went looking for my mother. I wanted to show her what her son had become—despite the neglect. She'd remained at that same trailer park but died six months before. Overdosed on heroin."

"I'm so sorry."

"I'm not. I wasn't sorry then either. She destroyed any affection I had for her. But I craved closure. I guess in a small way I wanted her to be healthy and to tell me how sorry she was." John stroked her collar bone as they sat in the dark. Ray snored softly beside them.

"It was all meant to be. I passed a recruitment center on my way out of Denver and signed up to join the Army, and the rest is history. Aside from Levi, my military brothers were the first family members I had. Men who truly cared about my welfare and had my back."

She stirred. "They're not the only ones who care for you."

"Lizbug, I'm not sure why a wealthy mining magnate would want me near his only daughter."

That irritating statement had her turning in his arms. "That mining magnate had a similar upbringing to yours. Maybe not quite as extreme, but my grandparents on my father's side were both alcoholics with gambling addictions. They'd go on month-long binges, and the system eventually placed my daddy with a foster family. They took him in for the foster money, but he was a fighter. He always vowed that he'd be the best dad in the world, never abandon his child or his family. It's because of his childhood that he is such an amazing person—just like you."

Her finger throbbed. She must have whacked it against something during her nightmare. Her shift to examine it had John swinging his attention to the healing joint. He cradled the joint so delicately, like he held butterfly wings. The pure love reflected in that action broke down the last of her walls.

"I love you, John."

Stiff granite suddenly became her mattress. She met his glittering eyes, loving the fire sizzling in his laser-like gaze.

"Repeat it."

"What? That I love you?"

He crushed her mouth to his, then immediately gentled the kiss. "God, baby. I love you too; you know I do."

Lizzy pulled back and cradled his cheek. "It's not enough."

"What do you mean?"

"I want us to be together, but I'm not ready. Not yet."

"Because of Nigeria?"

She rolled stiffly to her feet. "I'm tired. Let's go to bed."

"Talk to me."

Silence was the only answer she could give.

Two days later, Max and Donnie rolled out, headed for training at Camp Williams with the newest team member, Dylan Jenkins. A local Utahan sniper from the 19th Special Forces Group. Johnny admired the laid-back soldier. Aside from his Army career, the operator embodied a reckless, surfer-like attitude as a well-known snowboarder in Utah. It would be interesting to see how their uptight team leader handled the Owen Wilson wannabe. Dylan's long-range marksmanship and excellent skills in the field would make him a valuable MIT member—aside from the additional training lined up for him at MIT headquarters later in the month. At Max's insistence, Johnny stayed behind with Lizzy. As they were still evaluating Jenkins' skills, it wasn't essential for Johnny to be at Camp Williams. If they needed him, they'd call.

"I forget how hot the summers can get in some parts of the States, is late May supposed to be this warm?" Abby groaned from her prone position on the sofa. "I always tell people that Johannesburg summers can be mild in comparison."

The women had escaped the afternoon heat, but Gabe refused to come in and instead was playing soccer with John in the front yard. Lizzy dropped a slice of lemon in Abby's glass and topped it up with the rest of the soda water. "There are also creepier crawly bugs on this side of the Atlantic, at least compared to Jo'burg—Wyoming has swarms of flying critters. Do you miss South Africa?"

Like Lizzy, Abby was an American but spent a good chunk of

her young life in Southern Africa.

"Sometimes," Abby admitted. "But Utah is beautiful. Our house is surrounded by mountains and majestic views, although I need to get used to the snowy winters."

Lizzy handed the frosted glass to her exhausted friend before getting situated on the opposite sofa. Abby chatted about giving birth in the autumn, Lizzy half listened, instead gazing down at her amputation. The times it didn't hurt, when she wasn't looking at her hand, were the moments when the finger still felt like it was there. Then she'd glance down, and all the horror would come flooding back.

"Talk to me."

Lizzy jumped at Abby's firm tone.

"What's going on in that sweet head?"

Lizzy opened her mouth to reply, and nothing came out. She took a breath and tried again. It was time someone else knew her secret. She closed her eyes then took a bracing breath. "I'm married."

"O-kay," Abby said. "Married to John?"

"No."

Sitting up, Abby asked. "The doctor dude?"

"How do you know about the doctor dude?"

"Max told me. Says the surgeon has the hots for you."

Lizzy shook her head. "Garrison doesn't have the hots for me. He's just a friend and women aren't his thing—he has a boyfriend."

Abby placed her glass on the side table. "He does? Then who the heck are you married to?"

"The Scythian. Kris Muller is my husband."

◊ ◊ ◊

Grasping the edge of the sofa, Abby stared at her tiny friend. Lizzy sat so calmly, like she hadn't just dropped a verbal grenade.

Shivers ran down Abby's arms at the implications. Was Lizzy a victim of Stockholm Syndrome? Had she bonded with that monster? Were they still communicating?

Abby chose her next words carefully. "Do you want to be married to Kris Muller?"

Lizzy shook her head vehemently.

"Angel, were you a willing participant?"

"He forced me to marry him. Said that if I didn't, he'd kill Mason Clark—execute both of us the following day."

"Oh, honey—"

"Nobody else knows. The day I disappeared—when John arrived back at the farm before me—I visited with a lawyer in Salt Lake City, to see if I could get the marriage annulled. I haven't told John. He's battling with the idea of me as the Scythian's victim. How would he cope knowing I was the Horse Lord's wife, and that he rescued me on the wedding night? I've tried to tell him but I can't do it."

Abby went over to sit by her friend. "A wedding night where you were forced to marry your extremist captor—and you were beaten almost to death. It wasn't consensual and will never hold up in any court of law." She grasped Lizzy's hand. "Sweetie, forced to repeat vows while threatened with your life doesn't make you his wife. You're not married to anyone."

"That's what the lawyer said."

"That's not all that's bothering you?"

"We were married in his stables. He made me…made me…"

"Slow down; you don't have to tell me. If it's too much—"

"He made me wear a scalp coat."

"A what?"

Once she'd blurted it out, she couldn't stop. Lizzy's mind flew back to that terrifying day, and she told Abby as she'd remembered it.

Lizzy made her way slowly down the fortress passage on wobbly legs, following the guard out to the courtyard, then to the stables. He left her standing in the dim light before a large stall.

"The Scythian orders you to wait here."

Where did he think she'd go? She had nowhere to run, not in her weak state. Ten more steps and she'd collapse. A strong smell of hay and manure wafted on the warm breeze. Her stomach churned, and she knew she'd soon be sick. Her entire back throbbed, the pain spreading under her ribs.

Scuffling in the stall had her turning, and a huge black head emerged from the shadows. A stallion loomed above her. Its eyes—almost red in the afternoon light—rolled as it snorted. Lizzy stumbled back.

A voice whispered from behind. "His name is Atheas. He's a beauty, isn't he? An Akhal-Teke. The rarest breed you'll find."

Kris's strong hands gripped her shoulders. "Be careful. Don't get too close. He's a one-person horse. He hates strangers."

Lizzy tried to turn, but he held her in place. "Stay where you are. I like having my two beauties in one room."

Then his hands roamed. Lizzy sobbed as they slipped under the shirt and explored.

"Hush baby, don't cry." Fingers ran up her back, then through her hair. "I love your hair. It's like silk." He braided it, shook it loose, then gathered it into a high ponytail and twisted. "One day, it will be my prize scalp. I'll slice along here, here and here." He drew lines around her skull with his other hand. Then kissed her neck. "I've reserved a special place for it, on the back of my coat...so fokking pretty."

Terror had her panting as she stared at the still horse watching her from its stall.

"Don't be scared. I won't tire of you until we've had our fun. You're addictive. You smell so good. My sexy mini-muffin." He nibbled her ear, then whispered. "I have a gift for you—don't turn around, it's a surprise."

With one last kiss to her neck, Kris stepped in front of her, his mask in place. A guard walked up and grabbed her shoulders, holding her up as the red monster knelt before her, presenting a furry gift. Nausea leaped, and she jerked back.

"Wear my gift and ride alongside me as my wife. I made this especially for you—a matching coat for my Lizzy Liz."

She shrank away, not wanting what lay in his arms to touch her, her mind wading through the sticky nightmare.

"Say something."

"No. Never," she moaned, collapsing to her knees. She would've curled away, but the mercenary sidekick held her up.

The Scythian lost his temper, shoving the coat into her hands. "Take it or die. I'll kill the boy first, then it'll be your turn. Dead or alive, you will wear it."

Lizzy turned and vomited. Kris punched her in the side, and she threw up again.

"Say it. Say yes!"

"Yes." Choking out the word, she heaved again.

"Yes, who?"

"Yes...master."

They tore off the shirt she wore, then wrapped her in the coat. Tufts of hair sewn into rugged leather tickled her naked skin. Lizzy was wearing the scalps of those who'd died before her, literally wrapped in the horrors of the past.

The Scythian pulled her to him. "Do you know who you're

wearing?" He began to name the victims, and when he got to Jane's patch, Lizzy's vision faded to black.

Someone rocked her, and something else licked her ear. Lizzy jerked out of the flashback and found herself engulfed in Abby's arms. Ray nuzzled her neck.

"I'm so sorry, honey. I'm here. It's going to be okay. You're safe."

Lizzy clung to her friend and sucked in calming breaths. She wasn't safe. Kris Muller was still out there. John planned to hunt him down and that sat well with her. The sooner, the better.

◊ ◊ ◊

Handing over a cup of tea, Abby stroked her friend's shoulder. "Feeling better?"

Lizzy nodded. "He didn't…you know…after we were married. Kris took me to his bed, then spoke for hours about his creepy childhood. He made me sing for him. Then he tried, but he couldn't get it up. He got angrier and angrier, and then put the mask back on. Said that it would make him hard. But it didn't. I kept throwing up—couldn't stop—and Kris kept punching me, saying it was my fault."

Abby hugged her shaking friend, glad she'd survived that cruel night.

"One of his mercenary soldiers came in, and Kris walked out to speak with him. Kris returned to tie me up, saying he wasn't finished with me. That I was his. By that time, I was pretty out of it. I think that was when Kris received a call from an informant warning him that the American teams were moving in—that's when he ran."

They sat hugging each other until the front door swung open. Lizzy pulled away.

"You need to tell Johnny," Abby whispered.

Lizzy shook her head and turned to greet the sweaty boys at the door. Her looming giant toed off his shoes as a grubby tyke swung a stick around in chubby toddler hands. Abby smiled at her teeny warrior, then yelled for him to drop the wooden weapon.

◊ ◊ ◊

That night, after pausing to check on Lizzy and Ray, Johnny made his way back to his room. The house lay in silence as he brushed his teeth. It surprised Johnny how lively it got with just one small kid added to the mix. That toddler was like five SF men rolled into one volatile ball of energy.

After a quick shower, Johnny stepped out from the bathroom and paused. Lizzy sat on his bed. Her robe fell open around her naked breasts.

"Another nightmare?" he asked, looking away.

"No. I dreamt of you—of us. Of that day on my beanbag, in Kenya. When you turned me over and—"

"I know what I did, Lizzy." His dick stirred and Johnny cursed.

"I want you to do it again."

Sweat broke, and his rebellious member stood to attention. "You're not ready."

"I think I am." She stood. The robe fell, pooling on the floor.

"Lizbug, this isn't a joke. I could damage your progress." He stepped back as she walked forward. Her hips swayed, and he ran his gaze over the perfect apex between her thighs. *Look away, buddy.*

"Never. You're a healer. I've missed your strong hands touching me in all my happy places." That small smile accompanied by an old twinkle in her eyes had him reconsidering his options.

"Happy huh? We only do this if those places stay happy. If at any time you feel uncomfortable or scared…"

"I'll tell you to stop and you'll stop. Because you love me."

Small hands reached up to wind around his neck, and Johnny picked her up, his towel falling to the floor as she wrapped her legs around his waist. Her smooth, naked skin against his own had him pausing to savor the moment; it gave him an idea. Johnny stepped into the bathroom and grabbed a towel off the rack before walking them over to the bed and laying her down on the towel. "Turn on your stomach."

Next, he sheathed himself then ran back to snatch up the sweet almond oil from under the sink. He'd only ever used it in the winter as a remedy for chapped hands.

Johnny placed it on the bedside table and stood looking down at her. He ran a callused hand up her side, and she shivered.

"You still want this?"

She nodded. Fresh mountain air blew in from the open window.

"Are you warm enough?"

"I feel amazing."

The second run of his hand had her arching. Sitting beside her, he paid particular attention as he explored her exposed flesh with casual fingers. He followed each trace with a kiss, working his way along her back and over her pert butt cheeks. The backs of her knees and base of her spine were particularly sensitive. Next came the oil. He massaged her tight muscles with long strokes, and when her moans increased, Johnny allowed his hands to roam between her legs.

Lizzy spread herself wider and he rewarded her with a long lick. His tongue swirled briefly as his fingers massaged her buttocks. When she whispered his name, he worked his way up and down her thighs. The second time his mouth traced her opening, he paid more attention. Sucking and licking as she pushed to her knees.

Lizzy glanced back. "I want you inside."

He flipped her over. "Look at me as we fuck." He shoved a couple of pillows beneath her and positioned her at the edge of the bed, then pushed in steadily, making her gasp.

"You still good?"

Her eyes filled and he froze.

"I missed this. Missed feeling you inside me."

"I can be inside you whenever you want. Shit, you feel so good." Johnny eased out. "I love you." He thrust back in. "I've always loved you." He pumped his hips again. "I want you lying on my bed with my cock slamming into you—for all time." Thumbing her clit, he slowed his thrusts and stared down at his feisty princess. "Even if I couldn't be inside you, even if I never had this again, I'd be happy just standing by your side."

"I want that too, but I need this," Lizzy said breathlessly. "I want everything. I want us."

Johnny growled and rolled his thumb hard before slamming back in. She cried out, clenching around his pulsing cock. He rolled his hips, changing up the rhythm, thoroughly filling and grinding into her with every thrust.

Her hips bucked wildly, but he refused to let up, instead increasing pressure on her clit as his other hand gripped her in place. Her eyes grew wild as she came apart around him, driving him over the edge. He pounded his release, convulsing as he shouted her name.

He didn't let her recover, instead he worshipped her body. He could touch her again, and he never wanted to stop. He touched her through the night, everywhere with his tongue and fingers. He made her come and before she could float back down, he'd stroke her back up to orgasm.

Finally, when she curled into his shoulder with a sated moan, he pulled her close, not content to settle until they lay skin to skin. Johnny knew without a doubt that Lizzy was finally his—he'd waited so long for his girl to find her way back to him. He couldn't imagine ever letting this go.

◊ ◊ ◊

The mattress creaked, waking Lizzy. She didn't move, preferring to savor the safe moment. Cocooned in John's bed and his love, she'd slept through the night and woken feeling at peace. It wasn't quite morning, the hint of dawn scrubbed over by the sound of a storm sweeping in. Lizzy reached behind and felt the empty warmth as she heard John slam the window shut.

Ray shifted next to her chest, and Lizzy snuggled deeper. "What time is it?"

"Four thirty. I might as well get up; I need to check on the animals. This storm looks nasty," he said before brushing his teeth at the sink.

Lizzy dozed until the bed dipped, and he pulled his boots on. "Do you need help?"

"I'm all good, Lizbug. If you feel like getting up though, I hear Abby banging around in the kitchen. I think Gabe woke her."

The wind howled as rain pelted against the window. "Five more minutes," she growled. Her dog seemed just as wiped out as she was—after Gabe chased the puppy around the previous day for kisses.

Something crashed outside, jerking her awake.

John looked out the window and swore. "Shed door is open; lock must've broken. It's like a damn hurricane out there."

Ray whined, and John glanced over.

"Sorry about Ray being in the bed. It's my fault," Lizzy said as he walked over.

"Don't ever apologize. I like sleeping next to my two rays of sunshine." He gave them both a kiss on their heads.

"I'm not all sunshine at the moment," she said solemnly.

John rubbed her temple with a large thumb. "You'll always be my sunny angel, no matter what. Go back to sleep. Time for me to get muddied up—Wyoming style."

As he walked to the door, her heart thumped with unspoken emotions.

"John."

"Yes, angel?"

"I love you."

With a broad grin and a wink, John said, "I know you do." Then he was gone.

◊ ◊ ◊

She'd told him twice and Johnny finally believed her. She loved him. She fucking loved him. Unable to wipe the smile off his face, he breezed past Abby in the kitchen to grab his work gloves. She spoke on the phone with Max.

"There's a crazy storm this end. Johnny's doing damage control...sweetie, I'm fine. I swear. The baby woke me with an aerobics session...I'm resting. I slept a full six hours. Stop fussing."

Johnny mussed her hair as she hung up.

"He's like an old lady since I got preggers. You'd think I was the first woman on the planet ever to have a baby!"

"Give the Finnish bastard a break; he loves ya."

"What are you so cheerful about?"

"Lizzy loves me." He made a hip slide dance move, and Abby laughed.

"It would take a blind person not to see that; she's worshipped you from day one."

He rolled his eyes as he walked over to the door. "Bullshit. I screwed up in Johannesburg, and now I'm forgiven."

"She forgave you a long time ago. She's never forgiven herself for a lot of things."

Frowning, he walked into the pounding rain. What did she mean by that? Was she referring to Ivan? His attention quickly turned to the storm as the shed door swung back open, almost slamming off its hinges. The barn containing his sheep looked secure, and he moved towards the shed. A steel bucket bounced past as Johnny trudged through the thick mud. He ignored a toppling garbage can to the side of the door; instead he bent to pick up the broken lock.

Johnny went cold. Someone had cut the lock. It was cleanly sawn in half—not broken by the wind. Survival instincts kicked in a fraction too late as something slammed into the back of his head. He staggered, then fell, tried to right himself. Too late. The second blow had pain exploding behind his eyes. *The women. Gabe,* he thought before sliding into darkness.

Chapter Fifteen

Max hung up the call to his wife and strode into the meeting room. Abby wasn't resting or eating as well as she should. Screw trying ever again for a third kid. This pregnancy was the most stressful shit Max had ever experienced, and that included going head-to-head with suicidal extremist bastards.

Those worrying thoughts screeched to a halt as soon as Max saw his boss standing in the far corner. Max and Donnie had been pulled out of morning training and asked to meet one of their analysts—Jace Martin—on base. Jace was in the room but so was Colonel Jack Hearst. Was it to do with Slater's replacement? Max doubted it, as he stood at attention. Donnie fell in beside him. The look on the distinguished MIT mogul's face had Max's skin itching.

"Sir. It's good to see you. What brings you to Utah?"

"Erik, we've fucked up. Not just MIT but every agency in the northern hemisphere. Close the door and sit."

Okay then. Not what Max expected to hear. He'd never heard the colonel curse. The fact that Colonel Hearst used Max's first name meant there were more than just war games at stake. Max sat and regarded the men in the room. Two more analysts joined Jace. A spook stamped agent sat at the table, tapping away at his laptop.

An image flashed on the screen, and Max felt Donnie stiffen beside him. Max immediately recognized the man in the grainy security video. Kris Muller.

"Sir, where was this taken?"

"On American soil."

What the living hell? Had Max misheard him? "Come again?"

"It looks like Muller struck a deal with a Mexican drug lord and flew into Guatemala on a private plane. Muller then walked the Central American corridor over the Mexican border, then stole a car. Made good time getting over the border, but that's when his luck ran out. A gas station employee recognized him in Albuquerque."

"How long have we known this for?" Donnie asked, his tension echoing Max's rising blood pressure.

"Since this morning." Jace piped up. "The employee was found in a field behind the gas station, the night before last. Badly beaten and stabbed. He's in rough shape. Doubtful he'll make it, but he told the paramedics it was the Scythian who attacked him. He recognized Muller's photo from all the news channels."

The colonel stepped forward. "We only just received that intel. Once we were alerted, we traced back Kris Muller's journey to Mexico."

"How about tracing it forward?" Max said through gritted teeth. "Where's he heading? He has to know being in the States is a suicide mission."

"We're still figuring that out," Jace said. "He swapped out vehicles in Colorado."

"Where in Colorado?" Donnie and Max said at the same time.

"Alamosa."

Both men swore and were on their feet.

Max pulled out his phone, ignoring his superior's surprise. He barked at the colonel. "I need a bird. Now." Abby's number rang then went to voicemail. He tried again as Donnie briefed them on Johnny's location. Muller was after their women and Max was a four-hour drive away. An hour possibly by helicopter—and that excluded a briefing and their kitting up times.

◊ ◊ ◊

She'd drifted off to sleep again. The wind woke Lizzy, and she rolled off her lazy ass and stumbled into the shower. After a quick cleanup, she pulled a long-sleeved shirt over her shorts and searched for her sneakers. She looked around the messy guest room. John had the patience of ten saints when it came to her. It wasn't fair; she should be neater.

She remembered kicking them off near the bed and got down on all fours, reaching for the closest shoe. One down, one to go. The other sneaker sat, smack bang under the middle of the bed and she cursed her short stature for the millionth time. She crawled on her belly and stretched an arm out. No luck. Squeezing in a little more; her waist pinched against the bed base as she grasped the cursed sneaker. Ray growled, as a hand traced her ankle. John?

"Lizzy Liz. This is a damn fine view." The hand ran over her butt; she froze in terror. *It's another nightmare. I'll wake up soon. John is here, he'll keep me safe.*

The fingers trickled back down her inner thigh and over her calf before settling back on her ankle.

"Please, no," she begged.

Brutal fingers wrapped around and wrenched, skin tore off

her back, and her head slammed into the wooden base as Kris ripped her out from her sanctuary.

He rolled her over as she moaned in pain. "That's what happens to naughty wives who run away from their husbands."

◊ ◊ ◊

The nausea just wouldn't quit. *Leave me alone,* Johnny thought, pushing back into the murkiness. Another wave slammed in, and he twisted to get more comfortable. His shoulders and back screamed in pain. Something sticky coated his neck. What awkward campsite had his team picked this time? He'd slept in some shitty places, but this took the cake.

Someone yelped. A woman. She sounded familiar. She said something, but it sounded garbled. Did she speak another language? A kid cried. Someone shouted. Too much noise and Johnny pushed them away. He was used to napping in war zones, so he could easily shut out the chaos. A dog barked, incessantly, and that interrupted his strive for peace. *Someone shut that damn dog up*, he silently begged.

"I'll string up the furry bitch and skin her if you don't shut her up." The male voice had Johnny's arm hairs standing at attention. A door slammed, and the dog barks grew distant.

"Back here, now!" the man demanded. Footsteps echoed as someone ran up, then cried out in pain.

Muller...and Lizzy? Her cry felt like a slap to the face.

Johnny opened his eyes, looking frantically around. Everything seemed blurry. Double vision, a concussion. The earth-shifting pain pounding through his head confirmed that fact. He tried to call out to her, but his mouth was taped shut. He calmed enough to take stock of his situation. Lying on the living room floor. Arms and legs hogtied behind him. He shifted his wrists and his heart sank. Plastic ties—three sets—held his hands together. Muller knew what he was doing. Johnny didn't care, he'd twist the shit out of the ties and try to break free.

"Looks like your boyfriend's awake." Scuffed boots stepped into his line of vision and Johnny tried to roll onto his back.

Muller stood over him, the red mask in place. A filthy hand gripped the back of Lizzy's neck, as he waved a cricket bat in front of her. His soiled clothes were torn and worn away in places. He'd come a long way with little rest. That desperate mindset didn't bode well for his captives.

"You took your sweet time. We thought you were dead. I must've hit your giant noggin pretty hard. Gotta love a cricket bat—built for high impact. Shaped perfectly for smashing melons. I had to drag your heavy ass in here. I was about to start having fun with the ladies when I heard you whining."

The ladies. *Oh, God, Abby.* Johnny twisted, looking for his best friend's wife. Her head peeped out from behind the sofa. Dark hair sprawled across the floor. Gabe stroked his mother's unconscious face, crying softly. Johnny's gaze darted back to Lizzy, cataloging injuries. Blood on the side of her shirt. A scrape on her elbow. She looked determined, and that look in her eyes scared him more than the blood.

He noted a pistol jammed into the waistband of Muller's pants. Lizzy eyed it, and Johnny subtly shook his head. If she tried to wrestle a gun from a two-hundred-pound man, she'd end up very dead. There wasn't a damn thing Johnny could do to help. Helplessness like he'd never known before ate away at him.

Without a miracle, he'd watch them all die. That was Muller's plan. The smug bastard would make it personal for Johnny. A bullying coward would always want to be the biggest man in the room. He'd torture them all to get his last fix, and he'd start with Abby and Gabe. The woman who'd first betrayed him and her son.

"You've been sleeping with my wife."

What did Muller just say? His wife? Johnny eyed the masked son of a bitch as he slipped an arm around Lizzy's waist before running a hand under her breast.

"Did you enjoy her as much as I did?"

Johnny exploded at the implications. He fought the restraints, screaming through the muffled pain.

"He didn't know. Lizzy Liz, you never told him. Tell him you're my wife. C'mon, tell him!" Muller shoved her to her knees, pushing her face to Johnny's. Her sobs broke his heart.

When she buried her head in his shoulder, he rubbed his cheek against her downy hair, breathing in that familiar peachy scent. He infused the action with all the love he felt. Did she think he'd ever blame her for Muller's sick games?

Johnny's reaction angered Kris, and he kicked out at both of them, first catching Johnny's cheek then her waist. Johnny tried to shelter her but could do shit with his limbs tied up in a neat little back bow.

Instead, Lizzy sheltered him and got a blow to her thigh for her actions. Then Muller picked up the bat; Johnny felt restraints slicing through skin as he tried rolling over onto her.

Muller raised the weapon, then paused, instead wrenching her up by her hair. Lizzy struggled ineffectually against his firm grip. "I'll need to beat respect into you," he growled in her ear. "You ignore your husband for this piece of shit! Say you're sorry." He threw her to her knees as tremors of rage racked Johnny's body.

"I'm—I'm sorry."

"I'm sorry—who?"

"I'm sorry, mas...master."

Muller knelt and ran a hand over her head. "Why do you make me so angry? I've traveled all this way to find you. I had to drink kuk-ass river water, and I ate shitty MREs for weeks. Even ate geckos and a boa constrictor with my bare hands. Do you know what that does to a man? Have you ever eaten snake?"

"How...how did you find me?"

"Careful planning. After I kidnapped you—in Kenya—one of my men slipped into your apartment and planted a tracker—in that ratty stuffed toy on your bed. Also stuck one in your guitar. Figured if you ever got away or gave me trouble, I'd know where to find you or your family. You're too precious to take chances with." He stroked her cheek. "I tracked that toy all the way to Germany to the American hospital. Then to Frankfurt. Figured you were being taken back to the States by this bastard. It took time for my contacts to find the signal in Wyoming, but I was already on the way."

"You came here...for me?"

"Of course. You're all I have left, the first wife I've ever had. You're my mini-muffin, remember when I called you that, in the stables, when I stroked all this soft skin?"

Black rage pumped in time with Johnny's aching head as he envisioned the most painful way to kill the SOB.

"You will still be punished for the actions of your American soldiers. I lost my horse. Some asshole sheikh has it now, along with my cheetah. I lost everything!" He turned to Johnny. "Fok you!" Muller kicked him in the jaw.

Johnny tried not to pass out from pain, instead sucking bracing breaths through his nose.

Gabe's cries gathered momentum, and the masked monster turned his way. "Time for some fun. First, I kill the kid and his bitch betrayer of a mother. Then your soldier boy can watch me play with you."

Johnny was so caught up in the horror, that he nearly missed the flat look that washed over Lizzy's face.

"Do you want that again, master?"

Johnny turned to stone as the Scythian shifted. "Want what again? Don't play games with me, little wife."

"To stroke my skin? You're right, our wedding night was interrupted, but I had nothing to do with that. I love John, but I felt something for you too that night. When you laid with me, told me about your life on the farm and your uncle."

"How I murdered my uncle."

Lizzy was playing a dangerous game, but they had little choice. Gabe would be the first to die. Lizzy chose to sacrifice herself instead, and Johnny wanted to hurl. He worked a loose corner of his taped-up mouth over the woven carpet.

"Do you want me to touch you back?" Lizzy ran a hand down his thigh. "I was too afraid before. Now I feel... excited."

Muller growled, placed the bat on the kitchen counter and threw her against a wall, then shoved his tongue in her mouth. She'd bought them time. Johnny looked away, before the sick scene drove him over the edge of sanity, instead focusing on the other two occupants in the room.

Abby hadn't stirred, and Gabe tried to curl into her prone side, crying for his mommy and daddy. Johnny needed the little boy's help. The nearest weapon was in his go-bag which sat near the front door. Muller stood in the way. Johnny dragged his taped mouth over the rug once more, then looked around for anything to sever his restraints.

Muller came up for air. "Enjoy the show, Johnny boy?"

A muffled "fuck you" was the answer.

Lizzy stroked his chest. "I want you to myself first. Let's take this upstairs." She tried to saunter past and Muller grabbed her arm. "We're not going anywhere."

"Why? Are you afraid of what one small toddler can do? We won't be long." She rubbed a hand over Muller's crotch, and the resulting woody made Johnny's skin prickle.

It affected the douchebag and he turned to Johnny with dazed eyes, before pulling his gun and pointing it at Abby. "First I kill Evans. Your boyfriend and the kid can watch."

With one last swipe, Johnny pulled his lips free of the tape and yelled, causing Muller to turn. Lizzy picked up the bat and swung, catching Muller on the side of the head. She swung again, and he caught it in mid-air, wrestling it from her hands.

"Run, Lizzy!" Johnny yelled.

"It's me you want!" she shouted at Muller as she took off for the front door. Screaming obscenities, the prick staggered after her, shooting wildly. A bullet slammed into the wall, inches from her head. She threw the door open and launched out. He fired again.

Johnny heard him take off down the porch. Seconds later, a gunshot, then another echoed through the valley.

Johnny screamed out her name as he heard more pops. He'd failed her. He swore he'd protect her; instead he lay in a pool of blood as Muller hunted her. And Abby and Gabe? Max would never forgive Johnny for not protecting his family.

Chapter Sixteen

"The storm could've damaged the phone lines," Donnie yelled over the thrumming blades. Max ignored the logic, knowing in his gut that his family was in trouble and Johnny was either disabled or dead.

His teammate should've made mincemeat out of Muller's slimy ass and contacted Max by now. None of the mobile phones were being answered, and the landlines were dead.

The colonel's orders were to allow local law enforcement and the FBI to run the mission. But if Max was the first to arrive, he'd ignore that directive, just as he'd ignored the orders to stay on base until SOCOM briefed a fully manned black ops team.

Defying orders, Donnie and Max threw on battle rattle and relied on a friend and chopper pilot to give them a ride. Now MIT scrambled to cover their men's asses. They'd departed on a mission on American soil that was not fully authorized. Max didn't give a shit. His pregnant wife and child were stranded at an isolated farmhouse with a psychotic extremist. If anything happened to them, his job status would be an irrelevancy in the resulting bloodbath.

The bird landed two clicks out, and the two MIT2 soldiers took off over the fields, their M4's at the ready. They'd trained on Johnny's property over the years, and the exact layout was like coming home. They slipped over the fence running along the lower end of the farm and worked their way towards the house. Sporadic gunshots filled the air. Max pushed hard, racing towards the sounds. The damp air suddenly lay silent, interrupted by the occasional dripping of wet foliage.

Donnie positioned himself on the back porch. Max slowed as he rounded to the front. A police vehicle sat parked on the gravel, blue lights flashing in the misty rain. A deputy lay face down in the front yard, the muddy grass saturated with blood.

Max scanned the perimeter before edging forward, rifle at the ready. He felt for a pulse. Nothing. Turning the officer over revealed a gaping neck wound. The front door sat open, and Max approached it with trepidation, trying to keep his weapon steady against an onslaught of panic.

The first person he saw was Johnny. The man looked like a wild-eyed beast. His face streaked with blood as his eyes darted to the door. "Your kid is behind me. Help him! Help Gabe. The house is clear."

Johnny's words had Max's gut turn to water. Gabe. Was he injured? Max ran over as he gave Donnie the all clear.

Gabe's tear-streaked face popped up behind Johnny. "I usered the knife, daddy. Uncle Jay says it's okay. He has ouchies. The monsta ranned away."

"Gabe's uninjured!" Johnny said. "Muller's out there, hunting Lizzy."

Gabe held a penknife, see-sawing at the plastic cuffs that hog-tied his friend. Max pulled the knife from his tiny hands.

"My wife?" Max croaked out the words, spotting Abby at the same time as Johnny jerked his head over to the left.

"Behind the sofa—she's hurt."

Donnie slipped in. "Cut me free," Johnny yelled at their team analyst. "Lizzy's out there alone."

Max gathered up Gabe, then collapsed beside his wife. Her skin felt warm and her pulse thrummed steadily. Blood on her neck led to a lump on the back of her head. His exploration of the injury had her moaning.

"Abs, stay still. You're okay. Don't move, sweetheart. I've got you." Max heard Johnny cursing from behind as Donnie freed him, but all Max focused on was his injured woman.

"We need a damn ambulance!"

Johnny stumbled down next to him, trying to assess her injury. Blood drenched his shirt and he swayed on his knees. It looked like Muller had tried to de-brain the massive warrior.

"Shit, buddy, lie down. We've got this—"

"Muller's chasing Lizzy," Johnny slurred. "He may have killed her. I need to find them. Give me…gun." He staggered to his feet.

"No. You're not going out there," Donnie said. "You won't be shooting anyone in your state. I'll find her."

"Fuck it then. Don't need a gun. Donnie, take my personal rifle, be my backup. In the safe. Cover your asses." Johnny staggered to the door and Donnie tried to stop him. Shots echoed.

"Get out of my way. Cover me."

"Johnny, stand down," Max ordered as he tucked a blanket around his wife. It was too late—Johnny was out the door. Donnie used the keypad to let himself into Johnny's security room to access the safe. They all knew the combination. "He has a point. We can't use MIT weapons to shoot Muller on American soil."

"Kris did this?" Abby asked weakly.

Max ignored the question. "Donnie, go. Cover his concussed ass."

"No, wait! Stop." Abby grabbed Max's sleeve. "It needs to be you. This is personal. He's hurt our family for the last time."

"Honey, I'm not leaving you—"

"I'm fine; I have a hard head. Donnie will protect us. Go, Max. Kill the bastard; he tried to hurt our babies." She pulled Gabe from his arms with surprising strength. "Lizzy needs you."

With a nod, Max stood. Donnie handed Johnny's rifle over and Max exited the cabin. Distant movement up ahead indicated Johnny's progress towards the neighboring farm. The ranger was an excellent tracker and Max had little doubt that he was narrowing in on his unlucky prey.

◊ ◊ ◊

Swiping at her mud-caked vision, Lizzy stumbled through the fence towards Charlie's barn. When she'd flown off the porch steps, her immediate relief at seeing the deputy running towards her turned to horror when Muller's bullet sliced through the man's neck.

Lizzy veered, then stumbled as a second one zipped past her cheek.

Instead of heading for the road, she zigzagged across the field towards farm outbuildings that could provide cover. Her feet slipped, and she went down in the sloppy mud. Scrambling for purchase, she staggered towards the tree line before spotting the wooden barn. This time, tree bark shattered to the left of her, and she swung right, not daring to glance back.

The farm was a ghost town. Charlie and her foreman were up at the hospital for her father's third heart surgery. The rest of the staff had left early to set up a food stall at the Sunday farmer's market in town. Still, a farm hand popped out from behind a tree and took aim at the Scythian.

They exchanged fire; she heard the man cry out. Lizzy wanted desperately to stop and help, but that would sign her death warrant. She used the delay to race into the barn and slam the doors shut. The musky smell of hay brought back memories of her African stable wedding.

Charlie's sharp implements still hung on the far wall, and Lizzy chose her weapons carefully, before rushing to the opposite corner and burying them in the hay. Kris Muller rattled the doors, swinging them open as she sank to the straw-covered floor.

"Devious bitch." Kris ran assessing eyes over her cowering form.

"Screw you, Kris! You won't hurt my friends."

"After all we've been through. I told you all my childhood shit; I've never told anyone. You sang for me." He stood silhouetted in the doorway. All that separated them were dust motes, dancing in the morning light.

She swallowed back bile. He'd made her sing for him as she'd lain, trussed up, naked and bleeding on his canopied bed. Hours of singing, receiving punches and slaps whenever she'd drifted into a fevered haze. Feeling damp hands running over her body. A wedding night to a hooded, sadistic psychopath.

And his stories... Kris had spoken of how he'd tortured small animals. He'd explained in detail how he'd gutted his uncle with a butcher's knife, then how he'd murdered a small child from the local village. He continued the legacy by hunting new victims in the rural Botswanan community.

Killing came naturally to the Scythian from a young age. Lizzy had no clue how to defend herself against such a well-practiced opponent, but she wouldn't let him walk out of the barn—or return to her loved ones. She would die so that John could live.

Kris shoved the gun into the back of his pants before unzipping a side pocket and pulling out a sheathed hunting blade. Kris liked knives and she knew he was skilled at using them. Pulling off the cover, he examined the serrated edge. "I took your finger, but that wasn't enough. Now it's time to take your head." The burnished mask twisted into a maniacal grin, reinforcing the terror that statement evoked.

Lizzy flexed her fingers and buried them in the straw. Time for nine-fingered bravery.

"You're just an unloved, unlikeable and lonely little boy."

"What did you say?" He stepped forward.

"Let me guess, the kids in town never much liked you. I'm sure they sensed the evil sickness buried inside."

"Fok you. Nasty whore." Kris moved closer.

"Abby was your only friend, and now she can't bear to look at you. She thinks you're a twisted sickopath. In fact, the only home you ever found was with your fellow extremists. Lonely little men with delusions of grandeur."

Two more steps.

"You're a sad little psycho."

One last step. Kris loomed over her. "And you're a dead woman."

Straw flew as a machete whipped through the air, embedding itself in Muller's knee with a dull *thwack*. She wrenched it back and swung again, this time catching his thigh as he collapsed over her. His arm mashed her head into the ground as he screamed out the pain. She struggled against his weight, blinded by the dusty straw and his broad chest.

Kris grabbed her hair and slammed her head into the ground. Rolling his weight onto her shoulder, he twisted the weapon out of her grip. Lizzy groped with her other hand for the medieval-looking knife she'd hidden. She touched the handle before it skittered away. She used her thumb to claw him in the eye instead. He rolled sideways, and she was almost free of her monstrous prison when his elbow smashed into her chest and pinned her down into the crunchy mattress.

Lizzy screamed up at the spittle-covered mask. The Scythian wheezed out his pain. She reevaluated her fight plan as he placed the knife at her temple. A sharp prick, and blood trickled into her hairline. There was no fight plan. Just her last moments, looking up into the face that haunted her dreams. She flashed instead on John's face, remembered him cradling her under a shady oak on a sunny day next to a pretty lake.

"I've never driven a knife into a girl's temple before." The knife tip twisted. "Such a vulnerable part of the head. I wonder how far I'll have to drill this baby in, and if you'll die instantly. After that, I'll take your scalp."

Lizzy squeezed her eyes shut. The suffocating weight suddenly lifted, and she opened them to see Kris flying through the air before being slammed back to the earth. Then he took off again, jerked about like a floppy puppet. The puppeteer was John, madder than she'd ever seen him. He held the Scythian in a wrestler's grip and slammed him down over and over. It was like watching a WWE match, except way more violent.

John roared with each body slam. Then he ripped off the Scythian's mask and switched to punching—burying meaty fists in Muller's face. Lizzy watched, fascinated by the gory spectacle, feeling safer than she ever had before.

Only when John stood, staggered and fell did she remember

his head injury. He picked up the knife and tossed it away. Lizzy tried to roll to her knees; she got to one elbow as he crawled to her. His medic's eyes traced over her streaked face. "He hurt you…"

"You found me in time. I'm okay. It's going to be okay." She pulled his head to her muddied chest. John rolled them over, propping them against a bale of hay. They were both bleeding and soaked in dirt. Despite the terror, she smiled against his broad shoulder. She was where she belonged. This was home, burrowed into James "Johnny" Cane's chest—in a barn—on a rainy Sunday morning.

He stroked her hair as she stared at her brutal nemesis. Kris looked dead. Lizzy stretched out and nudged his foot. John pulled her back.

"Stay away. I need to take care of him."

John's words sounded slurred. He tried to sit up, falling sideways instead. Shouting his name, Lizzy got to her knees. "Don't you dare die. Focus on me!"

John tried, she held his face and stared into warm fiery eyes which flickered over her shoulder, then turned cold. John threw her to the side. The Scythian staggered to one knee, gun wavering in her direction. Blood poured from numerous wounds, he coughed then spat out teeth. John surged forward, in a blur of movement he wrapped an arm around Kris's neck, wrenching it as they both fell. The sound of a neck cracking, echoed through the damp air. Not letting go, John twisted even further, jerking the Scythian's head at an impossible angle.

When John finally rolled away, Kris fell to the floor with a *thunk*. Max stepped in and skirted the dead man, the shotgun aimed at the body. He kicked the gun away, then checked for hidden weapons.

John pulled himself back towards Lizzy as he waved an arm drunkenly in Kris's direction. "Told ya I didn't need a gun."

Max knelt next to the couple. "Rest up, brother. The ambulance should be arriving any minute. I have to get back to Abby."

"Muller shot one of Charlie's men," Lizzy said. "He's around the side of the barn. Please check on him."

With a nod, Max left, and Lizzy hovered as John's eyes drifted shut.

"Please don't leave me."

He gripped her fingers. "Never, Lizbug. Took me this long...win you over...not going anywhere. Stuck with my stubborn ass...forever."

Chapter Seventeen

John kept to his word. Two days later and he was ready to be checked out of the hospital. Lizzy giggled as he waddled over to the bathroom. The back of his gown left little to her imagination.

"Don't laugh. It's not funny. You'd think they'd have a larger gown for taller patients."

"I don't think it's your height, baby." Lizzy laughed. "You look like the incredible hulk, hulking out of teeny human clothes."

Donnie walked in, grinning at John's bare ass. "And the beard gives him a yeti vibe."

"I need clean clothes."

Lizzy spent a day in the ward, under observation. Charlie was kind enough to bring Lizzy a change of clothes the day before, but she'd mistakenly packed an old pair of John's pants that no longer fitted around his muscled waist.

"Relax, big man. I have your lumberjack clothing ready and waiting."

"Well, hand them over. We need to get to Abby's ward."

Donnie threw the large bag on the bed.

Lizzy's thoughts turned to her friend occupying the room on the floor below. Abigail wasn't faring as well, and Max was a literal mess.

Abby's head injury seemed okay. A concussive blow which needed time to heal. But when Kris Muller knocked her out—the fall to the floor in her third trimester—it caused uterine bleeding and tenderness. And then came the contractions. In her thirty-fourth week of pregnancy, she'd just been rushed into the operating room for an emergency cesarean.

After signing the discharge papers, they made their way to the maternity ward, and John hugged his teammate. Dark circles rimmed pale eyes. The haunted look on Max's face had Lizzy's stomach roiling. Hatred for a deceased man came easily to Lizzy. Not only was her friend fighting for her life but thanks to Kris Muller, Deputy Bill Thompson and Charlie's farmhand Jerry Carson were dead.

Both funerals were being held on the weekend. The FBI and MIT covered up the incident. As far as the townsfolk and local media knew, a drifter passing through town committed the break-in.

Charlie visited John's ward a couple of times and suspected there was more to the attack. When she started in with an interrogation, Donnie stepped in and shuttled her off to the cafeteria.

And now they waited to hear news on the emergency C-section. The tension emanating from the two large men had Lizzy taking a seat off to the side, but John linked his fingers with hers and pulled her close.

"Where's Gabe?" John asked quietly. Max's parents sat across the room, and Lizzy smiled at them.

"My brother took him home—with his wife and kids—to settle him back in a routine. Gabe isn't doing so good, first Cape Town, now this." Max rested his head in his hands, rocking slightly in his seat.

"This is my fault," John said.

Max's reply was immediate. "Bullshit."

"I should've protected your family," John whispered, keeping the conversation private.

"We had zero indication that Muller was on US soil," Max whispered back.

"I acted like a damn untrained sheep; he snuck up on me."

"You acted like a human. None of us are superheroes. This is all on that son of a bitch."

Silence fell, and Lizzy thought about Kris Muller's violent demise. It didn't bother her as much as she thought it would. Perhaps the endless violence she'd lived through had numbed her of all empathy. Except she wasn't numb, she felt content. Content that the red-masked man was finally gone and would no longer terrorize innocent civilians. Content that John sat safe and whole just a few feet away. Content that Abby had a man who loved her so. Her friend and their baby had to pull through because good things lay ahead.

"How are you feeling, Lizzy?" Max asked. "How's the hand?"

John answered for her. "She has a nasty scrape on her back that looks inflamed, and Lizzy isn't exercising the finger."

"Stop being so bossy! My back is fine. You're not taking care of your wrists either!"

John had already removed the dressings from his wrists, claiming the lacerations needed to dry out. "I'll stop being so bossy when you stop being so damn stubborn."

"Back to the bickering again." Max huffed. "I guess that means you're both doing fine."

Lizzy grinned at John, and he smiled back. A surgeon walked in, and they all stood.

"Erik Andersen?"

"That's me," Max said as he clenched his fists.

"Congratulations. Your wife and your little girl are both stable. Would you like to come in as we finish up? Your baby is at a low birthweight—just under five pounds. She's still at risk for respiratory distress syndrome, but we'll monitor her oxygen levels over the next couple of weeks."

"They're both going to be okay?" Max said through tears.

"Both healthy and strong."

After back thumps and congratulations, Max raced off to join Abby. Slumping back in her chair, Lizzy sighed out her relief.

"I could sleep for days," John said, as she rested her head on his shoulder.

"Me too."

He placed a hand on her leg. "Where's your hound?"

"With Charlie for the afternoon."

"How about we sneak over to the nearest hotel and grab a little R&R." John shot her a wink.

"Are you up for that?"

"I am if you are?"

"You're not angry with me?"

John turned and crouched at her feet. "Lizbug, why the hell would I be angry?"

"Because I lied to you. I didn't tell you about the marriage and—"

"Don't think for a moment that him forcing you to say those vows meant anything. It meant nothing! You were never married to the sick bastard."

"I felt so helpless when you were tied up and he threatened to hurt Gabe. I had to play along with him. I had to distract him."

John clenched his jaw and looked away. "You did. It was the bravest thing I've ever seen."

"You're not mad?"

"Only proud, baby." John reached out to cup her cheek. "I'm proud of my feisty firecracker."

"How about you rest that handsome head on the drive over, and if you behave, I might mount your feisty—and very large—firecracker."

John choked on a laugh as he grabbed her hand. "Then no granny driving. Pedal to the metal, baby. We're burning daylight."

Lizzy laughed as he swung her to her feet.

Epilogue

Wyoming
Three weeks later

Ray huffed out a snore as she rolled over to her side on the wooden porch. Scratching her velvety neck with his foot, Johnny took a swig of beer. The setting sun provided the perfect backdrop to Lizzy's sweet profile as she strummed softly on her guitar.

She paused, then swore. "Gosh, dang it."

"The finger again?"

"Or lack thereof."

"Don't push it. Give it time."

Lizzy stuck out her tongue, and Johnny grinned. She made a pretty picture, sitting cross-legged on the rocking chair with her hair twisted in a cute bun at the nape of her neck. Not quite long enough, tendrils fell around her face, dancing in the autumn breeze. Back to her normal weight with flushed cheeks—an outside observer would never guess at the trauma she'd experienced just a couple of months before. Dragging his chair closer, Johnny leaned in and kissed her cheek.

"What was that for?"

He didn't answer, instead staring into wide blue eyes. Placing the guitar down, Lizzy reached up and brushed at the scar on his temple before meeting his lips. Their tongues mated, and he cupped the back of her head for better access. Lizzy moaned in response. He reluctantly broke away and swiped a thumb over her pink lips.

"You taste like grapes."

"New lip balm."

"Jesus. We have a visitor, but I want to take you right here," he whispered.

She smiled wickedly. "Like you did this morning?"

He'd taken her all right. Johnny had woken her for an early morning walk, and they'd snuck out while it was still dark. At the top of the hiking trail—as the first sun rays traced the valley—he had given into temptation. With a wide oak at her back, Lizzy had curled her legs around his waist as he'd slowly pushed in and drawn back. The slow rhythm had driven them both crazy and Lizzy came twice before he'd laid her on the ground, lifted her ass and pounded out his release. Johnny smiled at the memory and leaned in to nibble her neck.

"I love getting dirty with you, Jay Jay. How about a walk to that small lake after dinner? I feel like a skinny dip."

"Shit, Lizbug. How am I supposed to concentrate on anything else until then?"

Lizzy shrugged and threaded fingers through his before settling back in the chair. "So, when do you leave?"

"Next Friday. After our move."

Johnny bought a second home in Utah, near Max. It meant that Lizzy would be closer to her therapist and the city. Not as isolated if anything went wrong while Johnny was deployed. He decided against selling his farm. Lizzy's parents would use it as a vacation home when they were in the States, and Lizzy and Johnny both still needed the sanctuary as an escape.

"How long will you be gone?"

He stretched out his legs as she traced circles on his arm. "Anything from three months to a year. Would you be okay with that?"

Lizzy also stretched out her legs. The difference in length was almost comical, he thought, examining their height difference as he raised the bottle to his lips.

"Of course. Why wouldn't I be? I'll see you there anyway."

He choked on the sip and shot her a confused glance.

"Oh, fudge. I forgot to tell you."

"Tell me what...Lizbug?" He drew out the nickname in warning.

"Mason Clark contacted me. His father thinks the Teens & Tots orphanage would be a great project for his son to work on— while he's finishing up with school. Mason wants to meet up with me and talk about what happened in Nigeria. He's doing better than he was."

"Do you think that's a good idea?" Johnny frowned.

"I think it'll help with our healing process. Mason's family will be in Jackson in two weeks."

"Lizbug, I'll be gone by then. I don't like you meeting him on your own."

She squeezed his large forearm. "What, am I five? Besides, His father will have a whole posse of bodyguards watching our backs. Plus, Mason wants to book a recording studio."

Placing his beer on the floor, Johnny turned to her. "A what?"

"I sang for him in Nigeria, after his mom died. He says he wants that same song professionally recorded. He thinks it will help him with his mom's passing."

"That's a huge deal. How did I not know about this?"

"He called yesterday when you were doing your PT training with the team. And Mason wants to market the girls' dressmaking skills in Kenya. Set up an online shop."

"It means you'd need to be there."

"Of course. I can do my photography and, at the same time, help the girls. Besides, I need to see Valentino. I miss him."

"Wait—go back—photography? Is that what you want to do?"

"I think I could be really good at it. Take photos of the kids, and build awareness for their plight."

"What about the nursing degree?"

"It's not my passion. Although I do love taking care of patients."

"For the love of God," Johnny muttered before getting up and stalking inside. He ignored her confused look and grabbed a notepad and a pen from a drawer, plonking back down beside her.

"What are you doing?"

"You need a life path—planning system—of some sort. Let's make a list." He flipped to a clean sheet. "So, you want to be a photographer?"

"Yep."

"And a fashion designer?"

"What are you talking about?"

"I gather that Clark teenager doesn't know much about cutting and sewing dresses, so I guess you'll be creating the designs."

"Fudge buckets. You're right. He wants to be a fashion designer, but for now I'm the most qualified."

"And you want to be a volunteer at the orphanage and a

singer but maybe not a nurse. Not that I have a problem with any of these. As long as you're happy, that's all that matters."

"Then what's the problem?"

"I thought you were all about finding yourself, wanting to find your true path in life?"

"Yeah, that's overrated and just so boring. Besides, I can create a job title for all of those."

Johnny laughed and shook his head. "And that would be?"

"A singing, dress-designing philanthropist with a camera."

"You're going to keep me on my damn toes, woman."

"I promise I won't bug you in Kenya. You won't even know I'm there."

"Fat chance." He snorted.

"What? It'll be fun having your wife work in the same city on your days off."

"My wife, huh?"

Lizzy blushed, and Johnny stroked a finger over the flush.

"I didn't mean—"

"Having you as my wife would make me the happiest man on the planet, no matter where we were."

A soft smile lit her face. "I have found my life path. All this time, I thought I was searching just for a purpose, but it was actually my heart—looking for its new home—right beside you."

"Fuck, baby." Too choked up to respond, he captured her mouth in his.

The porch steps creaked, and Donnie stepped out and cleared his throat. "Jeez, will you two get a room? If you're not squabbling, you're sticking tongues down each other's throats."

Johnny growled. "Be a good houseguest. Go hassle someone else. Like Charlie. You're good at getting her all riled up."

Donnie leaned against the door jamb and crossed his biker

boots. He was staying over for a week to help them pack. "How is she? How's her father?"

"Not doing so well. Charlie is going through a tough time. She's in the barn if you want to see her."

Staring out into the darkening dusk, Donnie swore and pushed off from the wall. "Take a cold shower, brother, while I'm gone. Your tented sword is scaring off the wildlife."

"Screw off, tech boy." Johnny picked up Ray, then carried her to her crate. He grabbed a couple of throws, then took Lizbug's hand and led her down a quiet path. They walked for over ten minutes in silence and arrived at a mossy clearing beneath a giant oak tree. Lizzy paused to admire the view. "I need to climb that woody beast."

"Not tonight."

Laying down the blanket, he pulled her to the fresh earth. The full moon cast her face in a glow as a breeze whispered through the trees. They lay, chatting and laughing. Hours later as he drove into her, he swiped away a smudge of dirt on his girl's cheek. This was home. Lizzy caught his hand and brought it to her lips, and Johnny's battle-scarred heart thundered out his love.

The End

Make sure to pick up "Fire in the Knight," book three of the Mobile Intelligence Series. Find out what happens to Charlotte Quinn and Donnie Wilson!

Fire in the Knight (MIT Book #3) is available for preorder.

Saint Julian's, Malta

With no sign of potential witnesses in the hall, the man pulled the apartment door shut with a soft click. He adjusted his hoodie and ran down the steps before stepping onto the damp pavement. The sun had set and on a wet November night in Malta, the streets surrounding Spinola Bay were practically deserted.

It was time to settle in and wait. The mark—Joseph da Silva—had only just sat down for dinner at one of the nearby restaurants. It would be at least an hour before he returned to his rental villa facing the water.

With quick and efficient movements, the assassin made his way to the docked speedboat. Villas and hotels pressed together around the inlet, stacked like LEGOs around the small cove. He ignored the colorful skiffs floating alongside his craft. Traditional Maltese Luzzu fishing boats painted a patchwork of color both on and off the water. Clambering onto a small speed boat, he adjusted the tarp that added additional concealment before settling in his seat. He glanced at his watch. Nineteen minutes and 28 seconds. The efficient time it took to gain access to the apartment—and to set the pressure switch—pleased him.

Setting up the Semtex charge inside the water tank took skill, but connecting the explosives to a double pressure switch between the toilet bowl and the seat had made him sweat. It was foolproof. Mr. Da Silva would return from his dinner. If he needed to piss, he'd raise the toilet seat which would trigger the switch and blow him to pieces. However, if Da Silva decided to sit on the crapper, the second pressure switch would also activate the water charge.

He reached into a packed cooler and pulled out a Tupperware filled with Bigilla, carrots and crackers. He loved the Maltese version of Hummus. No one made better Bigilla than his mama and he was grateful for the packed dinner.

Toilets were fool proof when it came to killing a mark. People may not use a fridge or an oven—mainly if they eat out or don't know how to cook—but at some point, everybody responded to the call of nature.

Cracking open a soda, he thought about the mark. This would be his fifth kill, not bad considering he'd only been in the killing game for ten months. He did the work that others were afraid to do, and his work was meticulous. Joseph da Silva shouldn't have asked questions. The private detective should've stayed in Italy. Instead he began investigating links between the Sicilian Mafia and wealthy Maltese families. Over the past decade, the police had made arrests, linking Maltese individuals to Libyan fuel smuggling and illegal gaming activities. But now that the dust had settled, new investigations would open a can of laundering worms.

The detective was bad for business. He had to die.

As the killer waited, he slipped a hand in his jacket pocket and pulled out his talisman, rolling it between his thumb and fingers. He took great care. One wrong move would mean death. He looked down at the small green object. The smallest grenade in the world. A replica of the V40 Fragmentation Grenade originally manufactured in the Netherlands. He carried the shell on every mission. It kept him alert and careful in the field.

The contained explosive energy lying in the palm of his hand, made his heart pump a little faster. Explosive devices fascinated him. That and the fires they caused, after ripping through space with shredded mayhem. He placed the fragmentation device carefully back in his pocket, opened a soda and returned to watching the apartment entrance.

Two hours later, the detective walked up the chilly street and then up the stairs. Rain pattered on the tarp, sounding peaceful as the sea gently rocked the boat. Ten minutes later, an explosion shattered the silence. Fiery missiles blew outwards, then showered onto the harbor below. The killer could feel the concussive blast from across the water and the sight energized him. Although he wanted to hang back and watch the flames flicker in the night's sky, it was time for him to leave. He turned on the motor and made his way towards the open water, blocking out the screams and never once looking back.

Fire in the Knight (MIT Book #3) is available for preorder here: https://www.louisedawnauthor.com/books/

Join my newsletter to find out first about
my latest releases, giveaways, sales and free books.
http://www.louisedawnauthor.com

Acknowledgments

Stain on the Earth was a satisfying book to write. Never has a plot flowed so easily or have my characters ever spoken to me this strongly. Lizzy Steyn makes me smile. Even writing her roughest moments, I could feel her quirky strength shining through. If she were a real person, she'd be my fun bestie, dragging me out on girl's nights out. Writing her character helped me in so many ways, and I'm grateful to have found her in my deepest imaginings. Elizma, I'm sure I threw a little of your happy soul into Lizzy's creation. Miss you girl.

I wanted to write about a Kenyan children's home as I had a similar experience volunteering my time with a remote orphanage near Harrismith, South Africa. A home that takes care of HIV orphans and who mentors the grannies in the rural community who foster these little tykes. The district is affected by structural poverty resulting in high unemployment rates and a community that is the poorest of the poor. That experience changed my life in so many small ways, and although I now live across the globe, I'll find a way to continue helping however I can.

Just a quick thanks to my beta readers – Jolene, Summer and Colleen—your loyalty and love floors me. You've helped me to get where I am. I love you girls. To my incredible parents, I love and miss you so much. Thanks for having faith in everything I do, no matter how crazy.

To my wonderful editors, Deb Nemeth and Joan Nichols. Thanks for making me look good on paper and wading through my messy drafts. Syd Gill—your beautiful cover designs make me so happy. I can't wait to see what you do with the rest of the series!

Louise Dawn writes heart pounding romantic suspense. She's also a corporate trainer in Utah. Louise loves travelling and has lived in many countries before choosing the States as her home. Her passion is reading and writing fast paced stories simmering in romance. If you enjoyed this book, consider leaving a review. It's appreciated by authors both new and established.

Chat with her on Facebook @
https://www.facebook.com/authorlouisedawn

Follow her on Twitter @
https://twitter.com/louisedawnwrite

Or check out her character's development on Pinterest @
https://www.pinterest.com/louisedawnwrite/boards/